South Jersey Casino Boy 2:

The Philly Connection

South Jersey Casino Boy 2: The Philly Connection

Chuck Turner

Copyright 2021 Horseshoe Crab Press

Amazon Paperback Edition

Acknowledgements

To everyone I know who has been willing to hear my ramblings, I am so very grateful. My wife possesses patience and love beyond what I thought our vows allowed for. Man, did I make the right choice. Our children continue to amaze me with their support and understanding regarding why I feel it so important to simply sit down and write, unlike the many years when I would be in a standing position and talking. I'm good at that. I'm a Turner -- we're all pretty good at it.

Thank you to my siblings as well. The Vernon Avenue world I present is one that they are familiar with (even though I've painted it with a different brush). They have inspired me to do this with the idea that, above all, redemption must always be in play.

I'm also very grateful to those of you who are willing to read the story and take a journey around South Jersey with me.

Finally, and more specifically, thanks to my Linda for editing and to our son Stephen for doing that and so much more. We've shared many laughs during the process and none so hearty as when I answered that all too common question from them: "Did that really happen?"

"Of course it did...wait...which part are you asking about, again?"

Table of Contents

Prologue

Ernie Tarsitano was, for me, South Jersey baseball's John Travolta. Travolta exploded onto the big screen in 1977 with an iconic role in *Saturday Night Fever.* Like Travolta, Ernie had perfect hair and good looks. He made me start thinking, "What if I could be that cool?"

My life, at the age of 16, included emulating cool people and trying to attract chicks. My brothers had gone to live their lives and pursue new conquests in other parts of the country. I quickly used up their advice on how to be a "just-cool-enough-lower-working-class-kid who is never going to college." I knew how to navigate the greater Mainland Regional High School territory and even branched out and dated a Holy Spirit High girl from Pleasantville.

In the summer of '78, I played center field for an Atlantic County League baseball team: "Linwood Toyota," named after our car dealership sponsor. Ernie Tarsitano was a left-handed first baseman for the Northfield team. He was easy-going, athletic, and a real good guy. On top of that, the man was riding around in a gorgeous frickin' Corvette…a CORVETTE. He couldn't have been cooler if he was Hugh Hefner's favorite nephew. Man, I wanted to be that guy.

Since a Corvette was out of the question, I decided to work on my game by asking lots of "meaning of life" questions to guys who I thought knew it all. At the very least, they were older than me and had sexy girlfriends. It was a start. So, that was "my move." The world was my classroom, and I was sitting at the front with a sharpened pencil and an arm waiting to shoot up and get the teacher's attention.

About the same time, the newly approved Casino Referendum had things percolating in the once-thriving town of Atlantic City. I wanted in on the action. As "Sin City East" was rising out of the ashes of a long-dead beach tourist town, Chuck Turner was preparing to take on the world. It was a harmonic convergence.

I tried a few different jobs, even working construction gigs for my cousin Albie, as I navigated the post-high school world. The work taught me some important lessons, such as the liberal use of the "F" word and that beer always pairs well with lunch. I took to it like Bruce Jenner in an Olympic event.

One day, I discovered that a good friend of the family was a Security Lieutenant at Bally's Park Place Casino. So, I headed over to fill out an application and set up a time to talk. The meeting with Ed Broome led to a Security Guard position at Bally's. I was "on my way" with a new career as an Atlantic City casino worker. Since we worked twelve-hour shifts for six days on and two days off, the immersion process was quick.

I will never forget the first week. I came home one morning to find Pop with the newspaper in front of his face (the usual). As I walked in, he asked, "How goes the new job? Lots of different girls there?" Pop understood that my main focus was meeting "new chicks' and expanding my dating horizon.

"It's like Baskin-Robbins' thirty-one flavors, Pop," I told him. "There are different women all over the place. It's unreal. I've never seen anything like it in my life. I held a door open for this one cocktail waitress and she kissed her fingers and touched my face. Then she said, 'You are a gentleman...and new here, huh?' and winked at me. She was gorgeous."

Pop chuckled and went back to reading his paper saying, "You'll do just fine."

Since I started the job before I received my New Jersey State Gaming License, I was typically stationed away from or just off the casino floor area. That meant that I had plenty of time to look in on the daily action and have conversations with folks as they went to and from their jobs. One particular shift, as I looked out onto the floor, I noticed a guy in a suit looking over at me. He gave me a small wave as he talked to what appeared to be a group of businessmen and their wives. It was Ernie Tarsitano with an employee badge attached to his jacket. I had no idea Ernie worked at Bally's. When we talked later, he explained that he was a Casino Host, which meant that he met with V.I.P guests (high rollers), showed them around and made sure they had what they needed to enjoy their time in the casino. Holy crap. I quickly realized how good life had been to me with Eddie Broome as my boss and Ernie Tarsitano setting the example for what "cool guys" do for a living in a casino. Nothing could surpass being a Casino Host...nothing. I decided that was where I was headed.

So, with information I received from Ernie and a conversation with Bally's H.R. department, I scheduled a meeting with the man who ran the whole she-bang. A couple of days later, during his paper reading/coffee time, I told Pop my plan. The paper slowly lowered as his eyes peered over the top and he said to me, "You're doing WHAT? Does your Mother know about this?" She didn't, but I told her next. I had scheduled a meeting with Ernie's boss, the man who could point me in the right direction and help get my career moving forward: MLB Hall-of-Famer and the 1953 American League MVP as a member of the Cleveland Indians, Mr. Al Rosen.

When the day came, I put on a suit and tie and was so damn nervous it felt like my clothes were strangling me. I headed into Al Rosen's office, hand extended and introduced myself with a big smile.

Al shook my hand and explained, "I have about 15 minutes for you today, so let's get to it. What brings you here?"

Before I continue, it's important to understand something about me: I'm not an autograph hound and not overawed by famous people. I never will be. I've gotten autographs here and there, but it was because the moment was right and I felt like I was giving a compliment to the person. Other than that, I treat famous people with respect and let them have some space. The approach served me well later in life as I worked in Hollywood and spent time in-studio and on location for Leonard Hill Productions (through West-Pac Security). I got some pretty cool assignments because well, I acted "cool."

The meeting with Al Rosen that day years ago was the first in a number of opportunities to interact with people whose world view was much wider than mine. I respected who Al was and where he had been in life. He asked me plenty of questions, but the one that stands out the most to this day is: "So, why do you want to be a Casino Host like your friend Ernie?"

I explained that I didn't want to be a security guard for long or be stuck in a basic job. At the time, I didn't think about the fact that I was presenting my goals in a pretty negative way.

"What's your badge say?" Mr. Rosen asked me.

I didn't understand the question. He couldn't see my employee badge, as I had buried it in my suit pocket the first chance I got. I told him, "Bally's Park Place."

Al smiled and told me, "It says Chuck, not Ernie. You work on you and make yourself better. Deal a few games and learn the casino business by being with customers, day in and day out. That's the best way to get better and find out what you want to do, understand? Work on you. Best advice I can give you." He was right. I thanked him with a strong handshake and left with the words as a guide for the rest of my life.

Weeks later, I received my license, began to deal Craps and stepped into some of the most intense moments of my life. My Linwood buddy and king of the eternal grin, Pete Dalzell, often describes his first Craps dealing days this way: "I know why they call it Craps: I shit my pants dealing it the day I started. I was scared to death." Pete accurately describes my feelings those first few days.

My first day, my Boxman (supervisor at the Craps table) saved me from drifting into a "fear coma" by describing, in detail, what to do every time I had to make a move. "Listen to me, Chucky: with your left hand, grab two white chips and with your right, grab one red chip." He walked me through payouts to customers and kept telling me to stand up straight and BREATHE. I ended the night at a local bar with some other "break-ins" (new dealers). We did flaming-shots of 151 rum. It was the start of a new "recreational approach" to life.

Every night offered the chance to let loose and be wild. That was an issue. Within a few months, I was arrested outside Bally's in a case of "being at the wrong place at the wrong time." It didn't matter. They nailed me and did so with quite a few Bally's employees coming down the escalator. Seeing me cuffed and taken away was not good. In fact, it was very bad. So bad that a few days later, a Pit Boss leaned into me while I was dealing and told me to "go find somewhere else to work." He was big and serious, so I took his advice. The very next day, I went to The Sands Casino (about a block away) and applied for a Craps dealer job there.

The young lady in the Sands HR office knew all about my incident and chuckled about it with me. When I thanked her for interviewing me and got up to leave, thinking this chance was lost, she smiled and said, "When can you come in for an audition?" Holy shit, I was in.

Bally's was in my rear-view mirror and the Sands was my new playground. As most the folks who worked there would say, it was a great place to be and you met some of the smartest, strangest, craziest, funniest, horniest, drugiest, riskiest and good-hearted people (to this day) in your life.

"First of all, say yes my man, know what I'm sayin'," my new-found Sands Casino buddy Gerry Florio would tell me. "Life is too short for being a 'mis-i-rab' and saying 'no' to everything. Don't be that guy." Since Gerry was from that far-away mystical place they call South Philly, I knew he was on to something. The Sands was my new home and my life got even crazier...much crazier.

It was awesome.

Introduction

"Sex is everything, Theodore. Period. Whatever is in second place is a pretty distant second. So, I would advise you, don't waste your time looking for love in a woman. Understand? It's only going to age you faster." What the hell kind of advice is that? Mom says that love is the most important thing. This is not Mom's approach.

"Do not look for love, mon amie," Aunt Ginny continued, "madness lies in this pursuit, comprenez vous? L'amour est…fleeting. Love is fleeting. Chercher la vie, eh? Look for LIFE. A woman who has life will bring you more than love. More, even than the world: la galaxie, oui? And all from the comfort of a warm bed."

Aunt Ginny has a way of saying things that get your attention. I think it has a lot to do with her French-Canadian accent slipping into the way she talks. I have to admit, it's pretty sexy. Occasionally she leaves the English language all together. This usually happens when she's trying to emphasize a point or gets past three glasses of wine. That happens often, I understand. Her ex-golf pro husband, Uncle Ralph, has a habit of kissing her on the neck and saying things like, "this is the greatest female on the face of this Earth" and "my Queen, command me." He slaps her butt a lot too. I think they're both a couple of horn balls.

Pop describes it in a much different and not very flattering way. I've heard him call Aunt Ginny the "French Wino Wench." I can't repeat what he calls Uncle Ralph, but I have heard Pop and Uncle Bone make jokes about where he uses his putter and such. Not only can't I repeat it, but I don't even want to think about it.

The fact of the matter is: Aunt Ginny and Uncle Ralph are different than most of the folks in South Jersey and they aren't afraid to make sure everyone knows. If you go to their house unannounced, as we have before, one of them might show up at the door in a robe that's barely closed…at 5:00…in the afternoon. Yikes.

One time, we went with them to dinner at a nice Italian place in Hammonton. They ordered lots of different things on the menu, even asked the waiter to bring smaller portions. Then it got a little weird. Aunt Ginny and Uncle Ralph started feeding each other, even reaching over to grab food off the other's plate and commenting about how "succulent" it was.

Pop leaned over to me and whispered, "Imagine reaching over onto Bone's plate? He'd stab you before your fork got halfway there!"

That made me laugh pretty hard. I told Pop, "Then he'd ask about your food and want a taste. Uncle Bone likes food, huh?" He's the one who taught me that twirly thing, the thing you do with pasta when you scoop it with your fork and spin it around into a big spoon. He showed me saying, "Do this Teddy Boy. This is the MOVE."

Aunt Ginny and Uncle Ralph didn't do that "move" at our dinner. They picked up spaghetti with their hands and dropped it into each other's mouths. The folks around us were staring and making comments. We don't go to dinner with them much anymore. By "much," I mean not at all and Pop says he won't ever go again, and I don't blame him.

Mom stopped joining their eating excursions after an incident last year at Aunt Ginny's friend's restaurant over on the bay in Margate. It was a Florida beach-themed place with waitresses wearing these butt-thong things kinda covered with see-through-ish skirts. They opened on Friday at 2:00 pm with a spring break theme. By 7:30 pm, the cops had to be called and, unfortunately Mom's picture was in the paper. She was trying to leave the madness when a drunk guy grabbed her. Mom threw an elbow and knocked him into the next time zone. The *Shore Times* was there to catch everything...and did. So, no more "dinners" with Aunt Gin and Uncle 'Rally." Actually, there is no more anything with those two right now. They kind of disappeared and Mom and Pop aren't saying much about it. Occasionally, when asked, Mom will answer, "Who knows with those two -- they're out exploring the Milky Way for all I know."

Today, I'm heading to Aunt Ginny and Uncle Ralph's house after finding a mysterious note on my car windshield yesterday afternoon. I opened the envelope and immediately saw a kissy-lip lipstick-signed ending. The note instructed me to be at Aunt Ginny's house at 1:00 pm and emphasized that I should keep the trip a secret. Since I followed the directive, it's just going to be me and the note-writer. Maybe the person will show up to an empty house to kill me and leave my body to be discovered, I consider as I'm driving. On the other hand, it might be the occupants themselves trying to have a meeting without anyone knowing. I have a feeling something is wrong and they're in trouble. If that's the case, I have to be there.

I get out of the car and grab the spare key from the secret back door of the birdhouse on the locust tree at the side of the house and enter. It's quiet but clean. Jazz music drifts through the air but there is no sign of the person that turned it on. I sit down and wait, expecting my aunt and uncle to make a grand entrance of some sort. That would be their style.

About ten minutes tick by when I hear an engine roar in the driveway and begin to pull up to the front door. The engine is revved a few more times and then stops. Footsteps approach the door and, without a knock it opens. In walks a familiar face: one I haven't seen since the Miss Atlantic County Pageant last year. "Hello Jess," I say, a grin on my face from ear-to-ear. "So... it's your kissy-lips on the note, huh?" I look behind her and notice her car. "Wow look at that 'Vette with the pink pinstriping. That's a cute touch. It looks pretty fast -- can we take it for a spin?"

Jessica looks at me and smiles, then tosses the keys in the air for me to catch. "Sure, I was hoping you'd want to," she tells me as she walks over. My God, does she smell wonderful.

"What are you wearing? I mean, what's that perfume? I mean, wow, that's really nice. Is it new?"

"Je Reviens," she tells me with a twinkle in her eye, "I thought you'd like it. It looks like you do."

"It got my attention…I mean, you have my attention. Man, I've never had a perfume do that before. You smell fantastic."

"Thank you, you're very sweet to say that. It means a lot to me." Jessica reaches into her purse, pulls out a book and hands it to me "Teddy," she continues, "read any good books lately?"

Not where my mind was going, but I actually have. "Well, I did just finish *Chariots of the Gods*. Does that count?" I ask as I look down to read the title of the book she handed me. "*Tao, Sensuality, Life. Heightening Your Pleasure*," I read out loud. We lock eyes and start to giggle a bit, enjoying the silliness of what I said.

She takes my hand and laughs a bit harder. "Sure, but I think you'll like this better." We stand there holding hands for a bit, our giggles slowly fading as we continue to look at each other. It is as if, any second now, one of us is going to spring toward the other. It's like the tension, the unreal electrical surge that comes over you when you are in the starting blocks for a 100-yard dash. The starting pistol sounds, you explode out of the blocks and everything becomes a blur. No drug...nothing can match it. It's the greatest feeling in the world. I know it's not love that I am feeling so it must be "life." It's what Aunt Ginny spoke about. She is absolutely right.

"So, is this foreplay?" I ask Jessica as I hold the book up and smile. I can feel my breathing getting slightly heavy. She steps closer to me, takes the book from my hand and tosses it on the floor beside her next to the purse she dropped.

"No, this is one-play." She walks over to the table that Aunt Ginny keeps wine on, pours out two glasses, returns to me and points to the couch. "Sit," she tells me. I do and she directs me to the center where I take my place, making sure not to spill any of the bright red wine. I'm betting this couch is way too expensive for stains. I'm an upholsterer's son: I know these things. Jessica holds her wine glass high, slides onto my lap, then slowly slides off to my left and into a comfortable position. "Be a good boy and take my heels off, will you?" I oblige, asking her if her feet hurt from wearing them. "Not at all, I just like watching you do things for me, that's all," she tells me.

My mind quickly surmises that, depending on how you're keeping score, there's either two more "plays" or three more moves to go. We hit "two" in mere moments. We clink glasses and take a drink. I'm almost tempted to guzzle down the wine to speed up this play section but quickly realize that would be, well, pretty stupid. Jessica moves her feet back and forth in a playful way as if she's thinking about silly things and funny little stories. It makes me chuckle a bit. She is playing this very cool and smiling at me like she knows something that I don't. I'm pretty sure that is the case.

"So, Teddy, tell me, what have you been up to since I last saw you? Anything exciting or interesting? Any secrets you can share?" I look down as I think about my "secrets" and quickly realize how uncomfortable they make me feel right now. I'm not sure what to say. Jessica continues, "Aha, a reaction. So, he is not wearing armor after all but, I knew that already. That's ok, neither am I and I can prove it. Hold my glass." She swings her legs up off mine and stands up, facing away from me. Reaching behind her, Jessica unhooks the lower middle of her dress. It quickly drops away and leaves her completely naked. Holy shit, that was fast and my "play counter" just broke.

Again, she slides onto my lap and then off to my left. "Glass," she commands. I hand it to her and she grins. "Armor is not necessary with me...ever. Shed your armor Teddy, it won't serve you. Let go. Just let go, and you will feel better. Does that make sense?"

"Well sure, but it does bring up a question."

"What's that," Jessica asks, looking a bit puzzled.

"Is this still two-play?"

She smiles. "It is until you take your clothes off, then we proceed from there. You'll like that part because that's when I use the stuff that's in the book I gave you. How's that sound?"

It's not something I have to think through for long. I stand up and undress about as fast as I can without falling down or bumping into something that would leave a bruise later. "Wow," Jessica says as she watches me, "if I didn't know better, I'd think you were wearing some sort of jumpsuit with your clothes all attached. It's coming off in a blur. Do you get dressed the same way?"

"Huh?"

"Teddy, slow down before you pull a groin. That would be most unfortunate."

I slow down but the damn right pant leg is stuck on my...oh shit...my right Puma is still on. I kicked off the left one without batting an eyelash, but somehow figured I could finesse things from there. Not quite.

"Ok," Jessica directs, a slight giggle in her voice, "sit next to me. Right here. Sit down. Let's fix this." I sit to her right and point my right leg at her. She unties the sneaker, pulls it off, then my sock and finally, the pant leg. I peel off my underwear and toss them far away.

"Freedom," I yell, both arms in the air.

We both laugh and Jessica repositions so she's sitting up against the opposite arm of the couch. She pats her upper chest, as if to point out where she wants me to lay my head. I slowly take my directed position. "Page 17," she tells me.

"Page 17?"

"Yes, page 17. Lovers should slow down and appreciate the moment. With that comes pages 21-22: talk, communicate. Start the process of feeling physical pleasure by allowing your mind to feel it first. You can talk to me and tell me anything. I mean, I love talking because I know it builds comfort, trust and even anticipation which is very important. So, you can tell me anything and it will always be just ours. Nobody else will get to hear it, ever. I promise. If you killed somebody, you could tell me although, I'm pretty sure we're not going to be talking about anything like that. I guess I should probably ask though: have you killed somebody?" Jessica gives a slight giggle as she says the words. I know she's simply making conversation to keep things interesting and light. I slide closer to her face, wanting to see her eyes as we continue to speak.

I'm not fully sure why, but I feel the need to say what is inside that has been eating at me all this time. I'm safe here and with her. It just makes sense. "What if I said yes?" I ask her. "I mean, what if I have killed someone? It sounds good to say we can talk about anything but if it's about someone being killed, that changes everything, don't you think? Doesn't that make it all different?"

She leans into me and kisses me slowly on the lips, holding my face with both her hands. As she pulls away, she gives me a slight smile. "Well, if I had to kill someone, I'd want them to be bad because enough good people die every day. It seems as though the bad ones have a habit of sticking around too long. You know, like a cold. So, if you did kill someone, I'd hope that they were a bad person and you just helped make the world a better place. Does that make sense?"

"It does." We kiss again. This time, it goes on a bit longer and we start to fade into each other. I know it's time to get off this couch and find more room. Anywhere. The floor will work.

Just before we begin to roll sideways toward our landing spot, Jessica stops me, and with a puzzled look on her face asks, "So, have you killed a bad guy?"

"Why don't we save that for the pillow talk?" I whisper.

This elicits a look of puzzlement, then a huge smile as she gives me a play slap on my face and begins to laugh, shaking her head from side to side. "Pillow talk? Teddy, how do you know about pillow talk? Just what are you reading besides *Chariots of the Gods*, huh?"

"As the youngest of eight in a pretty small house, I eventually figured stuff out over the years. What can I say? They've done most of the talking and I've done most of the listening." We complete the roll and onto the floor we go. Thank God. She has me wrapped in an intoxicating moment with her touch, her perfume and her voice. All of it. The thought of killing drifts far away as I become consumed by the power charging through both of us. This probably isn't love, it's simply a moment that we've found together.

Chapter 1

"Boobs. They're called boobs. Does that help?" I look up and into the eyes of the young lady with a slight Irish accent (I think it's Irish anyway) mucking cheques across from me. I'm pretty confused by what she just said. "These," she continues, "on the front of my upper body: boobs. I thought you'd like to know what they're called, since you keep staring at them. I'm just trying to be helpful here."

"Wait, what? Huh? I'm not, uh staring at your boobs. I don't...do that. I mean, I'm just mucking big chests. I mean...big chests...CHEQUES...like you are, that's all. That's it. I swear. I'm not staring at your big um...boobs." Yes, I am. She's wearing an open white button-up shirt with some sort of tank top underneath that says "The Philly Connection." I like it.

Luca leans into us and whispers, "Hey you two, Mr. Stav maniac-guy is gonna come back and hear you talking and we're all going to get our asses reamed, understand? What's the issue?"

Jesus Christ - it's day one of craps school and I'm already in a situation. There's only 30 minutes left to go in a class that's had me picking up and stacking different colored chips in piles of twenty. It's called "mucking cheques." She thinks I'm staring at her boobs. How the hell does this stuff happen to me? And now, Miss "staring at my boobs-redhead" is standing straight up, looking at me with a smile on her face and pointing as she speaks to both Luca and me.

"He owes me an apology," she tells Luca. "He's staring at my boobs. I want an apology and I want it now." Jesus Christ - I wasn't even looking at her and now she's making a scene. If the teacher, Pete Stavros, comes back and catches wind of any of this bullshit, that maniac will kick my ass out of class. Done. Finished. What the hell is going on with this girl?

Luca tries to calm the situation. "Ok...ok, listen. What's your name?"

"It's Margaret Shanahan. What's yours?"

"I'm Luca and this is…"

"I don't care what his name is. I want an apology. That's it. YOU apologize," she says with fire, looking directly into my eyes.

Luca puts his arm around me and whispers, "Just apologize and it will all be forgotten, ok? I know that you didn't do anything, but this crazy broad thinks you did. Let me handle it and follow my lead on this. I'll get you out of it. Just do as I say, capeesh?"

"Sure...whatever shuts her up."

Luca leans toward Margaret and says to her, "Ok Red, my friend here didn't mean to stare at those big tits of yours, okay? He can't help himself. He likes big tits. He's going to say that he's sorry. Will that work?" Oh no, thanks Luca. It isn't bad enough that she's pissed off at me for something I didn't even do. She demanded an apology and he's talking to her like she's some sort of floozy. We just went from bad to worse. She's going to punch him and slap me. Shit, how did it get to this point?

"That's fine. I want my apology. Give my boobs an apology. Since you stared at them, it's only fair you apologize to them," she tells me, calmly. My God, you have got to be kidding me with this bullshit. It feels like somebody just drove me to bizarro land. She's got me looking like Jack the Ripper and Luca is suddenly the charming UN negotiator. What the hell is going on?

"Ok, ok. I'm...VERY...sorry."

"No. Look at them and apologize."

I look at her chest and tell, um them, "I'm very sorry." This is a first. Ironically, it could also be a last. I mean, how often are you asked to apologize to body parts?

"AHA, you WERE staring at them, otherwise you wouldn't have apologized. I knew it." With that, she moves away from us to the end of the table, puts her head down and begins to muck cheques with another group.

"Luca what the hell just happened? Are you fucking kidding me? Is she psycho or am I going crazy?"

"Shh...take it easy. Give her a chance to cool off and when class is over, we'll revisit this. I promise you everything is going to be fine. Just trust me on this. You gotta trust me, understand?"

"Oh sure, Mr. 'He Can't Help Himself' and 'He Likes Big Tits.' Why the hell would you say something like that?"

"Like I said, don't worry about it. It'll all get solved after class." I return to mucking and keep my head down the rest of the time. Stav talks to us briefly when the half hour is up and dismisses us.

Luca approaches me. "Wait here for two minutes until everybody leaves then, come on out. She'll be gone by then. No chance of her stabbing you, know what I mean?" That's his plan? There is no resolution, just avoid her because she might be carrying a weapon. What the fuck?

I wait for a few minutes, walk down the stairs and out into the street to find Luca with his arm around Margaret. Both of them are laughing their asses off, practically howling, and wiping tears from their faces. Holy shit. Son-of-a-bitch: they got me. I don't know who she is but it's pretty obvious that she's in on this.

"Surprise! Look at your face. You came out thinking some big-boob crazy redhead was going to slash your throat, or even worse. That's fucking funny."

I walk up to them with my arms out, shrugging my shoulders and shaking my head back and forth. "Seriously, what the fuck is wrong with you two? Who is this?"

Luca takes care of the introductions. "Margaret Shanahan, meet my good friend Teddy Damian. Teddy, this is Margaret."

"Nice to meet you Margaret. You do this often?"

"Nope, it was Luca's idea. All I had to do was play along. It wasn't too hard. You're very sweet and I was told you're a good sport. Sorry about all this."

Luca found out that another buddy's ex-wife was going to take the same class we had signed up for. One thing led to the next: Luca and Margaret decided to pull a stunt on me. Like I said – they got me.

"Really Teddy, sorry about that. How can I make it up to you?" That's a good question. I'm not really sure I need her to do anything but maybe prove to me that she really doesn't have any weapons. "I'll tell you what, how about we go down to McShay's and have a few? I'll buy the first round. How's that?"

"Deal. Let's do it." We head to New York Avenue, just off the boardwalk, to Atlantic City's most famous Irish pub and restaurant. Across the street is Chez Eiffel: the hottest dance club in all of New Jersey, so I've been told. As we pull up, I ask Luca about it.

"That used to be a gay bar," Luca explains. "You're on New York Avenue, Teddy. This is the gay part of town, my man. Should we leave you here so you can roam around?"

"It's not just a gay bar, fellas. It's a disco," Margaret chimes in. "Everybody goes there: gay, straight, old, young. It's got a little bit of everything. Someday you should go check it out."

"Sure, right after I finish running the circuit of all the 'straight places.' Do they play Zappa or Zeppelin in there?" Disco isn't really my thing."

"It's not mine either but let me tell you, that is a party-place every night of the week. I like it there. You might like it too, Teddy." No way. There is not a chance in hell I'm going to a disco. Disco sucks: plain and simple.

We go into Mc Shay's. Margaret seems to know the few people there. It's smiles and introductions all around. She winks at the bartender and says, "Liam, set us up: three Guinness with Bushmills' back."

"Sure thing, Freckles. Good to see you, Lass." Freckles? I didn't notice that many freckles. Oh well, the drinks have been ordered, so I am happy.

We drink and laugh through a few rounds. Why not? Margaret tells me that she has worked at the bar for over 5 years: this place is like her second home. Maybe that was part of the problem in her marriage.

"I'm a bit friendly but that isn't a bad thing," she tells us. "Sean just wasn't a people person. When we first came to Philadelphia from Ireland, we were at the bars a lot getting drunk which led to an argument and sometimes, a fight. It got old and so did we. It happens. I moved down to the Shore to get away from all of that, you know? I do love it here, and now, I see that the real money will be out on that casino floor and I want in."

"Sure. I mean, I guess so. We're all gonna find out one way or the other, aren't we?"

Luca heads to the bathroom and Liam delivers yet another round for the table. This place is starting to grow on me.

"Hey, what's with the t-shirt? What's 'The Philly Connection?"

"A friend of mine has a boat and takes high-rollers out on fishing trips around here. He calls me 'eye-candy,' but I know my way around a boat. I did a bit of fishin' with my da' back home when I was a wee lass. I like the ocean. How about you?"

"It's great to look at and cool off in. After that, there's that shark thing...and sinking. I can't imagine anything worse than sinking and then having a shark attack you. Awful."

This elicits a laugh from Margaret. "Well, that would be an awful day. Good thing that doesn't happen a lot, huh? Hey, how about a toast?"

I hesitate for a second, "Shouldn't we wait for Luca? He hates missing out on these types of things."

"Nah, he'll be fine. C'mon now: drink a toast with me." We pick up our shot glasses and she asks, "What shall we drink to?"

I think for a moment, then come up with something. "My birthday! It's not for another week, but…"

Margaret cuts me off. "No, here's to big surprises," she tells me as she throws back her shot before I get a chance to move my hand from the table. I grab my shot, throw my head back and hear her glass slam onto the table. With a fast head snap back down, I go to slam my glass and realize she's showing me her "big surprises."

Wow...now I see why they call her "Freckles."

Chapter 2

It is 5 o'clock and Uncle Bone and Luca pull up in the Maverick. As usual, something comes with them: a tradition with the Bonparente men. Not every time, but more times than not, they like to bring a little something or other to add to the visit. They are very good at telling a story to go with whatever they have with them. One time, Uncle Bone brought a roll of toilet paper and tried to convince my dad that it was imported from Italy. He claimed it was much better than anything we had because small fibers of Egyptian cotton had been added to it. The discussion went on for hours. The punch line for the whole thing came when Uncle Bone told Pop, "There's only one way to find out how extra special soft it is. Go on, I'll wait. I'll bet you a buck it's the greatest you ever tried."

"You're on." Pop told him as he went inside and upstairs. Bone's serious face turned to a smile. He did the "shh" sign with his finger telling us, "I don't feel like stopping at the package goods place." With that, he snuck around the side of the house, got into his car and drove away with one of Pop's six packs of Schmidt's. Zing. He worked hard for that one, but the prize was much more than the buck he bet. The man is just funny - that's all there is to it. I wonder what they have today.

"Hey, Teddy, 'il duo dinamico e qui, eh?"

"Yep, you two sure are a dynamic pair. Where are your capes and masks?"

"We didn't bring them today. We do have a nice wine, though. Your Mom will like that. It's not that California swill either. It's where God himself planted the grapes with his own bare hands."

"What's God doing working in France?" I ask. I thought he was too busy for stuff like that."

"Italy, smart ass. He passes over the French, know what I'm saying? He stops once in a while, but I think that's just when it's 'wrath time.' There's not enough of that to give to them if you ask me." I take the wine and Uncle Bone heads out to the shop to visit with Pop. Luca and I head to the kitchen.

"I see in the papers they're talking about Johnny C leaving Bixby's, huh? They wait a whole week to say something. How's Lisa doing?"

"I don't know. I left messages and got one call back three days ago. She told me that they all need time with it."

"Yeah, tough break, man. It'll work out, Teddy - I'm sure it will."

"Well, she and I aren't exactly married you know, we just...."

"Yeah, you're just fun friends. I got all that. Whatever spices your meatballs, my friend. So, you wanna talk dice?"

"Yeah ok, let's do it," I tell Luca with a shake of my head. "Are you getting what Stav is yelling...I mean, telling us? Do you have your stuff memorized yet? Just when I think I do, I don't and it's fuckin' driving me crazy. How long is this shit gonna take, Gumba? This ain't like real math, am I right?"

"Yeah, it is a little weird. You got that felt, right? Lay it out and let's go over it." Most people learning to deal Craps do exactly what their instructors tell them to do: go out and buy at-home practice stuff. I bought a 'half felt' (half a Craps table -- the area directly in front of the dealer) and got some chips. Luca and I go up to my room. I have everything laid out on a nice little table Pop helped me throw together with some two by fours and plywood. It works.

"Ok, let's start from the top." As I pick up some chips to move them, Luca knocks them over with all the rest.

"If you want to start from the top, then we muck. That's most of the class, don't you think? That is all Stav likes to do, make us muck chips, curse and yell. I've never been called a monkey...ever. He does that and more. Remember when he first called you a 'fuckin stupid animal that's no better than a monkey to any gambler?' Christ, he said 'you're just a monkey so act like a monkey, dummy-up and deal.' He's not exactly charming, you know. He's just another one of those Nevada assholes, if you ask me. I'm getting tired of being a fuckin' mucker. I want to be a dealer." I have to agree with Luca. It seems like we spend more time doing shit work and listening to Stav bad mouth us than anything else.

Stav is an asshole and seems to revel in that fact. Is it really as bad as he says it is inside the casino? Will people be yelling and spitting at us while we try to do our jobs? Am I gonna get punched?

For now, we muck the chips into stacks of twenty and begin to practice our drop-cuts. I take a stack and drop two chips, then three, then four and then five, restack the whole thing and start again using both hands. My right hand is stronger than my left, yet my cuts are more accurate with the left. It's weird. Luca, well, he's just got a long way to go with both hands.

"Are you practicing?" I ask him.

"I am now. I'll get it eventually. This shit is hard." I have to agree with him. We keep working on it though because without a good or even decent touch, we won't be worth shit on the tables. As for odds and payoffs, I'm doing ok. I started out trying to understand the philosophy aspect of it (since Stav likes to teach it that way) and switched over to simple math. That makes it much easier for me. There are thirty-six possible combinations when two regular dice are rolled. The number seven is king of the combination roll with six ways the dice can hit. Numbers six and eight have five ways. Five and nine have four ways. Four and ten have three ways. The longer shots are three and eleven (two ways) and finally, two and twelve (one way). Everything revolves around these facts so understanding them sets everything else up. The bottom line is this: knowing the probabilities helps you understand the flow. In turn, that helps you understand the entire table lay-out. We have a lot more work to do before we really understand it all. I'm just glad I'm starting to get the basics.

We muck and compare notes for a while longer until we hear the call from Pop, "Boys, when are you heading to school?"

We head downstairs and Uncle Bone asks, "You two working on your dice game up there?"

"We're just getting a little practice time in before tonight," I answer. "You know, get the hands loose so that class goes well. Stav doesn't like it when you look clumsy. He said we should be practicing with coins to strengthen our fingers: silver dollars, quarters and such. He calls it the 'old Vegas Way.'"

"Sounds like he knows what he's talking about," Bone tells us.

We check the time and decide to head to the school early to get some practice in at the full-sized tables. We fly out the door and fire up...er...start up... the Maverick. This car is definitely underwhelming. I think Luca took it over from his Mom because he got punished or something. I can't imagine he chose it.

"Why did you get this thing again?" I ask as we start down the street.

"Don't start with me, Damian. You can always get out and walk. My Mom wanted a Cougar and rather than trade this baby in, it made sense for it to be my first car. That's it. If I take care of it, who knows? Maybe I score a Capri or a Mustang. Hey, a guy just has to play his cards right and see. That's what I'm doing with this whole thing, my man. Smile and say thank you and take care of what they give me. I'm counting my blessings and praying for more. That's the move on this right here." Luca's plan actually sounds good. He's not stupid - far from it. It's just fun telling him he drives a pussy car without actually saying it.

"It's still a pussy car." Whoops...I guess I did say it after all.

"I like my pussy car, I'm not gonna lie." We laugh and push each other on the shoulder, knowing we like busting each other's balls a bit here and there. I'm glad he's got the car.

We head over to Atlantic City and Casino Dealer Pros School by Mediterranean Avenue and North Kentucky. Parking sucks so any sort of early arrival just makes sense. Plus, we can spend some time together without Stav yelling at us and getting all worked up. Luca turns off Albany Avenue and heads north into the city.

"Hey Ted listen, I'm really hungry. How about we pop into Coletto's over by White House Subs and get a slice and a Coke, know what I mean? Quick in and out, easy peasy."

"Sure, that sounds good."

"Perfect we'll eat, and you can pound two Cokes to get the caffeine in your blood and get you pumped up a bit"

"Yep. I'm not a coffee guy, but Coke does it every time."

Ahh…Coletto's Pizzeria: a little jewel that serves up the thin crust stuff. I do like to chew a thicker crust but when a place does the crust thin and it crunches just right, it's worth it. Coletto's has been doing it for over fifty years. It's a nice place. The building is an old, converted house just off Mississippi so seating isn't great and, of course, neither is parking. They've painted it all white, added some black metal handrails going up the stairs and once you get inside, the smaller round tables have the red and white checkered tablecloths on them. They're plastic but they clean easier which just makes sense. We order our slices and Cokes and don't waste time eating, as is the tradition when eating a meal with a Bonparente. No exceptions. With our food gone and bellies full, it's off to class we go. Soon, the Maverick is placed in a tight spot-on Kentucky. Jesus -- parking here is just no fun at all.

"We're going to have the place all to ourselves. It'll be good to practice, right?" Luca asks as we head to the front door.

"Sure-thing Paissan, next time use some deodorant though. Working in close quarters with you is a bitch."

Luca smirks at me and fakes like he's going to backhand slap me. "Better my B.O. then the French whore toilet-water that you're wearing." We go in and up the stairs to the sound of cheques being mucked. What the hell? We get to the top of the stairs and, sure enough, pretty much everybody from our class is already there, bent over and mucking like it's a race. Shit, they look like they've been practicing.

"Where the fuck have you two been?" Pete Stavros yells at us like we're delivering his pizza late.

"Stav - we're an hour early. I mean, I'm pretty sure we're early, aren't we?"

Stav walks toward us shaking his head with a disgusted look on his face. I feel like I'm about to get sent to the principal's office or some shit like that. I can see Margaret smiling behind him doing that 'throat slash' move. I wish she wouldn't do it so gleefully. "You guys pay a grand each to learn something that took me twenty-five years to master: to figure out how not to trip over my dick and screw customers over while handling their money. And, if I did it right, I might get eye contact. It certainly didn't guarantee me any tips. Now geniuses, you have ten weeks left to figure out if you've got what it takes to step on the casino floor and handle the firing-squad they point at you every fucking night. You get me? Every...fucking...night," he says, pointing his fingers into Luca's shoulder. "You'll have good guys who lose and go crazy. You'll get assholes that treat you like shit for eight hours on a table. You got con men and scam artists looking to take you down. The casino puts YOU in charge to make sure that they don't 'get it on.' You got horny old broads distracting you because they just want to screw you. All that does is mess you up. Should I go on? Why the fuck are you here? Are you looking to take the easy way into a world that will fuck you over in a minute? Huh? You think this is a little kid's game? Is that what you think? You're both fucking wrong...dead wrong. Get your head out of your ass and understand that getting here on time means getting here early. No exceptions. I clearly said on the first day that I give extra time every day. Ninety minutes before your paid time, those doors are open. So, here's the deal: you guys stroll into my class one more time like you just did and I'm kicking you out. Go fucking learn how to deal Bingo, for all I care. Now, shut the fuck up and muck cheques."

Mr. Personality just destroyed us in front of the rest of the class. I'm not sure if I want my money or my ass back but he certainly made his point. I'm going to muck cheques. First, I head to the bathroom because I did drink a lot of Coke.

When I return, Luca has a spot next to him for me. I bend over the table and begin to muck cheques. I'm not going to lie - I hate this shit. Bending over strains my back. I doubt you need to do this for two hours straight when you're dealing. It feels more like Stav is making us pay physical dues for the short time we are with him: as if he intends to cram twenty-five years of his misery into our twelve weeks. Enjoy! I wonder if all those years of cigar and cigarette smoke mixed with watching gorgeous cocktail waitresses walk by that he had no shot with finally got to him. Like many of these Nevada guys, he traveled East so he could act like a big shot.

Stav is a Steubenville, Ohio Greek American. (I am told there are lots of those there.) He moved to Vegas when he was 16. His co-teacher is from the same place, a guy named Mik Timopolous. Mik teaches all the card games. I understand that Mik only curses every 9th word so he would be an improvement over Stav - not much though. I have no interest in cards. I decided my form of abuse would come at the hands of a maniacal craps teacher. What can I say? I'm a glutton for punishment.

"Let me fucking tell you something, all right? A fucking monkey could deal this game, understand? A monkey. That's just a dummy with a fucking tail. So, dummy up and deal. Don't think. Just muck the fucking cheques and be a monkey," he tells the class. "I have to go see a man about a horse. Don't burn the place down. It will only take me a few minutes. Keep mucking."

Thank God he left the room. Maybe some oxygen will return, and we can catch our breath. Stav is wearing me out with his Greek tough guy "you all suck" act. One thousand bucks for this bullshit. I'm looking forward to graduation night when he takes us all out for drinks and gives us the old, "Hey – I was just busting your balls, being tough with you guys to make you better dealers," speech. "I am not really an asshole. I just act that way every minute of the day." I bet that happens.

I tell this to Luca, and it cracks him up. "Five bucks says you're wrong," he tells me. "Guys like him don't act for shit, my man. Not a chance. This guy has seen some interesting times in his life. I'm thinking a lot of that stuff took place before he even got to Vegas, know what I'm saying? This guy is real -- he's not playing around. He could give two shits about you, me or anybody else in this room, know what I'm saying? I heard that he's got a big job waiting for him. As soon as Penthouse opens up, he's going to be running the show. Piss ants like you and me ain't got a shot to get a job with him when that happens if we keep fucking up, standing out like two sore thumbs and looking like we don't care. I seriously doubt we're gonna have drinks with him. When we're done here, he probably tells the whole class 'good luck' as he sits behind his desk, so he doesn't have to shake hands. This guy is all business. I'll take that bet. You sure you want to make it?"

"Yep, I'm sticking by what I said," I tell him. Inside, I'm slapping myself. That was stupid. The only reason I'm not backing out is because I'm hoping that I'm right not because what I said makes sense anymore. Luca is right: this guy is all business. We're certainly going to find out soon enough, aren't we? Or, as Stav might say "ten fucking weeks to go, monkeys." Ten weeks.

Chapter 3

After class last night, Luca and I headed to Geraghty's Bar in Somers Point. We decided raw clams would hit the spot.

"Try this." Our bartender, Greg Garrison (a fellow Mainland High graduate), decided to ply us with the latest new liquor samples his distributor provided that afternoon. So, last night we did a mixture of Tequilas. The last was called Mezcal. It was smokey and strong. I liked it. "Nobody else has this stuff right now," Greg confided. "You guys are the first to try it."

I did my usual routine: a glass of water for every booze drink. I pretty much doubled the water because who knows what the Mezcal will do to you later? You've got to water-up to keep the hang-over chances to a minimum. That's the move.

We also got paid a brief visit by a charter member of the "Bushman" - MRHS class of '79, Roy Foles. This guy has a story that can make the papers (he has made the papers...still does) and he and I are cool. It's him and Steve Scrafari who I get along with -- the rest of the Bushman Boys aren't exactly on my Christmas mailing list, but that's ok -- every cheesesteak isn't a good cheesesteak, some have ketchup and some have marinara sauce. Life goes on.

Roy walks by us with two stunningly foxy disco-chicks on his arms and has a grin from ear-to-ear. I feel like bowing to him because, well, this ain't no disco. Far from it. Roy just seems to dance to his own tune.

As he walks by, he whispers, "I just bought the place - come by more often," and winks as he pats me on the shoulder. He points at Greg behind the bar and does that finger whirl thing that indicates "this is on me" and tells him, "His money is no good here." George just rolls his eyes as he walks up to us.

"All drinks are free tonight, but the tips are double -- dip in, Damian, ok? I'm building my college fund. Get it started."

Luca laughs as Roy walks by. "That guy is the KING!"

"Prince. He's known as the Prince of this town"

"What? I don't care if he's the Duchess of Yorkshire, he's ok in my book. You guys pretty close?"

I take a sip of my Mezcal and tell him a story that's pretty famous at Mainland High. "New kid comes in from Nevada...you know...casino hot-shot's kid and he's fuckin' mouthy and disrespectful to pretty much everyone he's bumping into. He's trying to act too cool and it's getting old pretty fast, especially with me because somehow, someway, he found out that Coach Wingate liked to call me "Headcase" and decided he was gonna use that on me when we had a little disagreement in Algebra class one day.

It came out of nowhere, too. He leans over during a test and says "Hey, Headcase, breathe through your nose, not your mouth. You're fuckin' bothering me." As I went to say something back, Roy leaned in and asked what was going on, and I told him that this guy wanted to borrow an eraser, so Roy gave him his, and the guy says 'that's mighty white of you.' Wrong thing to say." Luca smiles, understanding how stupid that little saying is, but he asks about it anyway.

"Why is that?."

"Well, Roy is half Polyneesian, and considering how much shit he has gone through in his life over his parent's ugly divorce, that's a pretty fucked up thing to say."

"This guy is an asshole, for sure. You fight him after school or what?"

"Well, hold on, it got worse. When the substitute teacher asked what was going on, Mr. Cool decided to point at me and say, "He's talking to me and I'm trying to concentrate on my test. I got talked to, but I was allowed to continue on."

"Ok, so you beat him up later, or what?"

"Kinda, because remember I told you about Belhaven Ave School 7th grade, when I ratted out Chrissie Nommo for talking to me in English Class during a test...man I didn't like her at all...and then our school Bully Charlie Saricuzzo found out and challenged me to a fight? Remember that?"

"Yeah, I do. You wouldn't fight him -- told him you wouldn't meet him after school to fight, so he found you at lunch time in the cafeteria and punched you in the crotch! Took you down in front of hundreds! You both got suspended! That's funny right there!"

I wince a bit and decide Mezcal will ease my momentary feeling of discomfort down below. It can't hurt. "Real funny. Anyway...Algebra class ended. I held back a bit, not walking near him. The moment we got out of the classroom, I made a bee-line to him and quick-jump at him, grabbing his shirt and ripping it over his head. I punched him so many times, our class geek Daniel Ridgetown took the time to tally-up, and then report the massacre totals to me later.

"11 punches to his crotch. 3 to his head. 5 to his chest."

We tried to stuff him into Carol Kennedy's open locker and then Roy began to slam it on his head. By the time it was all done, we all got three days suspension and he transferred to Holy Spirit High. Jimmy Boswell was waiting for him with the info I fed him, so he didn't last long there, either. I hear he went back to Vegas to live with his sister. Good riddance."

"So...why so many punches below the belt, huh? That does seem a bit excessive, Pasiano, know what I'm saying?"

"You're damn right it was excessive, and it didn't have to be either. He laid out his little insult game, so a fight was gonna happen in the hallway or outside at some point, because I wasn't having this asshole come in and piss all over my existence, ok? Not happening -- can't have that shit and I suspect he's been bullying kids for a long time, so ..."

"You decided to punch a bully in the nose, huh? Is that it? Well that makes sense, but why did you 'go south' on him? Why not draw some blood and ruin his shirt, huh? That usually does the trick. A bloody nose tells the story, as far as I'm concerned. Enough blood and that's all the 'talkin' that's needed. Am I right?"

"You're right, but this guy is also a rat...a big fuckin' rat...and Charlie Saricuzzo taught me a valuable lesson that day a long time ago, and I didn't forget it. Rats get punched in the pants -- plain and simple. That's how it is. You punch a rat below the belt."

This conversation went back and forth for some time, and the drinks kept flowing. I agreed with Luca that the only reason I'm a pretty good fighter is because I'm usually pretty angry when I'm throwing fists and it helps me handle whatever is being thrown at me. Smiling and 'putting up dukes' like some half-assed gentleman will get me beat every time, so fighting for the fun of it will never be my best approach. If I feel the hate, I got a chance. On this night, I saw Roy and that always brings smiles. No hate here.

So, it's 7:47am. I am in bed with my alarm blaring and my head telling me that the water-up move kinda worked...but not completely. I kill the alarm and drift back into a quiet slumber.

A couple of hours later, I am woken by the sound of the front door opening as someone comes into the house. I roll over to put the pillow over my head as the phone adds to the cacophony.

"Teddy...phone!" Mom has her loud "Mom voice" working this morning. It's one of the "standard accessories" for that side of the parenting team. It seems like she never gets a sore throat or tries to yell quietly. Why is that? And why does she include details that shouldn't be shared with the general public (like folks three blocks away)?

One time, I got the "what are you eating, your underwear is a mess" shout-up as she sorted through the laundry. Unfortunately, this prompted me to return the shout and make things worse. I said something about how a "maid" should not be allowed to shout at me. Man, that was the WRONG thing to say...loudly... with the windows open. Sometimes, you end up inflicting your own wounds and you just learn the hard way.

This time, I'm going to play it cool and won't be shouting back any wise-ass comment. I learned my lesson. Whenever Mom does anything for me now, it is met with a big "thanks Mom" and a smile in my voice. Since the underwear disaster, it has been self-preservation. That day, Mom threw all my underwear into the garbage without a word to me about it. Whoops... A drawer without underwear is like Sunday without avoiding church. It's just not normal stuff for me.

"TEDDY," the voice sounds even louder. "For cripes sake, "ANSWER THE PHONE!"

"Sorry Mom." Quick afterthought. "THANKS!"

"How many times do I have to yell at you? Geeesh."

"I'm getting it now. Who is it, anyway?" Shit. I broke one of the basic rules of phone etiquette in our home. You only get to ask that question if you answered back in a timely fashion because the other person is in a just-answered-the-phone rhythm. Do things differently and you open yourself up to getting yelled at. Surprisingly, Mom keeps a civil tone and lets me know the info I seek. I slide by this time.

"It's a Mr. Smith from the HR Department at Bixby's -- he says he's following up on your interview. HURRY UP!" I hear her shuffling up the steps. Now I'm gonna get the look that says "get-a-move-on Mister!" I hate that look.

"Hey, move it! He is obviously calling you about a job. That's what you want, isn't it? Here you go!" Considering how awake I'm not at this moment, it's gonna be pretty hard to fake the excitement that she's looking for. I have to set expectations a bit lower for her. At least I'll try.

"Ok, but he might just be checking a few things on my application. No problem, let's see what he wants." Mom turns and picks up the upstairs receiver and hands it to me, all smiles like I just told her my 'wife' is pregnant with triplets. Back downstairs she goes. Thank God. I put the phone to my ear. "Hello, this is Ted."

"Well hello, Ted. It's Bob Smith from Bixby Casino Human Resources. How are you doing today?" says a husky voice from the other end.

"I'm fine Mr. Smith." I know I have not met Mr. Smith but I'm sure I have heard his voice before. Either that or he just has "one of those voices." I don't quite know. I'm not fully awake yet.

"Mr. Damian, we must have a bad connection. I hear a lot of static in the background, like pots and pans and things like that. Do you hear it also?" he asks.

"Yep, I'll take care of it!" I yell down to Mom to hang up the phone. After a few seconds, I hear the telltale 'click' of a receiver being placed back in the cradle.

"Ah, much better. I wouldn't want our private conversation interrupted. What I have to say is particularly important. I need to get to the point and be brief. Do you understand?"

Wow, I do now. The voice is one I last heard about a week ago during my interview. It's Agent Quaylz. "Let me get right to the point, you'll be asked about all of this, I'm sure. We are asking you to come in for a standard drug test for the job you've applied for next Wednesday at 10:30AM. We feel you are one of several good candidates for an open position and, although we don't have an exact start date, it could happen anytime within thirty days."

"Ok, I'll just shout down to my Mom now so that she knows I 'kinda' got a job. That will ease her concerns. You couldn't just call and say I got the job, huh?" It's quiet for several seconds. I am betting my smarmy response didn't go over well.

Agent Quaylz continues, "Mr. Damian, we've already covered a lot of ground with you. I'm doing this follow-up because I need to meet with you soon. I've given you everything you need to move forward. I suggest you cooperate on this. Am I clear?"

"Oh sure, clear as mud. Ok, we'll meet. Tell me what's next."

"Very good. Arrive at Bixby's and go to the same receptionist that you saw before. Tell her that you are there for a drug test. She'll be expecting you. Understand?"

"Yep, I understand. Ten-thirty at Bixby's. I got it."

Agent Quaylz continues, "Good. Tell your Mom that Mr. Smith enjoyed speaking with her and that I'm looking forward to seeing you next Wednesday,"

"Sure, I can do that."

"Very good. See you then."

Click.

Chapter 4

I am ready to return to the place where I went through the strangest interview ever. Actually, it really wasn't an interview at all: it was a recruitment. This "hunting" they told me about must be big. They want me in for good reasons - reasons that they tell me I'll find out "later." Before we go any further, I must tell them I'm ready. Today is just a standard HR process: pee in a cup. I can do that.

"Mom, seriously, what's the best thing to wear for this. It isn't an interview. I might sit down and talk with somebody, but I don't think so. He just said to come in for the drug test." I know I can't wear shorts and a Phillies t-shirt looking like I ran all the way there. I imagine some guys show up dripping with sweat and looking nervous. I'm not going to do that either. Besides, this casino is a big place with lots of chicks running around. I'll be damned if I'm going to walk in the building looking like a damp rag. That is definitely not the move.

"Wear powder honey."

"What?"

"I said to wear powder so that you don't show up dripping wet. You don't want that." Mom might not be a mind reader, but she is smart. Powder it is. I'm glad I don't have to wear a suit. Nothing is worse than a sweaty suit-wearing guy, begging for a job. Not only will there be no suit, there won't be any begging.

I head downstairs to the refrigerator. I'm pretty sure I saw a can of *Fresca*. Occasionally, Nana will come by and put a few in our fridge for her and mom. On visits, they'll both crack a can. They used to drink Tab, but Nana switched over to Fresca. That made everyone happy. Tab was never anyone's favorite. On a hot day, Fresca over ice is just about right. It still doesn't beat Coca-Cola, but it's a close second.

I grab the refrigerator door, slide it open and find the usual suspects occupying the inside shelves. You got your Wawa lunch meat, leftovers from last night's chili con carne, a bowl containing some of mom's famous tuna fish with pickle relish and hard-boiled egg (that's her secret recipe), and a couple of bottles of Schmidt's Beer. I put my hand in, reach way back to the back to find that, lo and behold, mom repopulated the refrigerator with cans of Tab. What the hell. "Mom, are you drinking Tab again? What happened to Fresca? I thought you switched over to Fresca full time. I don't drink Tab."

I hear a small chuckle and then from the stairway, "I know you don't honey so now I have a cold soda waiting for me when I want one. I suggest you tra-la-la yourself over to Cumberland Farms and get a Coca-Cola. How do you like them apples?" I don't like them apples at all. It would appear that Mom is trying out some of Pop's tactics when it comes to keeping the kids away from certain food items. It's like sardines. Pop knows I like them, so he hides them in his shop. Mom loves to make her special tuna recipe, but

Pop and I won't eat that. If I want a good tuna fish sandwich, I have to go to Lawton's Deli and pay for it. Nothing about this whole situation seems right. I'm being squeezed out here by these parental moves. They're smart.

"Okay Mom, I see what you guys are doing. That's fine. I'll just go to Hanks to grab a Coca-Cola and Hershey Bar. I can bring one back for you but by the time I get here, it will be all melted and everything. Of course, you can always stick it in the freezer, and it will be good as new. You just won't be able to read the word *Hershey* on it anymore. It will be like it was in a hobo's pocket and got dropped on the ground."

Mom smiles and waves her hand at me. "Theodore Joseph Damian, don't you have a doctor's appointment to get to? You seem to be wasting a lot of time young man."

"Test Mom...TEST...not appointment. There is a big difference."

Mom giggles and gives me a slap on the upper butt. "Test, appointment. Fletcher, Feltcher...whatever. The point is it's time for you to go. Good luck, honey!"

Yeah, good luck to me. I remember when I did the interview for my paper route. I was so nervous that day, I stayed in the bathroom for an hour. My sisters were really mad and pounded on the door to let me know. If Pop hadn't intervened, they would have broken it down.

The easiest job to get so far was with Lou V. I was over at Dori's house watching a Flyers game with him one night. During a commercial, he turned to me and said, "Teddy, stop being a bum.

Come work with me. I will make sure you get paid cash and I'll buy lunch once in a while. All you gotta do is do what I tell you. Capeesh?"

"Uhhh…yeah Lou V, that sounds cool. Will it be hard?" I asked.

"Yes and no. You will get to do construction and learn from some pretty good guys. We all watch out for each other. You get to work outside and we're always busy. If you want, you could even do some work on the weekend and make a little extra cash? It's a good deal."

I thought about it for a while. It did seem like a pretty good opportunity. Why would I not want to do it? "It sounds great, Lou. What's the downside? There is always a downside, right?" I remember how hard Lou V laughed when I asked the question, because he laughed for a long time. It was like I just told a great joke. "What's so funny?"

"Well Teddy, it's like this. You got your normal human beings like me and you. You know, we eat, sleep and use the bathroom correctly. Then you got your different class of people. We call them roofers. They are completely different from you and me. I could tell you that they're crazy but that would only be the half of it. I don't have much control over them, because they've got their own world. You just have to understand because then it becomes really simple. Stay away from roofers…period." The look in his eyes told me that I better listen to what he was saying. I kind of did.

Then I met this girl and trouble started. I guess I should have paid better attention to her when she told me. "Well, my ex-boyfriend's a little crazy but we're not going to see him any time soon. He's doing six months for petty theft." What she didn't tell me was that his six months was up in a week and that he was coming back to continue working as…a roofer. All I can say is that after our fourth shot, she seemed like the right girl for me. You know what they say: live and learn. I'm still alive.

Off I go to Hanks for the coveted Coca-Cola. I'll skip the Hershey bar for now because the last thing I need is to show up with chocolate all over. As I pull up in front of the store, I hear a loud whistle. "Teddy Damian, just where the hell did you get a gorgeous car like that? Holy shit, are you a doctor or something?" I turn to see a familiar face: Mr. Baez. He was one of the customers on my paper route. We used to talk a lot and tell each other jokes. He's a good family man and liked by all the neighbors. My favorite thing about him is his sense of humor. Mr. Baez always has a smile and something funny to say. He would crack me up almost every time I saw him. He always ended our little conversations with the same phrase: "Viva Puerto Rico!" Mr. Baez is an immensely proud man with a great management job at Prudential. "Not bad for a Puerto Rican, huh?" he would ask with a wink and chuckle. He received his business degree from Glassboro State College and liked to tell me how important it was to focus on my schooling to better myself.

I used to get a kick out of how Mr. Baez taught his kids to call me Mr. Teddy. "Luis, Mr. Teddy is here. Come kick the bad man in the shins." Sure enough, his son would come running out giggling and screaming. "Yay, we get to kick him. Sophia, Poppy says we can kick Mr. Teddy!" What a good man: raising his kids with love and humor. I respected him the first day I met him. His wife died in a car accident in Puerto Rico about five years ago. He mentions her almost every time I see him. I think part of his heart went with her, but he still makes the effort to make other people smile. It is almost as if he lives life for that purpose.

"Ok Teddy, spill the beans. You got a $100 bill tree growing in your backyard? Somebody stole mine. Did you take it? I'm looking at this car thinking yep, it's him." Mr. Baez slaps me on the shoulder and gives out a big laugh. "How the heck are you? My God what are your Mom and Pop feeding you, huh? You are all grown up!"

"Actually Mr. B, Mom and Pop have incorporated a new system to help me move out of the house sooner. These days they're hiding food. Just the other day I came down for dinner and Mom said, 'Do you want warm water or cold water with your stale bread?' All I get is bread and water. It's awful. I think we need some Puerto Rican influence in our house to improve our food. Things have gotten really tough!"

"My wife used to say, 'You don't eat, you don't walk. You don't walk, you don't work. No work, no money. You know what that means!' So, against my better judgment I ate all of the delicious food she made for me. I still haven't lost the weight." We talk a bit more about our families. I tell him the story of how I got the car, keeping the private stuff to myself. I don't think Mrs. Milchzek wants me blabbing our business to everybody so I try to keep it simple.

"She needed to get rid of the car because she wasn't using it anymore. She talked to my folks and Pop made some sort of deal. That means I owe my folks now! I'm looking for a steadier job."

As we talk, we walk inside the store and say our hellos to Hank. I grab my drink, pay Hank and head toward the door. "You should come over to the house sometime soon, Mr. B., so we can chat about baseball." We both love baseball.

"Ok Teddy, we'll see each other real soon. Probably not right after my Mets sweep your Phillies in New York this weekend! I'll give you some time to lick your wounds first." We both have a good laugh as I go out the door.

I climb back into the GTO and do my new favorite thing -- I peel out. It's pretty cool because the car jumps. You can't do that on a bicycle! I arrive at Shore Road, make a left and see another familiar face. This one doesn't look very good. It's Jake Goff, one of the richer kids in Linwood. He is sitting on a bench at a bus stop. With traffic coming up behind me, I can't pull over to talk to him, so I beep and give him a wave to see if he recognizes me. I don't think he does because he just… flips me the finger? Why the hell did he do that? Maybe he didn't see that it was me. I didn't know him well in high school, but we got along all right.

He used to talk about his Pop a lot. He hated that man. Jake's family runs Walton Flowers. Their greenhouses are situated at the back of their house alongside the end of the golf course. So, hanging out at his house meant we'd sneak onto the course all the time. We didn't do anything bad, but we knew we were breaking the rules and that felt pretty cool. If we were caught, we would get yelled at and told to get off the course. No big deal. When we hung out inside of his house, Jake's mom would offer us fresh chocolate chip cookies and her special iced sweet tea. That tea was ULTRA-sweet. I'm used to my mom's tea which is always hot with a little sugar. Big difference. Anyway, I don't know what's going on, but Jake just flipped me the bird. Oh well, maybe I'll catch up with him sometime soon to see why. For now, it's off to Atlantic City and my drug test at Bixby's.

Hmmm. I could go down to Pleasantville and jump on the Atlantic City Expressway. That way, I can open her up a bit maybe, get to 75, and hear that cool rumbling sound the engine makes. I dig that. Then again, I could also score a big fat speeding ticket. The hell with that. I'll just shoot across the Margate Blvd. Causeway. I'll cruise Margate and Ventnor to get to Atlantic City. There shouldn't be much traffic and since it's 9:35, I've got lots of time.

I'm a little nervous. Even though it's just a drug test, it does start the process again and I'm really not sure what the hell I'm going to be doing. I'm a bit in the dark. I haven't told anybody about what is really going on, because I can't. This sucks.

I find a parking spot on South Ohio Street close to Pacific Avenue. Wow, now that's what I call luck! There's so much construction going on here that most of the spots are either taken up or blocked off. This town is growing quickly. It could become bigger than Las Vegas. It would make sense: it's got an ocean and lots of people live close enough to drive here. How can it miss? I think it's a sure thing.

I walk up to the security entrance. No Carrie this time -- just some guy named Bruce. "Hello, my name is Ted Damian. I'm here for a drug test. Can you tell me where I go?"

Bruce shuffles through some papers and then tells me, "Yes, I have your name right here Mr. Damian. Security officer Devens will escort you. Come to the door." He pushes a button and a buzzer sounds. He points to the door as if to tell me to open it. I walk into the building to find another man waiting for me. He must be Devens. Together, we follow the now familiar path up to the floor where Endzone's office is. "Right through those doors. They are expecting you. Good luck."

I push open the big oak door on the right and see my old friend: "Not Barbara."

"Hi. I'm back for a drug test." "Not Barbara" smiles at me and stands up from her chair with several pieces of paper in her hand.

"I've been told to give this to you. Please take a seat and read it. I have to leave for a moment. Can I get you anything?"

I think for a moment. Would it be too much to ask for a Coke? There is something I do want. "I'd like to know your name. I think it would be rude if I called you 'not Barbara' all the time. I was raised better than that."

"Mr. Damian, I've come to realize that many men want to know my name. It's flattering. You can call me Jane."

"Ok, what's your last name?"

"Well, if you must know, it's White. Now that's all the time I have for questions." Jane turns and leaves the room. I get the funny feeling that's not her name. She's a little mysterious.

Oh well. I unfold the paperwork and see a note with instructions on it. "Meet me here at 11:30." The note is signed "Mr. Smith." I unfold the other piece of paper. To my great surprise, I see that I am supposed to meet Mr. Smith at the Brigantine Castle. Brigantine Castle? I'm going to take a drug test there? I don't think so. This is getting weird. Since my friend with a fake name isn't anywhere to be found, it's time to get going.

As I stand, Jane returns. "Mr. Damian, would you please follow me? We're going to have you exit this way." We walk down the hall to a set of stairs that lead onto the boardwalk. As I walk through the door and turn to say goodbye, I face a shut door with no knob.

So much for being a little nervous about a drug test. I shake my head. Nothing ventured, nothing gained. I return to the GTO, jump in and peel out for my meeting with Mr. Smith.

Chapter 5

The view driving over the Brigantine Bridge is gorgeous. Absecon Channel is back to the left with the Absecon Inlet and Atlantic Ocean to the right. I've heard Pop and others talk about fishing these waters up into Great Bay to the North where it connects with the Mullica River. It is so beautiful and peaceful to me. South Jersey is a special place for those who see and appreciate the various areas: The Pine Barrens just above the Mullica are another great example. My brother Jerry would take me with him on ice skating trips to the frozen cranberry bogs around the Pine Barrens. I skated a bit until I broke through some thin ice one day. That was that. I never wanted to put on a pair of skates again. Who would?

I look out onto the ocean. It seems to go on forever. I don't spend much time on the ocean. After you experience sea sickness, you never forget it. That's my excuse for not wanting to go out. Plus, I have heard about sharks and think it is best to avoid them as well. If I'm in a boat, I tend to stick to the back bays and the simple choppy waters. The fishing is easy, and you see land and the beach. The beach is where it all happens. I am usually in Longport or Ocean City. The first one is pretty calm. The second one is pretty hectic. I need both choices.

Coming over to Brigantine doesn't happen very often for me. It's a bit far away to just 'hop over to.' Pop reminisces about coming to the Seahorse Pier years ago to fish and hang out with some buddies. As he puts it, "grabbing a dime beer and shooting the shit." The pier was eaten up a few times by storms and eventually went away forever. The town lost one of its main tourist attractions. At the same time, seemingly billions of Greenheads, the scourge of the flying bug world, began to use the local marsh area as their breeding ground tainting everyone's perception of the city. "Greenhead City" is what Mom calls it, so it stuck for me.

Construction of the Castle was a pretty good idea. Since they first opened in 1976, a lot of people have been coming to Brigantine. It would have been fun to drive over for a little relaxation. Unfortunately, that is not going to be the case today.

I have a mystery meeting with a mystery man. On the plus side, since I'm not sweating, Mom helped me pick out the right clothes for whatever I'm about to walk into.

I pull up to the corner of 14th and Brigantine Avenue. There it is: the famous Brigantine Castle. It's pretty cool looking. I hope we're not going into the haunted section to have our meeting today. That would make today's events even stranger than they already are.

I pull the GTO into the parking lot and park right next to an AMC Pacer car. This one is red, just like all the others I've seen driving around. It's ugly. The owner of this particular one attempted to look cool by adorning the car with pinstriping. You've got to be kidding me. My car looks even better next to this clown car. Yuck. I can't lock my doors fast enough to get away. It feels like bad luck just being around it.

I walk across the street and up onto the entrance, wondering exactly where Mr. Smith is hiding himself. Maybe he grabbed a snow-cone? I mean it is a hot day. As I look to my right, a man wearing dark sunglasses and a Phillies hat approaches me. Sure enough, it's 'Mr. Smith' or, as I now think of him, Agent Quaylz.

"Ahh, hello Mr. Damian. Thank you for meeting with me today. I felt it would be a good idea to get out of that office setting, catch some fresh air and have a good discussion about what might be. Does that sound ok?" He's been steering this ship the whole time, so I can't see how I can really say no. I mean, I am here, and I do want to find out exactly what the hell is going on.

"Agent Quaylz…" Just as I begin my sentence, he puts his right hand up to stop me.

"Let's go with Bob for now. Please, just call me Bob. Also, when I speak about company business, that's what I'll call it: the company."

"Ok Bob, you got it. Here I am, all ready for my drug test. Imagine my surprise when your Jane...Smith handed me the information that told me I'd be coming here." I continued, "I'm right to assume that there's no doctor's office here or some sort of clinic with a nurse waiting for me. Is that right?"

"Bingo. I have no interest in drug testing you. That's just a waste of time. We have better things to do, and I couldn't think of a better place to do it than out here. I understand you're a pretty good mini golfer. Is that right?"

"Yep, I actually play both right-handed and left-handed and don't change clubs. It's something I learned from my brother. He used to hustle me for quarters playing on the Ocean City boardwalk, so I can handle any course. Are you telling me you're up for a game?"

"Sure, why don't we go play as we can talk about things. I think it would be a good idea. I'm not very pleased with the way we left things last time we were together. I want to apologize to you. I know we threw a lot at you pretty quickly. I want you to understand something: we weren't trying to pressure you." Agent Quaylz looks me directly in the eyes. "That was not my intent, and I know it's not Endzone's. So why don't we head up, get a game going and have a chat. I have some things I would like to share with you, and I have some questions as well. I know you've got some questions you would like to ask me. How does that sound?"

"Well Bob, I do love mini-golf so that's fine. Let's go play. This might be interesting."

We head up to the golf area and pay. I'm about to play 18 holes with a CIA agent who has yet to tell me what exactly he wants me to do for him. I'm surprisingly calm about it. "Put these on." Agent Quaylz hands me a pair of dark sunglasses. "It's just good practice when you're out in public," he explains.

"Do you always wear those glasses and your Phillies hat when you have these kinds of meetings?"

"It depends. We are in Phillies country so I'm wearing a Phillies hat. To tell you the truth, if it was up to me, I'd be wearing a Cubs hat. You can call this a disguise." That has me chuckling inside. Some disguise.

We finish the fifth hole and I'm up by one stroke. This is a fun little course. I like the tilted berms on the sides. You have to hit the ball up, have it curve, then drop the ball down a straight line toward a hole. It takes skill. I can tell that Agent Quaylz is an avid golfer because of the way he grips the club and follows through on his putt. He is smooth and consistent.

"I need your help. You have a basic idea of what we do but it's time I gave you more specifics so that you can make a solid decision going forward. That's only fair, don't you think?"

"I do. I'd really like to know what this is all about -- all of it."

With nobody behind us for three holes, we take a seat on a small bench and put our putters down to continue the conversation.

"It's pretty simple really: a little sad but still, quite simple." Agent Quaylz takes a breath, as if readying himself for what he is about to say. "A long time ago, our government got into the nasty business of training elite assassins. They were pure killers: dozens and dozens of them. Men who went beyond the normal level of violence for any conflict. They committed heinous acts in the name of Uncle Sam in locations around the world. It was done in secrecy and with the complete approval from the highest levels in Washington. You might say that they were considered a 'necessary evil,' especially given the fact that other world players were doing the very same thing."

"Evil, you mean like the Nazis?" I ask. "I can't imagine anything worse than those sons-a-bitches. Those guys lived to destroy other humans and got pretty good at it. You mean like that?"

"The Nazis were driven to destroy because they considered themselves a superior race. Therefore, they determined it was justified to wipe out those they considered 'substandard.' They were evil, but not necessary."

"And the guys you are talking about, the 'necessary evil guys,' are they still um, 'working'?"

"Excellent question," Quaylz tells me, as if approving a student's response. "As the years have gone by, the need for their 'talents' was greatly reduced. That meant the men had to be assimilated back into society because, let's face it, they would not fit in stateside...not even close. We needed a way to help them, to condition their minds away from the work they performed. That, my friend, was easier said than done."

"So," I hesitate, thinking that I might not want to know the answer to my next question. "Are these the monsters that you told me about because, if they are then, holy shit, this is a goddamn nightmare. So, are they the monsters?"

Quaylz stands up and nods for me to follow as he strolls toward the back of the course where the view of the ocean is wide and picturesque. As he leans against the railing, he takes a deep breath.

"You're on the right track but wrong train," he tells me. "So, let me explain things a little more for you. The easiest way is to say that Schumaker was definitely one of these monsters, but he was in the minority. Actually, he was an anomaly. Out of the many men who received treatment and conditioning, only a handful didn't respond at an acceptable level. The rest did better."

"That's good to hear," I tell him, feeling myself relax slightly. "And this conditioning stuff...what does that mean? What kind of conditioning? What was done to them?"

"An entire program was developed just for them. The men were brought to several facilities across the Delaware Valley and put through vigorous shock treatment and LSD mind enhancement therapy. This was followed by months of daily meditation sessions. The theory was that this approach would bring successful change. In essence, it worked. Most of the men were able to function at a calmer and somewhat peaceful level. Not every one of them mind you, but enough that the research was transferred to another area of focus, or should I say another group of men...different men."

"This is where the monsters come in, am I right? So, who are they?"

Quaylz turns to me and nods his head as he prepares to speak, then stops. He turns again toward the ocean and stares out at it, glancing from side to side as he does, catching the attention of a seagull as he moves his empty hand to grasp the railing.

"This is where things went sideways...real sideways. Sure, it all started with good and focused intentions. The ends truly justified the means, as far as I'm concerned but, the best laid plans of mice and men ..."

"Go sideways sometimes?"

"Yep exactly, sideways. In this case, worse than sideways. You see, the entire project, this new secret entity, needed a subject: a new group to apply the method to. The group had to present a challenge because the methods were pretty intense...pretty extreme. The project couldn't be used on a group of cigarette addicts who were trying to quit."

"So, not smokers. I got it...makes sense. This would be just a bit extreme for those people. Effective maybe but extreme. Ok, so who then?"

"They chose the worst members of society, in my opinion: men who sexually assault children. In some cases, men who were particularly violent when doing it. They found the worst of the worst for the project."

"Christ, they actually recruited the monsters? You gotta be fuckin' kidding me. Did they double the treatment? After all, if it didn't work, maybe it would have eliminated some of those pieces of shit. Tell me they killed off a few of the bastards in the process. That would be justice, in my book."

Quaylz walks back toward the bench, picks up his putter and motions for me to do the same. "C'mon, there's nobody around. Let's play on and talk. It's safe."

We walk to the next tee. Quaylz places his ball on the turf and lines up his putt. There are four penguins to navigate around and a sign that says, "Nome, this way." He laughs as he looks back at me, pointing to the penguins. "Funny, huh?"

I don't get it. "Penguins? Yeah, I guess so. The whole tuxedo thing and the waddling is pretty cute, according to my Mom. You know..."

"No, not that.," Quaylz tells me, shaking his head. "The sign, Ted. The sign says 'Nome' which is in Alaska, not too far from the Arctic Circle."

"So, penguins never visit Nome?" I ask him. "I'm sure they can't read but wouldn't they just use instinct to get there? That's nature, right?"

"Hardly because they never visit the Arctic. That's a long way from home for them. Basically, penguins are southern birds. You find them in the Antarctic and the southern waters that surround that area of the world. The sign is misleading."

The irony of taking something away from where it belongs is not lost on me. I look down and slowly shake my head. "There's always the zoo. They seem to live alright in a zoo."

"Until the zoo runs out of money, right? Then what?" Quaylz strokes smoothly and his ball navigates our nattily attired friends, ending up a foot from the hole. Great shot. "And there's where I come in," he continues. "You see, the zoo well, it did run out of money Ted. All secret funding was pulled from this project, ending it shortly after it started. About 75 men were brought into the area. They were provided with housing and new identities. Some of the men's' sentences were commuted with the understanding that, as long as they participated and 'passed' the program, they would be free with monthly monitoring."

I place my ball on the turf and putt, striking the third penguin who ironically has the most animated face of the bunch, seemingly joining in on the entire bizarre turn of our conversation. He's mocking us or, maybe just me. I'm not sure. "So, if the program ended where did the guys go? They couldn't just let them all go free, could they? Did they put them back in jail? Did they get back their old identities? What happened?"

A note of disgust enters Quaylz's voice. "There's no other way to say it. It doesn't make much sense but here it is anyway: they were given a free pass, each and every one of them. Just like that, the program dissolved without a trace. Some of the 'keepers of the files and information' have disappeared or are with the dead and dying. It's a crime without a criminal."

"Just like that?" I ask.

"Just like that," Quaylz tells me, the disgust apparent. "It would have stayed that way if things had remained calm and peaceful, especially in this region. Everything was fine for about 3 years but then, activity picked up. Bodies have begun to turn up and sooner or later, outside attention will be placed on them. Eventually, the truth will get exposed. That's not what anyone wants: not even close. It would be a disaster beyond what it already is: almost nuclear. That can't happen."

"So, what happens when you find these guys?" I ask, trying to sound casual. "You probably can't reason with them, so what, do you move them to Alcatraz Island or hell, Antarctica? What happens?"

Qualylz stands over his putter and eyes up the shot. He steps back, looks at me, gives me a slight smile and bends over to pick up his ball. "You go outside the rules," he tells me. "Although, quite frankly, there are none. At least none that have been discussed, written down or agreed to. So, I'm ruling this next shot as a gimmee. I'm picking up the ball and putting myself down for a score of 2. You see? I simply eliminated it and moved on. I saw an issue and eliminated it. Understand?"

"So, you're killing them."

"Well...that's a bit too of a statement so the answer is no. We have a major challenge on our hands: a difficult issue. Since not much thought was applied when the problem was created, I plan to handle it accordingly. I am focused on elimination: it is as simple as that. Having said that, the actions I take will demand intricate planning and coordination. Trust me when I tell you that a lot of time will be spent on risk assessment as we move forward. I want the highest odds possible when it comes to achieving the elimination goals." Quaylz stops talking and looks me directly in the eyes for several seconds, as if trying to read my thoughts. Finally, he continues. "There it is for you. Is that clear enough?"

"Sure, clear as mud, "I tell him. "But I get the overall gist. They...go away"

He looks relieved. I understand. It seems to have taken a lot out of him to tell me the first time. "Good," he tells me. "I'm working off the books on this. As I've told you before, I'm in the process of forming a new team and want you on it. That's all I can tell you right now. Take the next few days to consider what I've told you, then get back to me. By now, I'm sure you understand how contacting me works. Use those channels."

Quaylz motions for me to walk with him. I look back at the penguins and wonder for a moment about them living in a zoo and then, suddenly being released. What's the worst that could happen? On the other hand, the men we're talking about aren't penguins...not even close.

"This is where we part, Mr. Damian, " Quaylz tells me as he reaches to shake my hand. "Call me soon. Let me know if you are in or out, understood?"

"Sure," I tell him with a nod of my head, "but I have a quick question. Just a small one."

Quaylz turns to face me, looking side to side as he does. "Shoot."

"What if my decision is no? What if I don't want in?"

Quaylz chuckles at the question. As he looks at me, I see a sort of twinkle appear in his eyes, as if he sees into another time. He steps closer and puts his right hand on my left shoulder, patting it as he does. "I've been in your shoes before Ted. I'll tell you what a wise old man told me when I had to choose."

"I'd love to hear it," I tell him, secretly praying that it will help.

"Ok, here it is.: Let's just burn that bridge when we get to it, ok?"

I give him a puzzled look. "Don't you mean cross?"

"I do," he tells me. "But YOU mean burn -- two entirely different things. Think about it." He turns to go and then stops and looks back. "I'll look forward to hearing whether you'll be crossing or burning."

As Quaylz heads toward the parking lot, I stroll toward the back railing and look out over the Atlantic Ocean. It breaks and crashes onto the beach, scattering a couple who were holding hands and not paying attention. "Bridges," I say to myself. Hmm...how ironic. I crossed a few as I traveled to this very spot. The thought of them burning down makes me think about how I would have gotten here.

Silly thoughts. As the image of flames shoots through my head, I begin to chuckle a bit until...shit. I know what Quaylz was saying to me. I'm surprised that I didn't understand it at the time. It's really not complicated at all.

Join Quaylz and all will be fine. Say 'no' and the bridge I burn is the one that leads to a number of things, including Endzone. Shit.

I spend the next twenty minutes going through my options. My instincts lead to the same answer each time. As I reach into my pocket to pull out some change, I walk to the pay phone by the entrance and place the call I know that I need to make. He's probably not even back to the office just yet.

"Bob Smith's office: can I help you?"

"Hello Jane, it's Ted Damian. Can you take a message for me?"

"Yes, I can, Mr. Damian. What is your message?"

"Tell him I said...crossing."

Chapter 6

"Teddy, TEDDY! PHONE! IT'S LISA!" I spent the late afternoon after my conversation with Agent Quaylz running around to avoid coming home to talk about a drug test I never got. Since I returned, I've been hiding in my room playing a new Zappa record my buddy gave me. I guess she did need to shout this time.

"Thanks Mom," I call down the stairs. "I'll pick it up." It's 7:15 pm. I thought Lisa was working the dinner shift at The Fish Net. Maybe she's calling to let me know that Cappy is moving some choice lobsters out the back door again. Man, that's the deal of the century...every time.

Uncle Bone says that Cappy Green, the head cook, has a deal with the restaurant boss for a side business based on payoffs for winning bets. Cappy is lucky so he scores a lot of cash-making opportunities. It's a sweet deal. Cappy gets his money plus some of the restaurant's choice lobsters. The "traveling product" is written off as spoiled for the owner, Rob Sarinka, which helps him at tax time. I am not exactly sure how, but Uncle Bone tells me it is a "win-win" for everybody. When I asked about the government getting cheated regarding the tax thing, he laughed. "Let me tell you something young Theodore, and I want you to listen very carefully. What I am going to tell you ain't nobody gonna teach you, even in one of those fancy Ivy League schools. Uncle Sam is the biggest taker of them all. He oversees the biggest organized syndicate of all. If he wants money, he prints it. Now, listen to this part carefully," Uncle Bone leaned in closer to me. "When Uncle Sam wants more, he comes for yours. When you don't give enough, he tells you he wants more on top of the original amount. If that doesn't work, he sends people to come after you." I leaned away to look into Uncle Bone's eyes as he continued on, "Uncle Sam has plenty and always wants more. That is just the way it works. Out here in the real world, we have to make do with our basic smarts and our ability to hustle up a buck here and there. Some of us know how to do it well. Uncle Sam doesn't like that because now, we're competing with him. Well, it's a free country." Uncle Bone said with a shrug. "Competition is good because it keeps everyone on their toes. Giving away money like its water is for suckers. Sometimes in life, you gotta figure out how to go get it and take it before Uncle Sam gets it. I'm telling you now, don't worry about no lobsters going out some backdoor, capeesh? It's the way it's been, it's the way it is and it's the way it's always going to be… end of story."

That is what Uncle Bone thinks, and as crazy as it might sound, I know he has a point. It makes sense.

I pick up the phone and hear crying on the other end. "Lisa…Lisa...what's the matter?" She won't stop crying. I don't know what's going on or what to do. "Hey," I say gently into the phone, "I can hear you. I know you are there. What's going on? Why are you crying? Lisa come on, talk to me. What's going on?"

"Teddy," she finally gets out. "I need help. My stepdad…is in trouble. I…I…" Silence. "Lisa?"

"I need to see you!" she yells into the receiver, her voice starting to crack.

"Where are you Lisa?"

The words seem to start spilling out on top of each other. "I'm at work. Can you come now? I need you to come here now! I can't leave and I need your help! I need your help right now, Teddy! You've got to get here!"

"What's going on? What happened? Tell me what is going on? Can you tell me?"

"Oh my God no, not over the phone! Please get here as soon as you can! JUST GET HERE!"

Shit, something bad is going on and she can't even tell me what the hell it is! I better move my ass and get over to the Fish Net as fast as I can. Lisa is a tough Sicilian woman and can handle pretty much anything but hearing her this upset leads me to believe that things are pretty bad. I hang up the phone and start toward my room to change and head out the door.

The phone rings again. Mom starts chatting somebody up like she is on a long-distance Christmas call from a brother or sister. Since she is occupied, I can quickly change my shirt and head out. Good thing because Mom can smell trouble, even if a skunk came through first. Her nose is that good.

I switch my shirt to a cleaner one and try for a quick exit down the stairs. "Teddy. TEDDY! HEY, WAIT! Endzone is on the phone and says it is important. Talk to him. Here." Mom points the phone toward me and smiles like she can't wait to listen in to the conversation.

"Ok, but I have to run up and grab my car keys. I forgot them. I'll take it upstairs." I reply as I frantically make my way away from Mom.

"Ok dear, I'll let him know." Mom replies with a warm smile.

Christ, now what? I fly up the stairs and delay, acting like it's taking me some time to find my car keys (the very ones I had in my hand the whole time…did she notice?) and pick up the phone.

Mom must have heard the click on the line as I hear her say, "Goodbye Arnie. It was great talking with you. Stop by sometime soon, ok? We would love to have a coffee with you and catch up. Here's Teddy. Bye!" Thank goodness, there is the telltale click as Mom hangs up the phone.

What does Endzone want and why now, of all times, does he need to talk with me? I'm not ready for another chat about joining Agent Quaylz and right now, I don't have the time. "Hey, Endzone. How are you?"

"Teddy, is it just us or is your Mom still on the line? I don't want her angelic ears hearing us doing any cursing, you know?" Well played Endzone. That is all Mom would need to hear to "go away." He covered it well, just in case.

"It's just us. What's going on?" I ask.

"I need to cut to the chase here: it's your girlfriend, Lisa. Her dad is an issue right now and it is not good…not good at all. He just got fired and is blasted drunk out of his mind. He is a big problem for everybody here. I have him in my office, and he keeps babbling about you, saying things like, 'In the end, I can only trust that little Teddy bastard. Lisa was right. Lisa was right.' Then he mumbled, 'My friends fucked me over and now all I got is Teddy -- some punk kid my daughter loves. I can only trust him. So, fuck it - I want him to pick me up. If he's good enough for my Lisa, then he's going to have to be good enough for me. Fuck all of you. Get me Mr. Teddy!"

Christ, how the fuck did my world turn upside down? "Endzone, what the hell's going on with this guy? He hates me. What does he want me to do for him? I don't get it."

"Well Teddy, it sounds pretty simple. He won't leave my office until he gets a guarantee that you're going to come pick him up and take him home safely. He says he doesn't like you, but you're the only one he can trust right now. I am telling you, he's very drunk and even more determined. The guys with the power here don't want it to become a bigger scene than it already is. He is screaming that he is going to sue, Teddy. I have to get him out of here without a confrontation with my people. Can you come get him? You are the only one that can do it. If you don't come, I'll have no choice but to have him physically removed. That will be bad. Can you get here and do it now?" Endzone doesn't sound panicked but he doesn't sound calm either.

"I'll come over. There is something going on here too, but I can break free in about 30 minutes. That is the best I can do. Keep him in your office until I get there. I'll pick him up and get him home safe and sound." I reply.

Endzone sounds relieved. "It's a deal. We'll stay right here. I'll try to get some coffee into him. See you when you get here, Teddy. Make it quick."

It just went from bad to worse. Now I have to burst out of the house, fly over to see Lisa and then head over to pick up her dad. My guess is that she knows what I just found out. Man, this is going to be a bad night.

I sprint down the stairs and yell back to Mom, "I have to run. I'm already late. Girls hate that. Bye Mom -- love you!" I take the steps from the front door to the sidewalk in one jump, jam the key into the car door to unlock it, get inside, rev the engine and am on my way in seconds. Please Lord, don't let me get stopped for a speeding ticket.

I'm heading for the Linwood-Somers Point border: about nine minutes away.

Chapter 7

I pull into The Fish Net parking lot on the corner of New Road and Ocean Heights Avenue in record time. Lisa is outside waiting for me. She looks terrible. That's saying something because this woman *always* looks fantastic to me. I stop the car and walk around to her. "Are you ok? Tell me what's going on."

Lisa stares at me with tear-stained eyes. "It's my stepdad Teddy. He just got fired from the job they moved him here to do five months ago. It came out of the blue. Mom says he called her and kept going on and on about being set up. He said people played a dirty trick on him to get him to lose his job. He's drunk and won't leave Bixby's. Mom said the only way he's going to leave is if you come pick him up. It makes no sense to either of us." Lisa throws herself into me. "I'm scared Teddy!" As she buries her face in my shoulder, I hear her trying to make sense of it. "I know he can be mean. He's not a nice man but something's just not right. He has a solid reputation and everyone he has ever worked with trusts him. He is honest. He's tough, but he's honest." Lisa begins to cry again. "Something is wrong. Somebody did something bad to him. Mom is beside herself because he won't let her come over to get him. He's too embarrassed, and probably too drunk, to talk to her in a calm way."

Lisa pulls back and looks me dead in the eyes. "He wants you: not me and not my mom. I am asking you: please get him out of there before something bad happens. Something worse than this."

I place my hands on her shoulders. "Don't worry Lisa. I'll get him and bring him home. I'll take care of it. Can you go to the house to be with your mom, so you are both home when he gets there? Would you be able to do that?" I ask.

"Yes, Cappy said I don't have to stay. He said family is the most important thing. Cappy is a good guy." Lisa pulls me close to her again. "It hurts Teddy, it really hurts. All I know right now is that you're here and it makes me feel like this will be alright." I hold her for a bit more, then loosen my grip and kiss her on her cheek, wiping away her tears. She stares into my eyes as if willing me to stay fixed in one place and move at the same time. "Do this for me, please. Go get him and bring him home to my mom. She needs that and I need it too." Lisa says as she loosens her hold on me.

"I'm going. I'll see you at the house." I turn, jump back into the car and start toward Atlantic City. All I can see is the pain in Lisa's eyes. I want so much to make it go away.

First things first. Right now, I need to do whatever I can to get her dad out of Bixby's and home where he belongs. If he stays at the casino, an already terrible situation will get worse -- much worse. I am going to have to speed through Linwood. Well, maybe not "speed" as much as really pick up my pace. I mean, it is Linwood: tickets come easy here.

As I watch the rearview mirror for headlights, I try to think through how this could have happened to Lisa's dad or "Johnny C" as he's known around town. He was a big deal in Vegas and was offered ridiculous money and the opportunity to be part of the management group if he came to Atlantic City. Johnny C went from being a long-time pit boss at The Star Gazer on the Vegas Strip, to a consultant and then Casino Manager at Bixby's. None of the current events make sense. I don't talk to the man and he doesn't talk to me, but I know enough about him to know that he is one of Bixby's superstars.

Lisa told me her stepdad had been bringing lots of new customers to the casino, mostly "high rollers." It sounded like he has an Asian connection, mostly in the Hong Kong area. The connection was the major reason he rose so quickly through the ranks. Something must have gone terribly wrong. How does a man with so much influence and power end up stinking drunk in the Head of Security's office, refusing to leave and babbling about suing? This is a fucking mess.

I get through Pleasantville and see the sign for the Atlantic City Expressway. Fuck it. I need to push the GTO and hope the cops are busy with the real bad guys. One must have hope.

I merge left in third gear and onto the on ramp at 53 MPH. The engine is screaming at me, so I bang it into fourth as the car rockets down the road. I hit 80 and look up. "Hey, I need this one. Guide me there. I have to have it right now." I step on the gas pedal, hit 90 and realize the car in front of me is slowing down a bit. Shit. I weave right and then left to clear from the slower car and see my speedometer hit 95. The engine sounds like a lion, roaring with power and grace. Damn, it's smooth. I pull back to the right

lane and ease it to 85 as I get closer to Atlantic City. Incredible --
this car is all about speed. I wish I was doing this road test under
better circumstances. In the end, I guess it really doesn't matter. I
need to get there, and I must be fast and safe. Check and well,
"check."

The end of the expressway is straight ahead. Bixby's is close
by. All I can do is hope Johnny C will just get into my car and leave
like he says. I'm doing more than hoping as I keep looking up,
trying to draw in guidance and protection.

I shoot down Michigan Avenue, make a small turn in front of the
parking garage, pull up 50 feet from the valet parking booth, stop
and park. As I exit the car, I hear, "Hey sir, you can't park there.
It's for valet only. Please move your car." Valet guys work for tips.
There is no way they are going to let somebody park a car in front
without the old "palm greasing" move. It doesn't happen.

"Do you have a radio?" I yell back to him. "Radio security and
let Lieutenant Bloome know that Theodore has arrived. He's
expecting me. I'm supposed to leave my car here and go to his
office." The valet guy, Edward, isn't having any of it. Man, this guy
stands out like a sore thumb. He must be 6'4" and 185 pounds. If
there was a poster child for redheads, he would be it. He's got the
freckles and everything. He looks like he's 50 years old.

Edward frowns, laughs at me and shakes his head. "Either you
move the car, or I call for the stand-by tow truck. It will be here in 3
minutes. Put your car into the paid parking garage over there or it
is gone when you come out. Your choice, my friend."

"Edward, let me explain. I'm not here to gamble. I'm not here for dinner. I'm here to pick someone up. I'm running late and we're using my car. If you don't believe me, call Endzone right now."

This gets his attention. He stops in his tracks and throws me a puzzled look. "Wait, Endzone? How do you know to call him that? Nobody here calls him that. I mean, I do but nobody else. Who are you?"

"I'm a…friend. We know each other. I'm Ted Damian."

Edward stares at me, crosses his arms, shakes his head and cracks a small smile. "Get the fuck outta here… No way! Holy shit! I know you! Ok, toss me the keys. You have to get moving but we're gonna catch up real soon. Go."

I have no idea how this guy knows me -- absolutely none. I toss him the keys, jog into the building, turn toward the elevators and push the button for the fourth floor and Endzone's office. Now that I am here, I just have to get my man and get him to the car. Maybe Edward can help when I get Johnny C downstairs. I hope so. I'm betting they are going to turn him over to me and expect us to disappear quickly.

I step out of the elevator as Johnny C appears, stumbling toward me, babbling incoherently and weaving side to side as he walks. He's not alone: I see four security officers behind him, keeping a safe distance but making sure they keep him within their sights. Behind the security guards is Endzone. He waves at me with both hands and motions with his thumb as if to say, "get him out of here." Fuck, what happened? Why the hell isn't Johnny C in

Endzone's office? Jesus Christ, he is an absolute mess. It looks like he has vomit stains on his shirt. This is bad.

Johnny C continues to stumble forward. Finally, he looks up, sees me in front of him and gets a huge smile on his face. I think that's good. I hope that's good.

"Ah, the ever-elusive little boy who likes to play grown-up with my step-daughter." He's a mess and slurring his words. At least he's not angry with me. I take this as a sign that I won't get punched...I hope. "THERE HE IS! Excellent, EXCELLENT! I have great...WAIT...I have GOOD credit here. Yep, now it's just 'good' credit. So, let's get a drink in this shithole and discuss your intentions with our Lisa. HOW DOES THAT SOUND? Let's make this a special occasion!"

This could be rougher than I expected. First, I have to reason with a fuckin' drunk. That never works. On top of it, this particular drunk wants to talk about specifics and be my friend. Oof.

"Switch -- that's what all of this calls for. IT'S SWITCH TIME, TERRY! SWITCH! It's a big-time switch time, you see?" Johnny C asks.

"I think so, but what are we switching?" I reply.

"EVERYTHING! We are switching everything! Don't you see? It is as plain as the bulbous nose on that face of yours, my good man. You see, everything I thought was rock solid and real is all bullshit! It doesn't mean a goddamn thing, you understand. It is all gone - dead. All that work, all those people, and all that money don't mean shit anymore! You can take that to the bank! I can't because I lost it all." Johnny C screams at me.

"You still have your family and that's the most important thing." I reply calmly, trying to figure out how to keep him moving forward to the elevator.

Johnny C puts his arm around my shoulder and pulls me close. Wow, does he smell bad: a combination of alcohol, cigarettes, body odor, and whatever it is that's stained his shirt. It's so bad, I have to put my hand up to my nose.

"Family is great, yep family is just great. Money is better because if you don't have money, you can't do shit for a family. Where I come from, you gotta have money first. Since I just lost the way I make money, I came up with a brilliant idea. Do you want to hear it?" I'm not sure I have a choice. It's going to be a real doozy. Maybe we should sit down for this. Wait, bad idea. If we sit down, he might never get up again.

"I do want to hear it -- I really do. Let's take a walk and get some fresh air. You can tell me all about it then." As I talk, I see Endzone with his hands moving as if trying to push us out the door. What now? My hands are more than full, and Endzone needs me to mime a plan back to him. Here goes nothing.

I point directly at Endzone, give him the hand-to-the-mouth-and-ear sign (phone), point outside and back to me, then make a steering wheel movement with both hands. For all I know, he thinks I'm saying something about being driven crazy. That would be an acceptable answer, but it wouldn't be the correct one. At least, it is not the answer that would work right now.

Endzone signals back, empathically pointing to his watch and outside, followed by two thumbs up. This signal gets repeated even more emphatically. It would appear my not-so-familiar new acquaintance Edward made a call, and our chariot awaits. Time to find out.

"Ok Mr. C, let's go. Like you said, you're getting out of this shithole with me. We can talk and you can tell me your ideas. I brought my GTO. It is better than any piece of shit these people have. We'll ride in a little style. How about that?"

"GTO? Lisa said you drive a VW Bug. Didn't she say you drive a Bug? Or is that her other boyfriend?" Grr. I could just slap him right now.

"Nope, not a Bug. C'mon, let's go see it so I can prove to you that I drive a real man's car. You know, one that can reach the speed limit without going downhill. We'll get you buckled in and rocket the hell out of here." I confidently say as I lead the drunk buffoon to the front door.

"Yes, get me the fuck out of here. I WANT TO TELL YOU SOMETHING VERY IMPORTANT, TERRY." He lowers his voice and leans into me. "We should talk." Great...now he is 0 for 2 on my name. Three strikes and he'll need to do a "tuck-and-roll" at high speeds. Calm down, he's drunk. I am not sure he knows his own name right now. Besides, if they find his body on the road and he can still talk, that will be an issue. Cops must know who they're talking to if they are going to help. I need to cut him some slack. Let's just get the hell out of this place. I think the "good credit" that he is so sure about has closed out. He's persona-non-grata. Uncle Bone taught me that.

"Ok, Johnny, let's get comfortable. Hop in my car over there and we'll talk on the road. You can tell me everything." As we step outside, I see Edward by my car with the passenger door open. Keeping a straight face the whole time, he gives me a wink and a head nod. "Right this way, Mr. C. It's good to see you again."

Johnny looks up, sees Edward and begins to wag his finger at him. As a big smile spreads onto his face, he reaches into his pocket and pulls out his wallet. Wow. "Eddie...Eddie...my new old friend. Parting is such sweet sorrow: it really is. I give you this for your troubles and for your fine work. Spend it wisely." He hands him the wallet, opening it and showing him the wad of bills that are inside. My jaw drops. If my guess is right, there has to be a few thousand inside. Johnny C turns, slowly walks over to the GTO and slides himself into the passenger seat, smooth as can be. Just as smoothly, Edward picks three $100 bills out of the wallet and slides it back into Johnny's pocket without missing a beat.

"We're old pals so a few C-notes will do fine. Shh." Edward is full of surprises. Now is not the time, but sometime soon, I'm going to have a chat with him and find out how he knows me. I still can't place the guy. "Ok," he says to me, "You're up. Get him home safe before these snakes take another shot at him. What went down is pretty fucked up: that's all I can say. It's fucked up." Edwards shrugs his shoulders and points toward the exit. "You better get going, Mr. Damian. It's time for you to do your one good deed for the day."

I think that this good deed might cover me for a week, maybe even a month. Considering what Edward did with the wad of cash,

I'm thinking he's also good for a while. "Yep, time to say goodbye for now. Thanks for your help, man. Much appreciated." I climb in and speed away.

We head for the Atlantic City Expressway and back to the mainland to find peace and safety. I don't know if or when Johnny will make a return. I think he is pretty much done for now. I know I would be.

Chapter 8

"Hey...HEY...listen to me. Listen!" Oh brother, Johnny C doesn't understand that I don't really have a choice here. Wait a minute, maybe he does. Shit...he is really the one in control of this. I'm basically a limo driver. He leans over toward me and says, "I need to tell you something and I need you to pay attention, Terry. It's important that you hear me out on this. Are you listening?"

I'm listening and to tell the truth, I think it's about time he spills the beans on what it is that he wants to tell me. He's the reason I came so I hope there is a good explanation. Great, I'm looking to a drunk for sanity and reasoning. The irony of the situation hits me slowly. That makes me the real idiot in this equation. I begin to chuckle to myself and shake my head as I look slightly down. He got me. He roped me in and made me part of his insanity. How about that? He made a point of it to make sure I knew that he didn't think much of me on multiple occasions. My favorite was when we first met at his house.

"Ah, a local boy, huh? Have you chosen a community college yet or are you just moving to L.A. soon?" I didn't understand the reference, but I did later: not smart enough to go to a "real" university, and dumb enough to run away to what people called "The Land of Fruits and Nuts" (California). That is the Vegas-guy view of South Jersey people. Meanwhile, his type graduate from high school and run to dive casinos to learn how to be a dealer.

They work at that for 10 years, catch a break, and work in a bigger place. Not exactly a bunch of Mensas. He's kind of like me, just older and crusty around the edges. And what do you know? All his hard work brought him to New Jersey and his dream job. As for me: I still might make it to California, so I'll be two-for two when it comes to enjoying an ocean. I win.

Anyway, here we are on the road traveling through Pleasantville. I have about a half hour left with him. What can he possibly want to tell me? It's time to get to the bottom of this and find out just why the hell he chose me.

"Why me, Johnny? Why did you call for me? I think that's a fair question."

"Fair ain't got nothing to do with this: NO-THING. My friends screwed me over just like that." Johnny tries to snap his fingers, but they don't respond to his request. He continues on, "BANG!!! It's all gone so FUCK THEM! You...you haven't screwed me. Funny, huh?" I look over at Johnny and see him shaking his head. "Lisa and I well, we don't exactly see eye-to-eye, and some of her boyfriends..." He looks up and out the front window. "Hell, that stupid husband that was forced onto her by my wife's ex: Jesus Christ, what a fuckin' mess that was. That girl suffered. She's a fighter though, a real fighter. She's fought with me a few times about you. Since all this shit has gone down, it's given me some ideas."

Johnny shifts himself in the seat, stretching his legs and leaning his head back. He is beginning to show signs of fading. His voice is trailing off a bit, and his head is bobbing up and down. The night is beginning to take its toll. It's either that or, like a baby settling down during a car ride, he's settling down.

"So, these ideas: you want to hear them?" Johnny asks.

"Sure Johnny, I do. Shoot."

He starts to mumble something to me. It is almost as if he's whispering. All I can hear is that somebody is a "jerk-off." Great: in his line of work that could be quite a few people I imagine. It sounds like some of them were his friends--not anymore.

He stops talking and stays that way for a while as we drive down the road. I imagine he's sleeping so I leave him alone for a bit. A couple of minutes later, I hear: "I'm resting my eyes and it feels good because I got my eyes burned out today looking at something. Shh, I can't tell you what it was. Shh." Johnny insists.

"Johnny, I'm wondering," I answer in a serious tone, "who's this jerk-off you're talking about? You keep telling me about a 'jerk-off' or 'jerk-offs.' Who are they and why are you telling me this?" I ask.

"EXACTLY! You got it. That's...the...key..." Johnny tells me as he fumbles to put his words together.

This is not going well at all. Johnny wants to share something he thinks is important and I'm all ears but all I hear is slurred words. This is not working. "Ok Johnny, what else do you want to tell me? You started this and I want to hear what you have to say. Now's the time. Tell me the rest."

His head continues to bob, and he starts to mumble to himself. I swerve the car to jolt him. As his head smacks the door, he shouts, "FUCK'! Fly the plane straight, asshole!"

"I am flying straight and I'm going to get you home safe! That's the deal!" I tell him.

Johnny lifts his head and begins to wag his left finger in the air, giving out a big laugh while nodding his head up and down. "BINGO! You got it, or I should say, BLACKJACK! That's the DEAL! You now have it! YOU HAVE IT!" Johnny yells.

"I have what?" I ask.

"WHAT?" Johnny questions.

"What's the deal? You said I have the deal. What deal?" I ask.

"You need to deal yourself in, ok? Just deal yourself in. The team will deal you in. Join the team!" His head drops down. This time, he seems to be out. I reach over and push his shoulder. No reaction, not even a mumble. He is "resting" and probably won't wake back up until we get him back to his home. At least I can focus on my driving in some quiet for a while and try to make sense of this crap. I don't understand a thing about what he made a point to tell me. I wish I could decipher what he is trying to say. It is as foggy as he is right now. Maybe I'll understand later...maybe.

We're deep into Linwood as we turn off of Shore Road and onto West Patcong Avenue. I head down West Avenue and hang a left. At Ross Lane, I make another left toward Lisa's house. I've been here a number of times, either by sneaking in and out of her bedroom window or going through the front door. Each time, we were doing things her Mom didn't approve of. It didn't have anything to do with sex. Lisa's mom put her on birth control years ago and considers herself a "sex-positive "person as she was a wild-child of the sixties herself. No, it didn't have anything to do with the sex. Lisa's mom didn't like the fact that I was dating Lisa's good friend Terra when Lisa and I got together and started our own relationship. Lisa's mom works with Terra's mom at another casino and had to endure the anger.

It isn't like we planned it: it just happened. However, Lisa and I went a little overboard with the time we spent together. We were accused of being "overly-horny" and "completely irresponsible." Whoops.

So, Lisa's mom hated me then and doesn't like me much now. How is it going to work when I pull up to the house with her stinking drunk, now-out-of-a-big-job husband draped over my shoulders? Her husband is NOT a small boy. The man has some weight on his just under six-foot frame: I would guess near two forty. I might need help.

Up the long circular driveway I go, as the front door opens. Lisa and her mom walk out. They both look awful. Lisa's mom is crying and holding her hands to her face. Her hands drop as she seems to weep even harder, her body visibly shaking.

I stop the car in front of the door and take my time, gently talking to Johnny to try to wake him up. "Johnny, we're here. Johnny. we're home. JOHNNY!" That stirs him.

Lisa opens the door. He smiles and speaks to her, "Ah la mia palla di fuocco dal sole, eh?"

Lisa answers back, "Hmmm. Il toro in un negozio di porcellane torna a casa, eh?" and they both giggle.

Lisa's Mom chimes in, "Dio mi porta mio marito in sicurezza. Lodare Dio."

I learned quite a bit of Italian from hanging out with Uncle Bone. As he told me, "You need to speak a little Dago, kid. Learn that Hebe stuff, too." Later on, I discovered that the "Hebe stuff" was Yiddish.

The first stuff was about Lisa being a ray of sun, I think. She said the word "bull" and "porcellane" (china) so "bull-in-a-china-shop" would be about right. Her mom talked about "God, my husband, my door, and God" again. That's an easy one: "Thank God you're home." Italian isn't that hard if you pay attention. Lisa smiles at me and mouths "my hero." She gives her hand to her stepfather and says, "We can do this." I get out of the car and walk around to their side, giving them some room.

Slowly, Johnny gets out of the car and, with an arm around Lisa and her mom, walks toward the house. He seems to have found a second wind, or perhaps it is pride. Either way, he appears stronger. He needs it.

Lisa's mom turns to me as she wipes the tears rolling from her face. She crosses her arms in front of her, walks up to me and nods as she begins to talk, "He told me some things last week. I know everything. When he sobers up from all of this, we will need to talk. Do you understand? Something is wrong…very wrong. He called for you because he knew he could trust you." Lisa's mom hangs her head. "Now, you might be in danger."

Wait, WHAT? He put me in danger? Why the fuck would he do that? Jesus Christ, what the hell did I do to him…besides, of course, being with his stepdaughter? And to think, SHE picked ME up and got all of this started. Hold on…I don't regret that part at all.

"You make sure you come talk to us in a few days. We have a lot to talk about. He might not like it, but he owes you now. I'm going to make sure this gets settled one way or the other. Capeesh or no?" Lisa's mom asks.

"Si, capisco," I reply.

"Good." She returns to the house and closes the door. The family has some healing to do and I need to give them a little time to figure things out. This is going to be a long couple of days for me anyway.

As I get back into my car, I can't help but wonder what kind of danger she believes that Johnny put me in? I'm too tired to figure it out so I'm going to head home where I know I'll be safe…unless I did something wrong. Then, the wrath of Mom and Pop will be on me. Right now, I could use a break.

I turn up West Avenue, pass my old school at Belhaven Avenue and continue down Wabash Avenue past the ballfield. Man, life was so much simpler then. Truth is, it was not as long ago as it seems. How did I get here? I drive past Hank's and think about all the candy I bought there as a little kid. Soon, I'm passing Dee Lumber Woods and remember the great and not-so-great turtle hunts. Being that age and doing those things was incredible – it really was. They were simpler times.

At least, I think that way now. Whatever danger I'm in must be serious for Lisa's Mom to confide in me the way she did. The sooner I find out, the better but it's 9:50 and I've had enough for the day.

I'll hit the couch for a little while. Who knows, maybe I'll stay up for Carson. He's on at 11:30 and I really enjoy his monologues. I could use the laughs.

Things are quiet when I go through the front door, so I grab a Fresca and turn on the TV, watch some news and sure enough, I make it until Carson comes on. Soon after, I head upstairs and I'm out cold.

"Teddy, TEDDY...son wake up. Theodore, honey..." I look up to see Mom looking down at me with red eyes. She looks like she has been crying. I hope I didn't cause this. That would put me on Pop's shit list. Well, deeper on his list.

"Son come downstairs and talk with us. We need to talk with you. Come downstairs!" Pop calls to me.

I feel like I am trying to find my way out of a fog. Things look serious, so I better get myself moving, "I'll be right down! I'll just use the bathroom, ok?" Mom leaves the room as I stretch and let out a loud yawn. I slept like shit and had nightmares about...hmm...being in danger.

Oh yeah...the danger. Could my folks have found out about that? Shit...I need to get downstairs as soon as possible. Something is up and it's not good.

I move quickly. As I look out the window, I see a dark green Ford LTD pull up in front of our house and park. I know that car. What the fuck is Endzone doing here? Oh shit - somehow since last night, this crazy out-of-control thing has gotten...worse? Is this thing spiraling on me? What the fuck?

I get in and out of the bathroom and bound down the stairs wondering what I am walking into? We're moments away from Endzone joining us. "Endzone just pulled up," I call out.

Mom walks over to me, "Honey, come sit in the kitchen with us. We'll get the door."

I head to the kitchen and Pop is on the phone, speaking quietly. Mom greets Endzone at the door as he walks in and shakes my hand. "Teddy, last night was rough and I thank you for coming in and doing that."

This seems a surprise to everyone in the room. Pop hangs up the phone with a puzzled look on his face, "What did he do? What did you do, son?"

Endzone puts his hand on my shoulder and speaks up, "I asked him to come in and help with an issue because he knew the guy we were having a problem with. Quite frankly, the man wouldn't leave unless Teddy picked him up. It was getting out of hand."

"Who? What is going on here, Endzone? Why are you here right now?" Pop asks.

"Frank," Mom sharply shoots at him, "he is always welcome in our home, don't be that way."

Pop looks at Mom. "That's not what I am saying, and you know it." Then, he turns to Endzone. "What is the reason you came to our house like this, like something is going on? Tell us!" Pop says, anger boiling just below the surface.

"Our Casino Manager, Johnny Constantino..." Endzone begins.

"Jesus Christ, him?" This time, his glare turns to me. "Your part-time girlfriend's dad? That guy? What about him?" Pop questions.

Endzone motions to the seats and everyone sits down. "It's a tough story to tell Mr. D, but here it is. Johnny C got fired yesterday and things got out of hand quickly. He was drunk and wouldn't leave the building. I was instructed not to call the police, no matter what. Even with my contacts, I couldn't help. I had to stay with him the whole time." Endzone looks in my direction, "Then, he started asking for Teddy and wouldn't tell us why. I tried everything but he wasn't going to leave until Teddy showed up. I didn't understand why he was asking for Teddy, so I called, talked to Teddy about it, and…"

I interrupt Endzone, "Lisa had already called me, Pop. She asked me to go get him. She was really upset."

"Why didn't SHE or her Mom go get him, son? Are they too busy?" Pop sits back in his chair, "Oh, that's right, the guy you claim hates you needs you to bail him out? What the hell is going on here?" Pop questions.

"They wanted my help. I helped. It was the right thing to do." I explain.

The phone rings and Mom gets up to answer it. I hear, "Hello Nana." She is quiet for a bit and listening intently. Several seconds into the conversation, she looks over at me and begins to stare, "Oh my God, no. Oh no…I better go…"

Pop looks at her. "What now?"

"That was Nana. She heard the sirens down by Belhaven. Something has happened over there. She says she is hearing about a shooting...at a house. She's not sure where..." Mom trails off.

Endzone asks to use the phone, calls the Linwood Police Department and asks to talk to an individual. He speaks for a while, is quiet and listening, then hangs up and turns, "The shooting is at the Constantino house." He looks down and shakes his head. I stand up and feel my body freeze, as I became a statue of ice.

Numbness hits me quickly and Mom reaches over and puts her arms around my upper shoulder. "What...who...what?" I ask frantically.

"Lisa is alive Teddy, but it's not good over there. You can come with me. She's asking for you." Endzone says to me.

Pop blurts out, "WHAT? ENDZONE, what the hell now?"

Mom puts her hand over her mouth, and I hear her say, "No...oh, God no..."

"I'm sorry. Johnny C and his wife are dead. Lisa is alive. The early indication is that she didn't do it. It looks like she tried to prevent what happened and couldn't. I'm heading over there now." Endzone says.

"I'm going," I interrupt.

"Son...no...you..." Pop tries speaking up.

"I'm 19 Pop," I tell him, looking him straight in the eye as I do so. "I can go. I have to go, and you know it."

He waves his hand at me as if to dismiss me, then nods his head. "He's with you, Endzone. Go!"

Mom puts down her head and begins to cry as Pop holds her in his arms. We leave the house and speed down Wabash to Lisa's house.

When we get there, police and paramedics are everywhere, including some from the county and state. There must be at least 20 people on the scene.

Endzone walks up to one of the police officers, speaks briefly and is pointed to the house. He repeats the process at the door, and we are escorted into the kitchen. Lisa is sitting at the table with the front of her clothes covered in blood. I notice some on her face as well. She looks like she was in a bad fight. Her eyes stare forward at something that I can't see.

"Lisa...LISA!" I shout to try to get her attention.

She slowly looks up and reaches out to me. "Teddy...He told me...over and over: 'Tell Teddy to join the team and get in on the deal.' Over and over...he just kept saying that...over and..." She slowly looks over at the EMT that has been attending to her and tells him, "He said, 'He's different...Teddy is different. He'll get it. He will get it.'"

With that, she slumps forward and begins to cry and shake uncontrollably. I hold her as long as I can. I am told they need to get her to the hospital, but I can join her after she's checked in. I walk them to the ambulance.

As the doors close, Endzone waves to me to come back into the house. As I do, he asks me to sit in the living room so that we can talk. "I'm going to tell you what I know. I spoke with the homicide detective who was on the scene first and talked with Lisa.

Apparently, Johnny got up this morning and snapped. Somehow, he woke up early and started to drink again. At some point, he grabbed a gun and talked about killing himself. His wife struggled with him trying to get the gun. He lost control and the gun fired, killing his wife with a shot to the chest. When he realized what he had done, he turned the gun on himself. Lisa was up against him, wrestling with him as he pulled the trigger and shot himself up through his chin. That's it. He shot his wife by accident, and when he saw that he had killed her, he decided to kill himself. Lisa did everything she could. She really did. I'm sorry Teddy. I really am." Endzone looks me in the eyes with a kindness and sadness that I can't let take hold of me.

"I'm going to the hospital to stay with her. She needs me. I have to go!" I reply quickly.

"I think I can help you get a ride with one of these guys. I have to stay and talk with a few more people for my own report. Is that ok?" Endzone asks.

"Yes, that's fine." I reply, grateful for a chance to get away. "Thank you Endzone." I climb into a police car with a Linwood policeman who drives me to Shore Memorial Hospital. Lisa is alive, but her parents are dead. The nightmare has made its way into reality.

When I can gather my thoughts, when a few days or weeks have passed, I'm going to find out why Johnny C told Lisa to give me those strange instructions. I don't understand it right now but, I'll have to.

Something bad happened and everything went horribly wrong for Johnny C. He wants my help from the grave. I'm supposed to "join the team and get in on the deal."

What the hell does that mean?

Chapter 9

Lisa has been in seclusion since she left the hospital. Although we have talked several times, she keeps the conversations short. I visited once when she was staying with a friend, but it didn't go well. She told me she was leaving New Jersey and never returning because her real dad has decided to take her to Nevada to live with him. Lisa kissed me and said, "It's for the best Teddy., it really is. I'm going to need time: a lot of time. I have to go away." She handed me the Pinto keys and simply said, "It's yours. Take it. I don't want it anymore." After she left, I went over to her friend's house and picked her car up. Now it sits in front of my house. Every time I walk out the door, an orange clunker reminds me of the world that used to be. It sucks.

Tonight, I am heading back to craps school. Somehow, the people in our class nicknamed Luca "Mr. Hands-of-Stone." I think Margaret started it. She is crazy. I often question who is crazier: Margaret or my instructor, Stav. I am convinced that Stav holds the record for the most "F-words" used in a single breath. He's like the hot dog eating contest guys you hear about: he puts up big numbers. Guys like Luca and I aren't exactly prudes but Jesus Christ, I'd chip a tooth trying to keep up with Stav's pace. The guy is a maniac.

"Damian, Damian, Damian. Are you fucking kidding me?! I already said it like, I don't know, 20 times! Head down. Assholes and elbows are all I better see on this fucking job. Muck those cheques. They ain't gonna magically put themselves in piles of 20, now are they?" He pauses, as if any one of us would venture an answer. "I didn't think so! Put your fucking head down and be a monkey! Muck those cheques!"

I will admit, my hands are getting better. What I don't understand is why I seem to be better with my left hand than I am with my right. Weird. I use a fork in my left hand, but my right is dominant. I throw and write with the right hand. You would think I'd be better with the right hand. Also, the left does come in handy for other things. I'm not sure if that would affect this. I would hate to change any current habits to find out. Best to just leave that alone.

Today's a big day. After all the harassment at the hands of Mr. Stavros, he promised to quiz us on prop bet odds and payoffs. Finally, we get to apply some of the things learned outside the classroom, inside the class. It shouldn't be too hard: the odds are printed right on the felt. If you can't read or see, the least of your worries would be dealing craps. This ought to be fun. We have some "Nervous Nellies" in the room who are highly intimidated by the way Stav stomps around, yelling and cursing at us. Seriously, I don't give a fuck. The guy isn't coming to a family Christmas party anytime soon. I'm going to get my thousand dollars' worth and stick this school in my rearview mirror. That includes Peter Stavros. I won't look for a job at the Penthouse Casino anytime soon.

"Alright, alright. Stack 'em and rack 'em. Let's move it! We got work to do on the prop odds and something tells me we got folks in this class who are BURIED -- got NO clue!" It looks like he is setting the atmosphere for failure so he can jump on the most nervous person he sees. I'm just going to lean in and smile the whole time. There is no way he'll pick me.

As I finish that thought, Stav throws a cloth on to the table, covering up everything. "Quiz time. Damian is first. Twelve-dollar bet on the hard 4. It hits. What do you pay down?" Stav asks. I start doing the math in my head. Stav continues, "What are the odds, Damian?"

"Seven to one. He gets eighty-four," I reply.

Stav smiles and asks, "Who agrees with him?" Some raise their hand, and some don't. He goes after the ones that leave their hand down. "Okay, Parson. What's your answer?" Oh boy, Parsons thinks it's 144. Wrong.

He asks Paulson. She replies, "96."

"Correct. It pays 84, but I said 'down' so he also gets twelve dollars back."

"Trick question!" I tell him.

"TRICK FUCKING QUESTION? IN A FUCKING CASINO? NO SIR, MR. DAMIAN! You don't handle tricks: you handle CHEQUES, MONEY! You get it right or you go work as a SLOT TECH. UNDERSTAND?!" Stav stares at me and then looks around the room. "Anybody else here think that was a trick fucking question?" Back to staring at me, "Listen up Damian, because I'm going to give it to you straight. You want to be a dice croupier?

Fine. Get your head out of your ass. The felt tells the entire story. All you need to do is learn how to read it correctly. I am trying to get you to memorize a few things to show you that you can't take anything for granted. Do you know why? Do you have any fucking idea what I'm saying to you?" Stav asks me and then doesn't wait for a reply. "No, you don't. Here's why: it's called speed. Ever hear of it? If you haven't, you better learn because on a dice table, speed kills. Let me explain it to you. It's simple. First, when the dice start hitting and the players start winning, management wants those dice to speed up. They are chasing house odds. Sooner or later, they are going to get to the advantage position. If the dice slow down and numbers keep turning, the advantage goes to the player. It's ever so slight, but it's there. When that happens, the dice are sent back out faster and faster until that glorious 'seven out' is heard by management. You hear what I'm saying? That's just one aspect of how speed kills." Stav starts pacing around the room, picking up speed in what he is saying as he walks. "The second and most important aspect is about the dice croupier. When you are 'jam up,' when you are 'there,' everything moves in regular or slow-motion for you. You have your players covered. That's because you know what the fuck you're doing. Now if you don't, let's say you didn't really pay attention during class, then speed will kill you. That means no job and no money: you wasted your $1,000, Mr. Damian. That goes for the rest of you. Stop trying to act like we're all going to become friends and sing *kumbaya* around a campfire. That's a bunch of fucking bullshit. You're going to step out onto a casino floor filled with degenerates, mobsters, assholes, and generally mean people. They might not have started that way at daybreak but make no mistake about it, Mr. Damian," Stav continues making eye contact with me, "You go to pay somebody $84 on a $96 pay-and-down, I've seen a man try to choke the stick man after finding out he lost $12. The guy could have tens of thousands up in the rack. It doesn't matter. He could have doubled his whole rack. He still wants his 12 fucking dollars. Do you still think it's a trick question?"

Stav paces around the room a few more times as he continues the questions. "One more thing: if this seems like something that really doesn't work for you, it's no problem. You can switch over to cards, join the team and learn to deal in that class. That's my offer. If you don't want to keep going, go see the team next door. Tell them you want in on the deal. Okay, break time."

I'm frozen in place. The clue Johnny C spoke to me, the secret clue revealed itself, just like that. It came out of nowhere, without any investigative work on my part and jumped right in front of my face.

"What about you Damian, is that what you want to do? Damian? Are you listening to me?" Stav asks.

I can't find the words and stare back at Stav with what must look like a stupid grin on my face. I still can't believe it. "No Stav. I mean sure, I'll talk to Mik Tim. I mean, I might want to deal cards someday. I like craps. The dice suit me better, but I will take a look at cards as well." I manage to get out.

"Bullshit. The last thing Timopolous needs is a guy who isn't committed. Don't waste his time. Either you want to do it, or you don't." Stav replies.

"I won't waste his time. I'll ask a few questions because I have some friends that want to learn how to deal cards. I can throw some business this way," I continue.

"Sure...whatever. Go talk to him. What do I care?" Stav says.

I walk outside. Luca is smoking a cigarette and talking to some of the people in the class, "You two kiss and make up or what?"

"Nah, he just talked to me about blackjack. He's an ok guy. He's not getting a Christmas card, but he's ok," I reply.

"Sure, he is. All assholes like him are great people...to their moms. Am I right?" Luca responds.

We finish soon afterward as Stav has to leave early for an appointment with some casino executives, or so we're told. He's probably going to get laid. Who cares? I will finish up without him.

"Listen Luca, I'm on to something. I don't have any interest in dealing card games. I'm sure you know that already, right?" I ask.

"Yeah, you suck at cards anyway. What's up?" Luca replies.

"That thing Stav said earlier, do you remember? When he talked about dealing and the team? That thing?" I ask.

"Yeah, I know. He's talking about his partner, the Mik 'team.' That guy?" Luca asks.

"Yes, that guy: Mikalos Timopolous. Christ, why didn't I see it earlier? Mik Tim. His nickname sounds like 'TEAM.' Do you get it? That is what Johnny C was trying to tell me the whole time. He's the key to all this, at least I think he is. He's got to be.

There's a connection here somewhere. It's so obvious! I must be right: deal and team. Listen Goombah, this is the guy I need to talk to. I'm going in to talk to him."

"You want me to go with you? You know, for muscle and all that?" Luca asks.

"This doesn't call for brawn. I think it calls for brains so it's my job. You want to pick a bar and I'll meet you over there?"

"What, go walk in this neighborhood? Hell no, I'll sit in the car and wait. You go take care of business. Besides, I gotta get home so no bars for me tonight. Try not to make it a long meeting, capeesh?" Luca says, giving me a stern look.

"Sure, I'll keep it simple." I respond.

He heads to the car and I go through the back doorway to the other classrooms. One room says "Blackjack" and the other says "Baccarat." I think I see Mik in the blackjack room.

"Mik?" I ask the stranger.

"Yep, that's me. How can I help you? I'm cleaning up to close, so if you can make it fast, that would be helpful." Mik replies.

"I gave Johnny C a ride home the night before, you know, it all happened." Mik looks up from his seat and stares at me. He gets up and goes over to a table, taking a cigarette from the pack, and lights it. He takes a long drag, blows it out, then looks down kind of shuffling his left foot.

"Johnny C and I broke in together in Vegas. We were just kids. We didn't know our asses from a hole in the ground. Those days, you dealt to some rough customers. They were some bad people. I got punched a few times. Hey, I'm 5'6" and 140 soaking wet.

Johnny, well, he was a big boy. He was there the day a guy pulled a knife and tried to slash at me because he lost. It all happened so quickly. When I think about it, it's like it was in slow motion. The guy pulled the blade, Johnny saw it, tapped out for the cameras, showed his hands and leapt onto the guy. He beat the living crap out of him! Johnny was pulled off by Security and they took their turn. He looked out for me and was my best friend. Now he's gone. You ever lost a best friend?" Mik asks.

"I just did. It never should have happened...never. It's the worst feeling in the world," I tell him.

"You want a cigarette?" Mik asks. I take one from him as he lights it for me. We sit down, "I'm Ted Damian. I go out with Johnny C's stepdaughter, Lisa."

Mik smiles at me and laughs, "Man, he didn't like you for a while there. He talked about it. It's the way he gets sometimes. I know that all changed. I think Lisa yelled at him enough times that it got through his thick head that you weren't such a bad guy. He got the message. All he cared about was that she was happy. In the end, that's all that really mattered to him."

Mik walks into his office area, opens a drawer on his desk, pulls out a bottle and two glasses and walks them back over to where I am sitting. "Ouzo," he tells me. "I've heard about it. Greeks like to drink it. Ouzo has a strange licorice taste. I'm not sure if I'm going to like it, but you know they say, 'When in Athens...'"

"Yamas!" he toasts as we throw back our drinks.

Oof, it DOES taste like licorice. Too much of this stuff and I'm going to be sick. I don't do well with the real sweet alcohol drinks: Southern Comfort comes to mind.

"So, you said you gave Johnny a ride home. I'm betting he told you to come see me, huh? Do you have something to tell me? Johnny and I were all square: good friends until the end. I knew the guy like the back of my hand. So, tell me, what do you have for me?" Mik asks.

"That's just it Mik, I don't know what I have for you. He was rambling quite a bit about, you know, being fucked over and not having any friends left. He said he got screwed over and the safest person to trust was me. I didn't get it. Why me? He never really liked me. Even if he did, I certainly didn't think so. I still have no idea why he decided to tell me that stuff."

Mik pours two more short drinks. I am thankful that they are short. Wow, that stuff tastes bad. "Good stuff, huh? From the home country. I only drink the best, and this is it."

"Yes, it is -- you have good taste." I answer.

Mik raises his glass and says, "To Johnny C: the toughest son-of-a-bitch I've ever known. He was the real deal." We clink glasses and down our drinks again.

His toast gives me a thought. "Johnny said something to me in the car while we were driving home that night. He told me to join the 'team' and get in on the 'deal.' I figure he was talking about you, right? It all points to you. It's kind of the same thing Stav said earlier about learning how to deal cards. Doesn't that make sense to you?" I ask.

Mik rubs his forehead and looks around his classroom as if he's trying to find something, his eyes darting back and forth. "Let me tell you something: Johnny C was a smart man. The guy could figure things out quickly: no matter what. He was also good at playing practical jokes on me. One of the things he was good at was hiding stuff. He gave me clues. We were drunk half the time, but I got a kick out of it, you know? That was just one of his things. We were as close as they get. I think he came to you for a good reason and he knew that eventually you and I would get together. That's the way Johnny C thought. He was crafty. What did he say again?" Mik pauses for a minute and then says, as if to himself, "I know he was feeling uneasy about Zirkov,"

"Who?" I ask.

"Zirkov, Levee Zirkov: one of the casino managers he inherited when he took over. Zirkov is juiced up, you know what I'm saying? He's got powerful juice, all the way to the New York families. Everybody knows it but somehow, the Casino Control Commission doesn't have a clue. It's all bullshit. The guy is fully covered. It's bought and paid for. Non-Italians like yourself take over twice as long to get their license as some of the connected Italians. It's so obvious, it is starting to become an embarrassment for the State of New Jersey. Word has it, they can't speed up the process, but they can slow it down for the ones that seem to be getting rubber stamped. This Zirkov isn't to be fucked with."

"That's it. That's what he was saying. He wasn't saying 'jerk off,' he was saying Zirkov. That's got to be it, don't you think? He wanted us to talk because something went down with this Zirkov guy. Are you and I are supposed to do something about it?"

Mik snaps his fingers and smiles at me, wagging his left index finger up in the air, "Son-of-a-bitch, that crafty son-of-a-bitch. Come here." He takes me to a closet and shows me the supplies he keeps on hand. "I'll be damned. Johnny was in here before and pointed something out to me. Look: that pack right there. He said something like, 'Christ Tim, this one looks bent. I'll put it on top for safekeeping and you pull it out for a special occasion…only a special occasion.' When I told him, I would just toss it, he put his arm around me and said, 'Trust me, you'll have a special occasion soon enough.' I didn't think anything of it. Go ahead and grab that pack," Mik tells me.

I reach up to grab it and it suddenly becomes apparent that there isn't a deck of cards inside. I think we just found our clue. "I'll be goddamn." I tell him.

Mik shakes his head and tells me, "Before you open it, I need to pour another drink. There could be a treasure map in there, for all I know!"

I pull the box down and walk back over to the table as Mik pours himself a big one and downs it. He looks at me and exhales strongly, "Ok, go ahead and open it. Let's see we he left us."

I open the pack and find a folded piece of paper inside. What the hell? Maybe it is a treasure map. "A piece of paper? What does it say?" Mik asks. I unfold the paper and in cursive writing are the words, "My house…second bedroom…closet ceiling."

Mik takes it from my hand and reads it out loud again. "Holy shit. Holy… shit. What are we waiting for?!"

"What do you mean? What do you want to do?" Suddenly, a car horn starts blaring loudly outside. "Oh shit: LUCA! I forgot about Luca. My friend is outside waiting. I have to go tell him."

"Listen, it's simple. You can tell your friend to come along or you can tell him to go ahead home and then you come with me. I have a spare key and I'm going to that house. I'm going to get whatever it is he left for us. Are you in?" Mik asks.

"I'm in. Let me go tell Luca to go without me." I run down and explain to Luca that Mik is working with me on craps and will give me a ride. "Go ahead without me Luca. I'll catch up later." Luca takes off.

Soon, Mik and I are in his 'vette heading over the Atlantic City Expressway on our way to Linwood and the Constantino house. He is not shy about driving fast, so we do a bit of weaving in and out of traffic until we get to Shore Road where he dials it down a bit. He leans over and says to me, "Look for cops. I'm going to push the speed." Fuck, he's not being subtle about it.

"Hey Mik, are you trying to get noticed? I ask.

"Really? Cops got nothing better to do than pull over a pretty Corvette going 10 miles over the speed limit?" Mik responds.

"More like 20. You might want to dial it back a tad."

Wrong suggestion. He pumps the accelerator and whips past the car in front of us and into oncoming traffic. "Haven't crashed once…don't plan to now. You might want to hold on because I get the feeling we're about to run this red light. Let me know if you see any cars pulling out from a side street. Hitting them would put us on the front page and we don't want that." Mik tells me.

No, we sure wouldn't. When the police officer asks us why we're doing 78 in a 45 in the first place, I'd have to tell him, "Nothing important, just on our way to sneak into a closed crime scene."

Chapter 10

Mik and I fly through Northfield in his '77 red Corvette entering Linwood. Not a cop in sight. "Cops take days off just like you and me, know what I mean?" No, I have no idea what he means -- I grew up in Linwood and cops are basically everywhere. They could run a taxi service.

We turn off of Shore Road as we get to our street. "Mik, I'm not sure if this is still considered a crime scene but I can imagine the neighbors are keeping their eyes open for any activity, know what I'm saying? A red Corvette showing up is bound to catch someone's eye. Let's take a different approach." I suggest.

"Ok, what do you have in mind?"

"Hook back around where we came from, out by that bike path. I'll show you". As he does, I give him the plan. He agrees and drops me off. Now I just have to be careful I'm not seen. I head south down the bike path about 100 yards then cut in through the woods to the backyard of the house. So far, no barking dogs. I scale the back fence, run across the yard and slide up to the back door. The key works: I'm in the house! Up the stairs and to the second bedroom I go. Luckily, the hallway is lit up with nightlights. The place has been cleaned up a little, but the possessions are still here. I open the closet door and reach up. I can feel an envelope taped to the ceiling. I got it! That was simple.

As I head back down the stairs, I hear voices outside in front of the house. I peek around the corner and the streetlight shows me a man and woman walking a dog within the driveway circle of the house. Christ, a neighbor must have decided it's sightseeing time at the local crime scene.

I try to move quietly toward the back door. Fuck - the dog heard me and starts barking, "Is somebody in the house?" a voice calls out shakily. "You're not supposed to be in there! We're going to call the police! We have a weapon and we're not afraid to use it!"

I hear them arguing about not having a weapon. He asks for her can of mace and rape whistle so he can get help. She hisses back that she forgot to bring it. I shake my head with a smile. The two are not exactly organized.

As I quietly close the back door behind me, I pick up a rock and throw it as hard as I can to the right of the house so that it lands away from them toward the side of the house that I'm going away from. Hopefully, it will distract the visitors and their dog. Now's my chance.

Over the back fence, through the woods, and back onto the bike path I go. I have 300 yards until I get to the end where I should find Mik waiting for me in his 'vette. As I run onto the street, I see headlights coming up the road. Mik must have cruised around, parked and then sat waiting. Smart move,

"You got it?" Mik asks as I jump into the car.

"I got it. Let's see what we have." I open up the envelope to find another envelope marked "OPEN LAST" and a small piece of paper with a key taped to it that says, "OPEN FIRST" The second envelope also has a name and address. I turn to Mik, "E. Roth, 2 Thieler Lane, S. P. Does it ring any bells?"

"I'm not exactly sure. How about for you?" Mik questions.

I stare at the piece of paper for a while. "The address is in Somers Point. I'm fairly sure it's down by the south bay, past the Crab Pot." All of the sudden it dawns on me. "Yep, I know it: it's a park-and-make-out area. Do you want to check it out?"

Mik shakes his head, "And what, knock on the door at this time of night? Do you think that's a good idea?" He has a point. We need to feel this one out. Who knows what we could be walking into? "Let's drive by and see what's there," Mik suggests.

As we drive back to Shore Road, Mik looks over and asks, "You said this was a make out area?"

"Yeah, you didn't have make-out areas in Vegas?" I ask.

"No, not in Vegas. We would drive out to the desert and bring a blanket and some booze. Nobody ever bothered us. Cops didn't have time for that bullshit, know what I mean? Besides, it ain't called Sin City for nothing," Mik says with a chuckle.

"Yeah well, it's a little different here, as you probably noticed. We have blue laws. You can't buy booze in Ocean City and most of the shops are closed on Sunday. It's supposed to give families a chance to walk around and talk to each other, like the old days. Sunday is not the best day in Ocean City," I explain.

"No shit? They got blue laws here? Man, New Jersey is never going to be anything close to Nevada. I figured that out already but now I'm absolutely convinced," Mik tells me.

We arrive at 2 Thieler Lane and park in front of a small house. A woman is sitting on the front porch smoking a cigarette and enjoying the late evening breeze. A little girl is sitting next to her with her head in a book. The woman turns and directs the girl to go into the house and watch TV as we get out of the car and walk toward the porch.

When we get to the front gate, I hear Mik mutter under his breath, "Uh oh…"

"What's the matter?" I ask.

The woman stands up, puts her left hand on her hip and takes a long drag from her cigarette, "Hello Mik. We were bound to run into each other at some point, weren't we?"

Mik glances over at me and rolls his eyes and then turns back to the woman. "Hello Tabatha, still babysitting I see?" He leans my way and whispers, "She can't have children -- doesn't like them much anyway." Turning back to the woman with a steely glare Mik shoots back, "When were you planning to tell me that you were in town?"

"I don't have to report anything to you. That ended a long time ago. What's it been, seven years?" Tabatha replies, disdain dripping from every word.

"It's been three. The divorce feels like it happened just yesterday though," Mik answers. Great, I just walked into a hornet's nest and judging by the way things are going, somebody's about to start kicking. That's generally a very bad idea. Best to say as little as possible.

"Who's your friend?" Tabatha asks. I detect a slight slurring of her words. She could be on her fourth Scotch. It smells like more.

"My name is Ted Damian. I knew Johnny C," I respond.

"Is that right? Were you a good friend of my cousin?" Tabatha asks.

That brings a big smile to my face as I point my finger at her, then back at Mik and then up in the air and twirl my finger. "Ahh.... you guys. Now I see it. How about that? It is a small world isn't it?" I reply.

"It sure is Terry," Tabatha says.

"It's Teddy," I remind her, "but that's okay." I turn to Mik. "Mik, why don't you take the lead? All I want to know is why Johnny C sent us here?"

Tabatha doesn't give him a chance to respond. A note of anger turns her already sarcastic voice up a level. "It's simple," she tells us. "My son-of-a-bitch cousin, God rest his soul, decided that he would involve my husband in whatever scheme he was involved in. How nice of him." She begins to shake her head. "He just couldn't leave Edward out of this. Come on up boys. Why don't we share a smoke? You can tell me what you came for and we can get this over and move on with our lives. Edward is at work but I'm pretty sure I'll be able to help you."

We step up onto the porch and a thought crosses my mind. I ask Tabatha, "Edward...does he work over at Bixby's?"

"Bingo genius, he sure does." She says dismissively and then turns to Mik, "Mik, why don't you tell Terry here our fun little story? I'm sure he's curious." Tabatha instructs.

Mik takes a deep drag from his cigarette, "Long time ago Tabatha...a *very* long time ago. Why don't we save that for now?" he suggests.

"Oh no, please you can't get off that easy. You see..." Tabatha points at me, searching for her next word.

"Ted. Please, just call me Ted," I offer.

"Ok just Ted, Mik here decided early on that we were going to have an open marriage: *very open*. I'm talking about high school girls sneaking into the casino, cocktail waitresses, fellow dealers. Hell, he was even screwing the wife of a prominent local minister. I know what you're thinking," she says, pointing at me with a shaky finger. "Yes, there are churches in Vegas. Anyway, Mik failed to let his wife know that we had an open marriage. Funny thing, huh? It just slipped his mind." She stares straight at Mik and continues. "One day, 18-year-old Yolanda shows up at my front door -- pregnant. I'm sure you can imagine my surprise. Now to be fair, because I am a fair person, the baby turned out not to be Mik's. Yolanda figured that since Mik had fun with her, he was her best bet for getting the big money. The real father bolted town and went back to Fresno. Do I have the story right, Mik?" Tabatha asks.

Mik flicks his finished cigarette out and on to her lawn.

I decide to interject. "So, if I can take a moment to suggest something. You know, help move this along a little bit."

Tabatha laughs, "Sure, did you bring the key? You did bring the key, right? The box sits in the back room in a closet, buried underneath a whole bunch of shit. Edward figured that would be the best place to keep it. That was our part: Johnny gave Edward something to hide. Your part must be to open it. You got a key or what?"

I hold the key up to show her. Tabatha nods her head toward the door, "I told you where it is. I don't want to know what's inside nor do I want to see it. Take the box and go and please, be quick about it. I expect that this will be the first and last visit I'll get from you, Mik. Let's keep it that way. Go ahead: mi casa es tu casa."

Tabatha lights another cigarette. We go inside and find a TV playing for no one. As we work our way toward the back, I see the little girl standing in the hallway, staring into the big bedroom. There's a huge bed with an ornate wood headboard that looks like it was hand carved.

Tabatha appears at my side, ice cubes clinking in her glass, "You like that TV? Nice, huh? Unlike Mr. Cheap Ass over there, my new hubby gets me nice things. He even promised to take me deep sea fishing in a couple of weeks. The man is not afraid to buy me what I like. He's nothing like old Mik-shit." Edward must be raking in the tips parking cars. Maybe I should work in valet rather than security.

Tabatha points to the little girl. "This one here, she's basically deaf and mute. She's my neighbor's kid. Her mom is pulling all-nighters waitressing at Caesars, so I got kid duty."

"Well, you're a good friend to help her out, I'll say that," I reply.

Tabatha laughs and takes another swig of Scotch, "Who said we were friends? She's a cash box and I have nothing but time. I know how to make a little hustle money. That's an important thing to know in this world, Terry." I wish she'd just call me Joe -- it would be less painful. Terry is just too close.

Mik finds what we're looking for in the small bedroom closet: a metal box that requires a key to open. He grabs a manila folder thick with paperwork. With a lowered voice he tells me, "Let's get out of here before she shoots and stabs me. She's done it before. If you push hard enough, a butter knife can be pretty painful." We take the envelope and head back to the front door.

I turn to Tabatha to thank her but, before the words get out, she says to me, "Don't bother. Johnny and I weren't close and the piece of shit you're hanging out with now ain't much better. Do us all a favor and don't ever come back here. Leave Edward and I alone. Is that clear?" Tabatha asks.

"It is," I respond.

"Good, now get the fuck off my porch and take your scumbag friend with you." Tabatha says as she points, urging us to leave.

We jump back in the car. Mik turns to me and says, "She wasn't in high school. She was in a community college. Also, it wasn't a minister's wife: it was his mom. She has the stories all wrong. She always does."

I don't really want to get into it, but I'm tempted to anyway. My inner questioning beast is just screaming to get out, so I ask, "What about the 18-year-old girl? Is that true?"

"Oh yeah, that was true. There were two of those. She only knows about one of them." Mik winks at me and turns to the road.

"Mik, I've got a stupid question. Tell me if I am crossing a line here. I feel we're getting to know each other fairly quickly. You might say we are friends now. Anyway, I just gotta ask: don't you use condoms?"

"What are you, stupid? Why would I use condoms? Do you know how much time that wastes? I mean, really? Condoms? What are you, 16? I've been married 3 times - never once needed one," Mik tells me.

"Forget it Mik: stupid question." I quickly change the subject, "Why don't we go to the Prime Diner and grab a back booth? Let's see what Johnny left us," I suggest.

"Do they serve booze there? I mean, it is a diner, right? Are you craving a BLT right now? I need a strong drink. God knows what we're about to be told from the grave. How about some drinks?" Mik asks.

"Ok, I got a place. We'll go to Bi-Bi's down the street. It's got a good bar and is a little dark. We'll have privacy." I respond.

We walk into Bi-Bi's and find a good spot in a side booth. Mik heads to the bar. "Do you like tequila?" he asks.

"I've had it a few times. Is it as good as Ouzo to you?" I reply.

This makes Mik laugh, "Ouzo is very different, Ted. The only reason I drink it is because I'm fucking Greek. It's for the soul -- not the taste buds. You drink it to balance your soul. Still, Ouzo isn't whiskey."

This man is complicated. I need to drink just to keep myself centered around him. He's what you might call a "different cat." We drink our shots and Schmidt's as I begin to untie the string that keeps the manila envelope closed. "Are you ready?" I ask him.

"No but go ahead anyway." Mik replies.

I reach into the envelope and pull-out papers, some photographs and another smaller sealed envelope. We begin to go through them. "Who are those guys?" I ask Mik. I recognize one of them for sure: he makes the papers once in a while.

"That's that mob guy: Fat Freddy Callo. The other guy looks familiar. Do you know who he is?" I ask Mik.

Mik takes the photograph to take a closer look. He shakes his head. "That's Levee Zirkov. It's not a great picture but that's him with Fat Freddy." He points to the building in the background. "Do you recognize the place they're coming out of? Does it look familiar?" He points to a place above the two men. "Look at that giant bird. What is that…an eagle above the door?"

I take the picture and look at it closely. It's familiar but I can't seem to place it. Wait a minute…I know this place! I've been by it. I've never been inside, but I know where it is.

Mik continues, "Who puts a big fuckin' bird over the front entrance? What kind of tacky shit is that for a restaurant, huh? Isn't that weird? I mean, who does that?"

There is only one place that it could be. "Ed Zaberer does that, that's who," I tell him. "That's Zaberer's restaurant in Wildwood. They also have one closer. I've been to that one. You should see the place. It's like a museum of the absurd. People seem to love it, you know?" I tell him.

"No, I don't know. I'm Greek: we make good food consistently, every day, over and over again. Greeks don't need big birds to sell their food. If it's a Greek place, it's gonna' be pretty damn good. That's how we are." Mik replies proudly.

We go through more pictures. Most of them are of Zirkov and Callo with a couple of other guys. "It looks like Zirkov is pretty mobbed-up," I tell Mik.

"You think? Jesus Christ stay far away from this guy." Mik says sternly.

I find the first sealed envelope we got at Johnny C's house and rip it open. Several pictures fall out. At first, we can't tell what is going on in the pictures because they landed sideways and upside down on the table. As I pick them up so we can take a closer look, we freeze. Mik blurts out, "Jesus Christ in heaven. God help us!"

I quickly gather the photos to stack them, covering them with my hands as the server checks in with us to see if we need anything else. "Two shots... of Ouzo."

We're both quiet. Mik breaks out his cigarettes and offers me one. We light them and smoke in silence. The pictures are shocking. We continue to sit in absolute silence.

As the waitress puts down the shot glasses, she tells us, "I don't know how you guys drink that stuff. It's different. It tastes like a jellybean."

Mik looks up at her and explains, "I'm Greek -- we drink Ouzo for our souls. Yamas," Mik cheers.

We pick up our glasses and shoot them down. Yikes. "Bring us two more!" I tell her.

I look over at Mik. "My soul needs it as well." I stare at him and he stares back. Where do we start?

"Something is wrong here. I know Johnny C. I know him and I'm telling you, he wouldn't do that, ok? He wouldn't. That's disgusting. He's not a man that would ever lower himself to something like that. He loved his wife with all of his heart! I'm telling you they were very happy together: very happy. He ain't going to do anything behind her like that, and he's definitely not gonna do it with…" Mik says.

"…a little girl?" I interrupt.

Mik looks down at his beer and slowly spins the glass around with his fingers. He appears to have tears in his eyes. He wipes his eyes and takes a drink, "He wouldn't do that! I'm telling you, he wouldn't! Johnny C was a 'stand up' guy all the way! 100 %." Mik continues.

I break out the pictures again and Mik looks at me and motions with his hands. "Put them away," he tells me, the disgust evident in his voice. "I don't want to see them anymore!"

"You think I do? I don't but we have to figure this out! We have to Mik! It's not right so we gotta find a way to make it right! He left the pictures for a reason." I tell him.

I lay the pictures out on the table, making sure no one is around or approaching. I tell Mik that I need his help to figure this out, "Look at them. He left these for us to see. It's not about him telling us he's doing something bad, Mik. If something is wrong, then we…"

Before I have a chance to finish, he grabs my arm and squeezes. "His eyes," he whispers as he points to the picture. "His eyes are closed. Look: six pictures and his eyes aren't open in any of them. Do you see?" Mik asks.

He's absolutely right. "There's only one way this happens Ted, ONE WAY. They drugged him and set him up. That's it. It's gotta be it. That's what happened. He's been knocked out. They fuckin' drugged him and got pictures… oh… shit…" Mik trails off.

As he says this, I'm thinking what he is thinking. "They found out about him snooping on them: about the pictures he got of Zirkov and Callo, right?" Mik continues. "Johnny found out that Zirkov was more than dirty - he was filthy. That meant trouble was coming his way. Johnny was gathering evidence to make his move against Zirkov and was discovered. They decided not to kill him because that would raise suspicion and place heat on the game they were running. It makes sense. They set him up and then let him remove himself after blackmailing him."

"This is sick." I push the pictures back together and jam them into the envelope. "I mean, this is some pretty sick shit right here, you know? Who the fuck does this?"

"Zirkov does. It's his specialty. He runs little boys and girls out of Eastern Europe." Mik tells me.

"How? How does this guy get away with doing it? How do children get shipped across the world for this kind of stuff? I mean, it just doesn't make sense." I say, shaking my head in disbelief. I stare at the table, lost in thought. "I don't know how he does it but if I can find out and not get killed, that would be something. This fucking piece of shit is the lowest life form walking on this planet. He's a no-good scumbag… he is…"

"…a monster." Mik interrupts. "This guy is a monster Teddy. Am I right?"

"You're exactly right, Mik. A guy who does this kind of thing can only be called one thing: a monster."

Chapter 11

I roll over and look at my alarm clock. Crap, I've got to get to work! Although I probably won't be on this job much longer, I owe it to Lou V to work like I said I would for the next week or so. I run through the shower, get dressed as fast as I can, run out to my car and peel out for work. Shit, I'll have to speed again. I pull up to the jobsite parking lot to see Lou V waving at me like I'm bringing the winning lottery ticket. Maybe he thinks I stopped to get him one of the extra-large coffees he seems to be drinking most of the day. The man is a coffee fiend.

"Teddy, bring that sweet ride over here man! Let me get a look!" Lou V shouts as he continues to wave at me. "God DAMN, A GTO?! I'll be damned, man. WOW! You really scored a sweet ride here, my friend, a real sweet ride. Unreal. You got one of the hottest cars on this site, that's for sure!"

I get out and toss him the keys like he's a valet. "Here, take 'er for a spin. If you like what you feel, make me an offer. Let's start at, say, twenty-five thousand?"

"Sure thing...but if your sister even catches a whiff of this test-drive, I'll catch hell like you wouldn't believe, know what I'm saying? Let's keep all this right here, my man." He climbs in, slips into first gear and wheels out giving a loud yell and kicking up a dust cloud behind him. Damn, I just washed it too. Oh well.

After a quick 5-minute ride, he pulls back into the parking area and is stopped by a couple of guys getting out of their vehicles by the entrance. Shit, I recognize the first three guys: they're the same roofers I ran into before. I gotta think they didn't forget me. I know I haven't forgotten them. There is a fourth guy with the group that I don't recognize. Although, considering how much trouble these idiots get into, I wouldn't be surprised if they had to find a replacement for someone who pushed his luck with the boss too many times. Roofers are all nuts. That's just the way it is, at least in my experience.

They start pointing at me with the guy I don't recognize laughing and shaking his head. I'm sure Lou V will fill me in. Lou V finally pulls away and cruises the car over, parks it and tosses the keys back to me, "Fantastic car, Teddy, really. You scored big time right there. Make sure you take care of her like a good woman, you know? She'll take care of you too." Lou V advises as he gives me a wink. Sound advice from a man known for the way he treats his own car. More importantly, his woman (my sister). I respect what he has to say.

"Speaking of women and such, that guy over there said that you and he have a little something in common." Lou V continues.

Oh shit, now I know why he was pointing and laughing. Crap. "So, Teddy I think you might remember his old girlfriend. You remember her, well I mean, you know l'hai scpata, eh?"

He makes that motion with his hands that Italians are famous for when depicting sex: a backwards closed fist moved back and forth just above waist level. Yep, I remember, and I regret it to this day.

"Don't worry about nothin', ok? They ain't together anymore. Besides, he's out on parole so if he farts side-ways he'll have to go back in. That one better be like a Boy Scout, hear what I'm sayin'? He knows it and I know it. We ain't enemies, but we ain't friends neither. He knows the deal: he stays on his side of the 'work street' and everybody stays calm. If he gets stupid and asks for trouble, I'll be his answer. Listen to me, the guy is an asshole and he cheated on her with every slut he could find in every bar he wasn't gettin' thrown out of, so I don't give two shits about him. Stick with me and keep away from Mr. Piece of Shit, hear me?" Lou V explains as he looks me squarely in the eyes.

"Yep, I hear you," I tell him, trying to look as sincere as I know he is. "I'm here to work and get paid. He can work through his own failures as a human with some other sucker. So, framework today?"

Lou V puts me on supply detail meaning I get to drive around most of the day in the company pick-up. Not bad, not bad at all. This should be easy. I'll just need to make a bunch of back-and-forth trips to the local Rickel for all kinds of shit: screws to plumbing supplies and everything in-between. No roofing supplies: those guys are under a whole separate contract and get their own stuff. Good thing: I wouldn't give them spit if they were thirsty in the desert. Fuck those guys. I'm going to make sure I have a good day doing what Lou V needs me to do: nothing more, nothing less.

I need to stay out of trouble. That starts with avoiding those fuckin' roofers. Especially 'Mr. Boyfriend' guy.

"Teddy! Food run, my man. Come here!" Lou V shouts out to me. He hands me a list of subs he wants picked up at a local place and tells me 'Corner Liquor' in Pleasantville is the place to go.

"A liquor store? Subs? What kind of place is this? You're saying they're good, huh?" I ask. He hands me cash. I glance at the list. Each sub is basically the same, some just have more hot pepper relish than the others: capicola/provolone with extra 'juice' (olive oil and vinegar), Frank's black cherry soda and Herr's potato chips.

"Get whatever you want for yourself, Teddy. I'm telling you, the old man there does a great job. He's got some of the best meat around. I like to make sure he gets my business, you know. He makes his subs FAT for us - the guy doesn't skimp. He's the best around." Lou V explains.

"Ok, I'll grab them now. See you soon!" I reply.

I jump back into the truck and head toward the street. As I pull down the dirt path, I see the roofer standing in the middle, waving his hands. What the fuck does this guy want?

He walks up to the side of the truck and holds a screw up for me to see. "We're all out and I figured since you're making a supply run, you could do this for us. My friend over here is out of screws. Can you make sure my friend gets the right screw? You'll give a guys' friend a screw when it's needed, won't you?"

I look in the rear-view mirror to see Lou V running our way. Fuck it. What do I really have to lose with this 145-pound weakling? He looks like a punk because that's exactly what he is.

"I'm not supposed to buy stuff for you guys. Something about insurance regulations and all of that, Lou V tells me, BUT I can help you on this one. Tell your friend to do it himself. He needs a screw; he should do it himself. You too. That would be the best advice I can give you." I reply.

"Can't hear you, my man. How about coming closer so I can get a better idea what you are saying? Climb out and talk to me."

I open the door just as Lou V runs up and pushes it closed. "You...Drew, don't you have work to do or do I gotta give your boss a call and talk to him about it? Huh? Go on... get moving!" Lou V ushers him aside.

Asshole Drew smirks at me and then tells Lou V, "We were just getting acquainted, you know? Just makin' friends here. You can never have enough friends. Calm down man, calm down. Jesus Christ! See you guys later."

As the asshole leaves us to crawl back to his shit-for-a life existence I ask Lou V, "What the fuck was that guy in for, anyway? Is he some kind of a badass? He doesn't look it."

Lou V pulls out a pack of cigarettes, flips one up to his mouth and offers the pack to me. "Here, let's take a walk."

I grab one. Even though I haven't fully developed the habit, I smoke one once in a while. I understand from talking with Lou V that he is the same way.

"He is and he isn't. I've heard the stories. The guy is a drifter and has been accused of some serious shit - not caught, just accused. Cops have talked with him and here he is. It's sick shit: I don't even like talking about it. I think he got hired because his company is slammed busy. They need the bodies." Lou V explains.

Lou lights up his cigarette and offers me the same. He takes a deep draw. I don't like doing that, so mine is shallow, like they do in the movies when it looks like the guy really isn't a smoker and is just trying to be cool. Smoking is not my thing unless I'm drinking.

"The guy drinks and smacks around women, like that girlfriend of his you got to know. How you got together with her is beyond me - didn't I tell you to stay away? Remember I said that there was nothing but trouble there? She comes from a biker family. Her dad is in jail right now and her mom is a mess. That's what I've heard, but I don't know the whole story and I'm sure it doesn't get any better." Lou V shakes his head sadly. "That guy? The last time he got busted was for trespassing. He was caught trying to break into a house... into the little girl's room. Word has it he pled down and got six months. I don't know if he's some kind of fucked-up perv-ee or just a drunk who makes for a stupid burglar. I don't give two shits about him. I do about you though, so listen to me and stay away from that idiot. You hear me? I'm telling you to STAY AWAY. This time listen to me."

Lou V pats me on my shoulder and points to the road. "Go get those award-winning subs before the fuckin' place goes out of business. Otherwise, we have to eat mud sandwiches and drink the ditch water they have flowing through the hose over there. Go on!"

As I head toward the truck, I catch my new friend talking to his buddies and staring at me. He waves his finger at me, breaks into laughter and then turns and walks away. It looks like he is going to be trouble for a while. I may have to go head-to-head with him and just get it all over with. The question is, when and how? Until then, I got subs to pick up.

Eating lunch with the guys is pretty cool: they act like they are eating a meal prepared by a four-star restaurant. Billie is one of Lou V's plumbers. He is a BIG boy and can eat a lot of food, "This capicola is like nothing else you get around here, you know? Where does this guy get his meat? Man, it's tasty. I should'a got two. Damn." I'm thinking it's a good thing he's a plumber, because wow, do I feel sorry for his home plumbing. Yikes.

"Teddy, these are pretty good subs, right? Man, I could eat these every day!" Lou V has obviously found his place.

"Yep, these are pretty damn good. I'm giving your guy lots of credit, I'll tell you that right now," I reply.

Lunch finishes and I run back and forth to Rickel for more supplies. I was kinda hoping that asshole would stop me again so I could slam the car door into his side. At his weight though, I might break his hip and put him out of commission for a long time. Maybe that's what the idiot needs. I can dream, can't I? Oh, if only...

At the end of the workday, Lou V and I go over to Bolden's for a quick beer or two. Bolden's is perfect for the kid who wants to buy beer illegally. You go in through the 'Package Goods' door, ask for your stuff, pay and get out. It works great for sixteen-year-old kids. If they try to sit and get served well, now you're insulting everyone's intelligence. Those types get tossed out and receive a lifetime ban... like my brother Jerry. He would score beer for his surfing runs and nobody gave two shits about it. Unfortunately, Jerry pushed his luck one day when he wanted a pitcher of Schmidt's with a sandwich he was eating. Dumb move. He was seventeen and the owner, Mr. Grimes, told Uncle Bone all about it. Uncle Bone got a kick out of the story because he knew my Pop didn't care UNLESS you get caught. Then, he expects you to 'man up' and take your punishment.

Pop talked to Jerry and Jerry did the right thing. He said. "I fucked up - it's my fault." That was enough for Pop, so no punishment was given. He figured the lifetime ban was enough. I think Pop is right on this stuff. Rules get broken all the time, that's just how life is. If you're breaking them and don't get caught, you are way ahead. When you get caught, you go back to 'even' in life. No big deal, it's just fun while it lasts.

Anyway, nobody is going to bother two construction guys having a beer, no matter what. The cops don't sweat you either. At least not until you get behind the wheel. Then, they have you. Plenty of idiots think it's ok to get blasted and try to drive home. I'm glad we have cops, because without them, things would get bad. Gotta have order.

Me and Lou V have a couple of Schmidt's and shoot the shit. "I called the house but no answer. Dori is probably out with your Mom right now," Lou V tells me before taking a swig of his

Schmidt's. "Your sister tells me she's having those dreams again, you know? I call it the 'happy haunting' dreams. In these dreams, she tells me people visit her from the past. I have dreams too but most of them involve making more money. Does that make me selfish? I think I spend so much time focusing on it during the day, it shows up again when I try to sleep. Your sister well, she just has more interesting dreams than me. What do you think?" Lou V asks.

Considering the weird dreams I've had lately, I'm not so sure about any of it. Lou V and I finish our beers and head out the door and back to the work site so I can get my car. It's the end of a productive day.

As he pulls onto the construction site, Lou V stops and stares me squarely in the eye. "Stay away from that idiot no matter what. No bull shit, understand?"

"Yes sir, no bull shit of any kind. You can count on me, Lou V. No problem." I tell him.

"I gotta go. Dori gets worried if I'm running late. See ya!"

He drops me off near my car, speeds up and goes out onto the road without stopping. As I start to put my key in to unlock the door. I hear a car coming from behind the building we worked on. It approaches me, drives by slowly, stops quickly, then backs up as the passenger side window lowers. Asshole and his roofer buddy look out with big smiles. "Hey, no hard feelings man. I'm sure we can get along just fine and get our work done, you know? I'm not trying to cause any issues. I'm on parole so I gotta keep my nose clean. You understand, right?"

Sure, peeping Tom, I completely relate to you and your idiot friends. "Oh yeah, I do. It's no problem on my end," I answer.

"Hey, nice car. It looks fast. How is the engine? Can you give it a rev and let me hear her? This Nova I got is pretty tame, you know?" As I rev the engine easy, he says, "Man, if only I had one of those," he tells me and then turns to his buddy and says, "might be a pain." I can't really tell, but I'm trying to get along, so I rev the engine harder and let it roar a bit, pumping my foot down several times like I'm making it talk. They both smile and nod their heads in approval. "That sounds nice. That baby is the real deal! All I got is the Nova, but it runs. That's the important thing: you gotta just find a reliable car. Looks like you got one. Alright, man take it easy. We're outta here!" With a laugh and some dust, they pull away. Good, making small talk with those two is like being at the dentist's office.

As I stop before pulling onto the street, I see Dori and Mom driving toward me in the Cutlass. They pull up and lower the window. Mom sticks her head out. "You two probably grabbed a Coke after work?" she asks.

"Yep, ready to head home now." I tell her.

Mom puts her hand out. "Listen, we think Lou V forgot it's quilting night at our house, so Dori left him a note and a plate of food for dinner. Are you heading straight home?"

"Yep. I heard Pop say something this morning about making his clam chowder. I'm not missing that!" I tell her.

Mom and Dori laugh. "Hey little brother, how about letting the ladies take your hot-rod for a spin home? We'll be gentle." Dori asks, a huge smile on her face.

"You think you can handle it?" I taunt. Dori dated a guy with a Chevelle in high school. He let her drive it around all the time. She knows her way around a muscle-stick better than most guys I know.

"I'll give it a try," she tells me with a wink. "We'll hit the Parkway and see if it's got any real guts. I'll give Mom here a thrill."

Mom has a worried look on her face as she opens her door to get out. "Keep it under 100. I'm not in THAT big of a hurry."

We switch cars and in a second, Dori is behind the wheel, spins out and takes off. No sense trying to keep up. She can handle herself and the car.

"Ok, buckle up Mom!" Dori instructs. "We're gonna launch out of Absecon, shoot to the Parkway and open this baby up a bit. I'll hit some high speed in the areas where I know the troopers don't have good hiding spots." Dori settles in, drives onto the White Horse Pike and over to the Garden State Parkway. As she enters the Parkway, she gives the accelerator a little push and gets a roaring response. Dori's eyes light up as she looks around, changes lanes and works the gears to pass slower cars. At 75 mph, she hears her mother screaming at her. "Slow down!"

Dori shakes her head and pushes down slightly on the brakes to find…nothing. She tries again. This time, the pedal goes all the way to the floor. A couple of deep breaths later and a hundred yards down the road, she tries again. The engine sputters and then explodes with a loud BANG! Thick, putrid black smoke pours out from under the hood, eclipsing any possibility of seeing any part of the road. As the sputtering grows louder, Dori realizes that she's losing power. She reaches over, swearing as she grabs for the stick and pops the car out of gear. The engine dies. As the car starts to coast, Dori feels the wind on her face and hears a calm voice telling her from the passenger seat, "No cars -- you can veer right and get to the side honey."

The car limping forward, Dori checks the rearview mirror for cars behind her and pulls toward the right side of the road. With wide eyes, she looks at her Mom. "What the hell is happening?!"

Dori pops the hood latch, grabs her sweater and quickly exits the car, yelling at her mother to do the same. Black smokes billow around them. She wraps the sweater around her hand and reaches down to unhook the latch. As she backs up, she yells at her mom, "Christ, it's like I just lifted the barbeque lid! It's on fire, Mom! There's no way to put it out. Run Mom, it's on fire!"

Further away, they find each other in the clearer air and stop to look back. In frustration, Dori bends down into a catcher's position and stares at the car. What the hell happened? As she tries to think through the past 5 minutes, she glances at the bottom of the car and realizes that the fire is not only shooting from the area beneath the hood but seems to be engulfing the car from underneath as well. Holy shit!

As if from a distance, she hears her mother's frightened voice. "I can't believe this! We could have been killed! I can't believe this is happening! Oh, Teddy's car! Oh my God!"

A siren pierces the moment and Dori looks up to see a state trooper's car flying by them on the other side of the road. She shakes her head. "They're probably heading for the turn-around spot about a half mile down the road," she thinks to herself. "It doesn't matter how long it takes him to get to them, there is nothing he'll be able to do." A few moments later, the trooper pulls up and parks far enough behind the car to divert traffic to the farthest lane.

As he gets out of his vehicle, a second BANG splits the air. The GTO is engulfed in a fireball. Seconds later, the GTO is no more.

Chapter 12

I wake up confused. Somehow, Connie and I ended up in a bed. Whoops…she's on the floor now. I'm guessing we drank a lot.

Connie is a cocktail waitress at Caesar's. She came into the bar to meet a friend and the friend ended up leaving early. We must have spent the whole night talking considering we are both fully clothed and my shoes are on my feet. I assume we just slept. Sleep is good, although personally, I need just enough to recharge my batteries, especially after one of my early-morning adventures. This time, I needed to blow off some steam: big time.

Three days ago, my car burned up with my sister driving and Mom along for the ride. Although they weren't injured, it was pretty bad. To top it off, I lost the car that Mrs. Milchzek gave me in honor of her husband. I feel like I let everyone down.

I went to the bar last night to meet Luca although he never showed. Instead, I met Connie. We drank, got high in the alley and it kept going from there. It was cool. She was funny as hell, laughing through the disaster that is her crumbling marriage. Meanwhile, I was trying to laugh through my dream car going bye-bye.

Connie's situation sucks. Her husband seems to be a real asshole. Her phone rings as someone starts banging on my door.

I lean over the side of the bed and try to reach her.

"Connie...CONNIE! Answer your phone. Are you dead?" I don't think she is although she's not moving and whoever is banging on the door is none too happy right now. "Connie, come on. Someone is banging on the door?" She barely moves so I fall over the side and start shaking her. "Connie, someone is banging on the door!"

She opens one eye, cringes as if in pain and yells, "Who the fuck is banging on the door?"

"I am! Answer the phone, will you? It keeps ringing and it's not for me. JESUS CHRIST answer your damn phone!" the stranger shouts.

"That's William, my sister's husband," Connie tells me. Then, she seems to come back to life. "SHIT! We're at my sister's house! How did we get here?!"

I scratch my head and frown at her. "From what I remember, you directed me here. It's about the best we could do. I'm not kidding." I do know that last night we got a bit blasted and were getting tired of the crowd at the bar. Most of the guys were in their late thirties and had lots of stories...LONG stories. I get tired of that stuff pretty quickly.

Surprisingly though, the night didn't turn out as a total loss. There is a woman in bed with me. Well, she's not actually 'in' the bed and she *is* fully clothed so that's not really a win either.

As far as William is concerned, it doesn't really matter, now does it? He just wants the phone answered. "Ok, I'll get the phone," Connie yells at the door. "I'll get it."

A minute later, the phone rings again. Connie answers it and hands the phone to me. "It's for you -- some Luca person." I reach over and grab the phone. Before I get it close to my ear, I can hear Luca yelling at me. "I gotta send a fuckin' carrier pigeon over with a bucket of water to dump on your head or what? Answer your fuckin' phone, will ya? Christ!" Luca sounds pissed.

"How did you get this number?" I ask.

"You called me last night and gave it to me. THIS IS THE WAKE-UP CALL YOU ASKED FOR!" Luca shouts back.

"Ok Gumba, I'm up." I tell him.

"Good. Listen to me: our friend is in town and wants to meet about that 'thing.' How soon can you be ready?" I take quick showers and move at a good pace, so I give Luca a 15-minute estimate. "Ok, let's meet in Margate. I'll give you the address of a family friend. We can have privacy there. Take down this address and we'll meet there"

Luca gives me the address and I hang up only to have the phone ring again. "What now Luca?" There is dead quiet on the other end. I feel a hand reach up and Ginny grabs the phone. "Hello." she listens for a moment and then continues. "None of your business, Cal. I said, NONE OF YOUR BUSINESS."

Oops. I think I just spoke with her estranged husband. Yikes. Why the hell I picked up the phone is beyond me. I obviously wasn't thinking. Shit. Connie continues, "Go take a leap, Cal. It wouldn't be your first one." SLAM...and Connie slides back into her sleeping position. Wow, she handled that pretty well.

I gotta get moving. Although, that's not generally a problem. I'm not a big "bathroom guy." Pop always says, "The bathroom is a business place, not a social place. You wanna be social, go to the kitchen. Chances are you won't have anybody waiting on you there. Plus, you stay out of the way. They should put timers on bathroom doors, and when your time is up, the door springs open. That would really change things." I think he's right. He has good ideas now and then - just ask him.

I pick up a pillow and toss it at Connie. She doesn't budge. Should I try a bucket of water? Nah, that would be pretty uncool - the epitome of what people might call a "dick move." Which, now that I think about it, is the opposite of the reaction a guy wants when his penis is involved in any interaction with a woman.

"Uhhh…" I look over as I hear Connie begin to moan. She is starting to stir. "Oh shit, my head." Connie looks up at me. "Did you make coffee? I think I smell coffee somewhere. I need coffee. Please tell me that you made coffee and a nice hot pot is waiting for me at…" she glances at the clock, "1:30 PM??? Oh… shit!"

"I don't live here. I didn't make any coffee." I tell her.

"Oh…wait…Oren must have a fresh pot going. I think it's a Western Pennsylvania thing," Connie tells me as she heads toward the door. "I gotta get some coffee. This bathroom is all yours."

Good. I need to take a leak, shower, get dressed and get the hell out of here. I flush and turn on the shower. As I step in and start to lather up, I hear a knock at the door. "Teddy, someone's in the other bathroom and I REALLY GOTTA… just… you know…

pee. Can we act…you know…married…and share? I'm really sorry. I really am."

This will be a first for me. Mom and Pop don't do that and I'm very sure I don't want to even act married right now, or any time soon for that matter. This is a real weird moment. What if she sits down and starts to… "PLEASE! I'M SORRY… but I GOTTA GO!" Connie pleads through the closed door.

"Uhm…sure. Go ahead." I hear the door open and close. She lets out a little laugh and pulls back the shower curtain. Connie is naked and smiling as she steps in.

We embrace as she tells me, "So, you got me here safe and didn't even try to fuck me, huh? Am I right? Does that mean you don't find me attractive? Are you just being a gentleman? What's the story, hmmm?" She kisses me gently on the lips and pulls away, wiping the water from her face. She grabs the bar of soap from me and starts washing herself with it. "This is the better part of 'acting married,' don't you think? So, which one is it, huh? Am I not attractive enough for you?" she asks as she starts rubbing soap on me. I'm really going to have a hard time saying 'no' to her. I would have even if we weren't showering together. I do like her, and we had a lot of fun together.

We laugh and I turn her face up so I can look her squarely in the eyes. "What if I just told you that I'm not a rapist? Would that suffice? I don't do that to drunk women. I brought you here because I felt that I had to. You told me to come here. Second, you were basically passed out in my car. That's why you are here.

That's all. Now this is a fresh start, don't you think? Should we start over… and introduce ourselves?" I ask her.

She pulls my head down to hers and our kiss starts to get deeper. So does our 'introduction.'

I just might be late for my meeting with Luca.

"Bye Teddy, take care," Connie says as we stand beside my car door.

"Sure Connie. Next time I'm at El Amigos I'll look for the girl biting on the cactus, right?"

"Maybe -- we'll see. Life is like that sometimes. So long for now. I might not see you anytime soon but, you never know,"

The woman is pretty smart about her approach to this. We had a good time and understand that that is good enough. She has too many attachments and, as she put it, likes to "keep moving." There's no time to reflect and make plans together. I feel the same way. We're cool.

Connie winks and heads down the street to her house by Birch Grove Park. She still lives with her husband--it's a little bit of an odd situation-- but is staying safely away from him most of the time. They are like angry roommates until they decide to figure out how to end it all. Apparently, he started it by cheating with another woman he claimed to have fallen in love with. Interestingly enough though, he also ended the relationship with the new one. "I guess she did some new things for him that I wasn't doing," Connie told me. "Then, he found out she was doing the same thing with other guys while she was dating him. So, his party with her ended. I've moved on, so he can't have me back."

When I shared that she didn't exactly seem like a sexual 'prude' with me, she laughed and said, "Oh sweetheart, it's a brand-new day for me. I have seen the light and I'm finally relaxing my mind and body. You know, out with the old and in with the new. I'm gonna be just fine." I believe her.

So, I'm finally off to my meeting with Luca and Geno. I haven't seen Geno in a very long time. It will be good to see him. He's exactly who we need right now.

Chapter 13

I drive Mill Road to Jerome Avenue in Margate, down to Atlantic Ave, take a right on the one-way Washington, and back around onto Decatur. I see the Maverick, so I know Luca is here. I park the Cutlass and go up to the door.

A big smile is waiting for me at the door. "Ted!" Geno yells with his arms extended.

"Geno!" I reply, going up to embrace him.

He hugs me and slaps my back hard, "Christ, you got older… and Luca got fatter. How does that work?" Geno asked.

"The fuckin' guy brushes his teeth with bacon, for Christ sakes. Every time he picks up a fork, he acts like it is exercise time. He counts off like he's in the gym, you know. I don't think it's working." I reply.

That gets a good laugh as Luca asks, "Where the fuck you been?"

"Helping an old friend in need, that's all," Geno tells him, with a wink at me.

"I have no doubt she was old. I will give five dollars right now if you can look me in the eye and tell me she was…eighteen…no… nineteen. Was she nineteen?" Luca asks.

"Kiss and tell, Luca? This shit is beneath you, Gumba." I reply.

"What can I say, huh? This guy has a thing for a certain type. Less twinkle in the eyes and more crinkle on the skin. He likes them old," Luca tells Geno.

"Bullshit, I just don't like little girls with little girl attitudes. Who the fuck doesn't want a good woman who knows how to handle herself? It takes away a lot of the game playing, man. You," I say, pointing at Luca with a smile on my face, "you're looking for a South Philly Italian wildcat to lead you around by your balls that she'll be constantly squeezing. That's your type."

Geno throws up his hands like a referee and says, "Enough already with you two. Jesus Christ, get laid and get happy. Nobody really cares about your types, alright?" We all have a good laugh.

Geno motions to the kitchen area where I see an enclosed outside patio where he put out a pitcher of water and glasses. We sit down and Geno puts his hands out toward us, palms up, "Ok, I'm here, so let's talk. Tell me what's going on."

Luca and I take turns talking as he pulls out a pack of cigarettes and passes them around. The discussion starts with Dori and Mom driving my car. I talk through the connecting dots, including the insurance investigator's report that it looked like the brake lines were cut and something dumped into the gas tank to catch fire.

Luca gives me a soft punch on the shoulder, "When were you gonna tell me this? They cut your brake lines?"

"Yep. Pop knows the guy, so he got the word fast," I reply.

Geno leans in, 'You're pretty sure about this roofer, huh?"

"I'm pretty sure. He definitely doesn't like me, and I get that. We had some words back and forth recently. I'm telling you it adds up like we are describing it. It does. Look Geno, I don't know this guy's full story. I know he's bad news and tried to break into a house by going through a little girl's window. Lou V says he had some issues in the past and skated on them because they didn't have enough proof. I think this sicko fuck is a weirdo- perv." I reply, my face boiling with frustration.

"Lou V hired this guy?" Geno asks. "I thought he didn't have roofers. Isn't that another company that does that stuff?"

"Lou V told me it is Jones Roofing out of Altoona. The two idiots haven't been back to the worksite since they set up my car. So, they either left town or found another gig somewhere. Who knows? Have you heard of this Jones Roofing company?" I ask.

Geno smiles and nods his head at us both. "Yep, I know a guy. I'll make some calls here in a few minutes, alright? I've got some work to do and I'll need some time to put things together, capeesh?"

We sit smoking as a calm quiet descends over the table. Luca clears his throat like he wants to say something but then just takes a drag on his cigarette. A couple of minutes later, he starts staring upward, as if looking for an idea that will miraculously appear on the ceiling. Since he isn't saying anything, I do. "Geno. These pieces of shit fucked with my car. Dori and my Mom were in it. They could have been killed."

Geno gets up and signals for us to do the same. "Fellas, sometimes harsh words and a little rough handling do the trick, like it did with our friend in Florida. Do you know what I'm saying? Sometimes though, you gotta do more. I'll be around for a few days. I'll take care of a few things and then be in touch. I need you both to sit tight. Can you make sure your Mom and Dori are safe until then?"

"Yep, they'll be fine," I reassure Geno.

"Alright, now listen carefully. DON'T SAY NOTHING to NOBODY...PERIOD...Got it? We understand each other?" Luca and I are perfectly clear that no matter what, our conversation can't leave the room...EVER! It is clear and simple.

We hug and say our so-longs. Geno pulls me in closer and speaks directly into my ear. "Not from nothin' but between you and me, you might wanna consider finding your own place. I'm just saying." He stands back and stares me dead in the eyes. "You hear me?"

"I hear you." I reply. He gives me a slight slap on my face and winks at me. I know he's right, for a lot of reasons.

As Luca and I leave, Geno returns to the house and walks into the back room where an old man sits in front of a TV, smoking a cigarette. Phillip "Philly" Silver has lived in this house almost two thirds of his life. He moved back from Florida years ago with his wife because she needed a special medical treatment which, at the time, was only available here. She passed away seven years ago, leaving him with the house and wonderful memories.

Philly knows Bone and Geno very well, so they are always welcome at his house. In earlier days, he ran a couple successful businesses (not all legit) and semi-retired. At the age of 79, he doesn't get around as much as he used to but that's ok: he gets plenty of visitors. Some of them "conduct business" at his home. He is happy to accommodate and keeps clear of most conversations. He's just an easy-going old man with friends.

"So, Geno... everything ok? Phillip asks.

"Yep Mr. S, wonderful. I was just talking to some of my friends. We were thinking of doing a little fishing, you know. Maybe soon – it is a little up in the air right now. It would be good to get out in the salt air and maybe catch something. What do you think?" Geno asks.

Phillip thinks a lot and knows a lot: he just doesn't always say a lot. Most of the time, he just goes along with the conversation, even when dealing with friends. One thing he knows for sure: Geno is no fisherman - not even close. That's fine. It's none of his business.

"Mr. S, may I use the boat? I'll take care of everything. I'll even pay you for it. I wanna make sure this all goes well for my friends and I, you know?" Geno asks.

"Sure, sure -- take the boat, not a problem. I don't want any money, just put fuel in it and most importantly," Philly turns to look Geno in the eyes, "make sure it's clean when you bring it back in. Guys go fishing, it gets busy with all those big fish you got on board, and before you know it, there's blood to be cleaned up. Having blood all over attracts flies."

Geno stops and looks at Mr. S, thinking through what to say next. Before he has a chance to respond, Philly continues. "The worst thing you can do when taking a joy ride, I mean a fishing boat

ride, is leave all that blood, 'farshteyn?' You don't want that, and I
don't want that."

Geno understands very well, even when Philly moves between
speaking Yiddish and Italian. Mr. S. will tell you, "I can keep up
with Jews and Dagos alike." He's a mensch and a Gumba.

"I'll make sure that's taken care of." Geno tells him.

"Good: we understand each other. The boat keys are hidden
behind the cookie jar in the kitchen. One last thing: if you don't
think you can pull off this 'captain of the boat' thing, let me know.
I'm always available because," he turns a bit more and leans in, "gli
affari di famiglia sono solo affari nostri, capisci?"

"Si, l'impresa familiare e la prima impresa," Geno answers.

They understand each other. Family business comes first, and
it's 'nobody else's.'

"So, come and go with the boat as you please." Philly ends the
conversation with a wave of his hand.

Perfect--Philly signed off on the first part of the plan. Geno
knows, it might be soon, or it might be a way down the road.
Eventually, he will be taking the boat out again. This time, it will be
deeper water than the bay...much deeper.

Chapter 14

I received a call to meet Quaylz and Endzone. For everyone's sake, I no longer worry about Mom or Pop fielding calls from "Bob Smith" or Arnie Bloome who has to act all folksy and "awe shucks" with my parents. If Arnie calls me, it's because we need to discuss business that goes beyond anything Mom and Pop would consider normal. "You're going to have to get your own place, Ted. There is no way we can conduct business with your parents as innocent go-betweens, do you agree?" I got the speech directly from Endzone. Later, Agent Quaylz followed up with a similar talk. "You are going to have to move out of your parent's house: I suggest you start picking out a new place sooner rather than later."

Finding the place wasn't that difficult since Steve was pushing me to move in with him. Considering it was only three blocks away from the house I grew up in, it was perfect. All I had to do was add an answering machine to the phone. Bingo, issued solved.

"Hello Mr. Damian, it's Bob. Call me at the office so we can discuss your policy further." That is what they came up with as the new approach. Agent Quaylz poses as an insurance agent and, if anybody asks, I tell them that he is working on my auto insurance claim and is working hard to upsell me with more insurance. "He knows my folks," I tell people, "so I try to be nice to him and throw him a bone here and there with some follow-up conversation. The guy's not going to stop so I do my folks a favor and act cool with him. No big deal."

I return the latest call and am instructed to meet Quaylz and Endzone at a restaurant in Brigantine. Quaylz assures me the city is safe for meetings. "We scoped it out because it doesn't have a lot of outsiders living in town. There are plenty of locals but not the transient casino workers that seem to be invading Ventnor, Margate and Longport. For now, it's our go to 'locale.'"

My instructions are to meet them at a place called *Bobby Soc's* on the corner of Brigantine Avenue and 12th Street. "Park around back, come through the kitchen entrance, and go around to the front dining area. It will be just the three of us. You may see somebody in the kitchen. Don't worry they are not involved and don't speak English anyway. See you at 8 am."

Endzone insinuated that I would be receiving a message, telling me to make sure to go directly home after my shift and check the answer machine. "Timing might be tight, so hustle up and don't stop anywhere on the way home."

I went home, took a hot shower and put on the best disguise I have: a Phillies cap, my sunglasses, basic jeans, Pumas and a t-shirt advertising the Poconos. I looked in the mirror before I left. "I guess I'm ready."

One more time, I pay a visit to the city of Brigantine. Who knows? Maybe someday I'll end up moving there and become a part-time beach bum. That's what Mom and Pop say my brother Jerry is, somewhere in Mexico. It's Baja, or something like that.

I see the sign for Bobby Soc's, turn right on 12th Avenue and drive around to the back. The restaurant is owned by the Soccomano family and named after their oldest kid Roberto, who played in the Canadian football league for 14 years. Bobby came off the South Philly streets and, without time spent in a major college, developed into one hell of a football player. He played as a quarterback and receiver. Bobby's blue-collar-style success story is legend in Ottawa and, of course, these parts.

Bobby Soc's doesn't serve breakfast or lunch so I'm thinking we won't be bothered at all. As I walk through the kitchen, I see an older man tending to his food preparation work. Wow, it smells great! Running a good restaurant takes hard work and lots of love. I smile at him and say, "Odora magnifico signore." He smiles at me and says, "Grazie, e gentile."

I speak some Italian. Learning languages comes to me easily. It is best if I am around folks to hear it for a bit as I pick it up but, after a while, I can communicate pretty well.

I push the swinging door that leads from the kitchen to the restaurant and see both gentlemen sitting at the table drinking coffee. Endzone greets me, "Good morning Teddy."

"Endzone, Agent Quaylz," I reply.

"Damian, have a seat," Agent Quaylz directs. "Coffee?" he asks and pushes the carafe toward an empty cup that was obviously left for me.

"No thank you. My engine runs fine without it," I reply. This brings a laugh. "I figured as much, but I thought I'd offer anyway. So, do you want some hot tea?" Agent Quaylz asks.

"Nope, I'll stick with Coca-Cola. It's kind of my go-to and, quite frankly, I can drink it warm or ice cold." I tell him.

As I take a seat, both men pick up their coffee cup and take a sip. I notice Endzone is looking over at Agent Quaylz indicating that he will be leading this round of conversation. "Ted," Agent Quaylz begins, "thanks for coming over and meeting us."

"No problem," I tell him. Might as well keep it easy-going.

Arnie smiles at me "Ted, what you did that night with Johnny C. went way beyond what was expected. The situation was spinning out of control and I had to make the call. Hell, he didn't give me a choice and neither did the main decision makers in the building. Do you understand? That was a no-win situation for everyone."

"Your involvement was highly appreciated," Agent Quaylz quickly adds.

"I did what I had to do." I am not going to tell them that I saw Lisa before I headed over to help Arnie. They don't need to know everything. Besides, that might not go over too well.

"Mr. Bloome and I were discussing that very issue before you got here. The John Constantino situation raises a particular challenge for us, don't you think? Although your actions were warranted and welcomed, it causes a problem. We no longer have you entering the building 'fresh.' Your appearance means we added the element of familiarity to the equation. When you start the job, people are going to recognize you. Do you agree? Security guards and even that worthless valet guy spoke with you. So, we need to buy a little time and let things settle down," Agent Quaylz explains.

"Why did you call him worthless?" I ask. I was thinking the same thing about the man who, after my little visit with Tabatha, I now understand is named Edward.

"He's playing stupid with everyone, including the police. He has a bad memory when he is questioned and acts like he doesn't know anything. He has been zero help. That means he's a liar or really stupid." Agent Quaylz pauses for a second then looks at me with a smile. "I think he's both." A light moment. I needed that. "We're going to delay your start and work on a plan to bring you in as soon as possible. In the meantime, nothing changes. We'll meet occasionally and keep you in the loop on activities. In short, the project is on hold until further notice." Agent Quaylz puts his hand on my shoulder. "We need you to lay low and wait things out until we're satisfied the timing is right. That's how we're going to proceed. Understood?"

"Sure, I understand," I tell him, the anger creeping into my voice. "We're back to square one." Here I am, ready to start crossing the bridge and they tell me to "stay off." In a matter of minutes, my plans go from jumping into a new life to keeping the one I have…sort of.

"It's important that you lay low." Endzone sounds apologetic. "Stay away from Atlantic City and out of trouble until we formulate the right approach. Maintain what you are doing: no major changes. Does that make sense to you?"

"Sure, it does." I tell him. What I really think is that it sucks. These guys have their program and I'm still not in it. Fine. While I wait for them to figure everything out, I'm going to stay on my own program. I have other fish to fry.

Chapter 15

Even though I was frustrated that it took me two months to start the job at Bixby's as a security guard, it did offer the opportunity to begin the process of moving out of Mom and Pop's house. "Begin" being the operative word here, simply stated, I have been staying over at my buddy Steve's house as much as I can. I haven't "officially" moved as I first planned. Mom's ok with it. Pop well, not so much.

Last night, I decided to crash at the parental house. Steve is planning to pick me up for work in a couple of minutes. Man, Steve Zucker loves his new AMC Javelin. It's black with a black interior. Steve speeds around town in it, especially if he's going to or from work. We pull three twelves these days, from 4:00 pm until 4:00 am. Steve has been driving us both because, to my chagrin, I am now using Lisa's orange Pinto to get around town. It's not a celebratory moment but I gotta do what I gotta do right now, including keeping it parked more than driving it. Borrowing another car or getting rides is my move for now. There was no love lost for the Pinto when Lisa owned it and it certainly hasn't gained status when she gave it to me.

I pick up the ringing phone and it's Steve, just as I expected. "Damian… ride? We can get a White House sub after work. I got some Billy Joel, so we'll blare that a bit. You ridin' with me or what?"

"Yep, pick me up at 2:45. Come in and say hi to my folks too. That stuff is important to Mom. You know the deal."

"Got it. See you then."

With White House open 24 hours, that's going to be our breakfast. Works for me. Steve is a fellow Mainlander, two classes above me. We were in shop class together. He didn't play sports: he was a drummer in the band. Steve was always the best at pulling pranks, both small and large. He was known for gluing stuff, like lockers and sports equipment, although none of it was attributed to him until after he graduated. Steve was amazing at talking his way out of situations. "I'll tell you one of my secrets," he told me once. "You can't use 'I swear to God' because that's been worn out. No one believes it anymore. Adults see right through that shit. You're wasting time. The trick is to have them repeat what happened over and over and then side with them. You know, tell them how bad that stuff is and how 'whoever did it should come forward.' Crap like that. You know, make it like you are one of them. You feel bad, just like they do, like it happened to you as well. That shit works."

You have to like this guy's style. He figured out the best way to work himself out of a jam and keep people looking the other way. I respect that. The adults around us in high school never stood a chance. Things are a bit different at Bixby's but not by much. Steve learned a few more tricks. He loves to do them when he can, like putting salt in people's coffee and switching out their fresh radio batteries with weak ones. Childish stuff for sure, but fun. He's a good guy who wouldn't hurt a fly. We're buddies.

"Teddy, come down here for a moment, will you? Your Father and I want to talk to you."

Uh oh, Mom just used the magic word: Father. Usually, he's Pop. When it's serious (and sometimes it's really serious), she says Father. Something's up.

"Coming!" What the hell did I do now? I've stayed away from doing laundry here like I usually do so it can't be that. I'm in the dark here.

I start with my usual bound down the steps with a sort of happy-to-be-here approach. I don't want to show fear. It's always best to look strong. If you show weakness when the two team up, wham - they catch you off guard and you are toast. I hate when that shit happens.

"What's up?"

"What do mean, 'what's up?' We should be asking you that question Theodore, don't you think?"

Damn, this isn't starting well at all. "What do you mean...I mean, what did I do? Since I'm using the Pinto and other rides, I'm not using your wheels, right? That can't be it."

"No, that's not it." Mom shakes her head and stares at me. "Are you finally moving out? When, Theodore, did you plan to tell us about that? Was it just going to come up out of the blue as you take stuff out of the house? Are you tying your bed to the top of your car? We would probably notice that and would have to ask you what is going on. Don't we have a right to know what your plans are? We do and do for you and this is the thanks we get? Would you like to explain yourself?"

Oh brother. I am way off-guard right now and the dial on their Teddy toaster is set at burn to a crisp. How the hell did I get stuck in this situation? I can only hope that some of that Steve Zucker magic rubbed off me and I can do the old "I know how you feel, I would be upset too" thing that he's really good at. "Ok, before you guys get really upset about this, let me tell you what's going on. So…"

"You're damn right you'll tell us what's going on," Pop interrupts me. "How about you let the two head honchos here at your happy hotel know just what the hell is happening? We had to hear this from Nana. Explain that."

Damn, Nana ratted me out on this. Shit. It doesn't seem right. Although, I didn't get the "Nana guarantee" I usually get when we talk about stuff like this. "It's just you, me and God" is one of her favorite sayings when I let her in some of the secret doins' in the world of one Theodore Damian. I should have gotten that guarantee. If she brings God into it, I know the information is locked down. That's how well involving God works, or at least it does with Nana.

"I never told Nana that I was moving anywhere. Now I can see why you guys are upset. It makes sense. If I were you, I would be a little miffed too. This all just a big misunderstanding. Sorry about that."

"So, you're not moving, is that it? Nana had the story wrong this whole time, huh?" Mom asks. "How did that happen? We would love to hear this one."

As would I. I'm just stalling for time and without the benefit of Steve Zucker whispering ideas into my ear or making notes and passing them to me. I am winging it here. Ah, Steve Zucker…there it is. I've got this now. "I told Nana that Steve Zucker is looking for a part-time buddy for the place he's renting by the golf course. The couple he expected to move in backed out at the last minute. He's alone until he finds a replacement, so he asked me if I wanted to come in and help with the rent. He's got another buddy who will be looking for a place in a few months so until then, he needs someone to join him. I told him I'd help him as much as I could for now. After all, he's a friend and a good guy. We work and drive together so he asked me to at least stay once in a while and hang out with him. He needs to know what I can do sooner rather than later. I was going to talk to you two about it today, but I guess Nana took care of that. She's funny."

This isn't working. Their faces look like stone. It's important to know why it's like this. It's pretty simple, actually. Mom is upset for several reasons; however, the main one is that it appears her baby plans to move out of the house without "official notice." I think she's going to be pissed or upset either way: it's "standard Mom operating procedure." I get that.

For Pop, this is a "Pop self-preservation moment" because what goes bad for Mom does more than trickle down to Pop. Sometimes, it hits him like a tidal wave. He hates that shit. He's not really upset if I move out. He can live with that. He just wants to know how much of this crap will affect his day-to-day ability to do the stuff he likes, like talking to Mom without her crying. He's got everything figured out already. Pop likes his world just the way it is, with him fully in control and doing whatever he wants to do when he wants to do it. He's got it made unless Mom gets upset and changes it.

Mom steps closer to me and grabs my left hand as she gives a big smile. "Honey, I thought we agreed that you wouldn't make any big changes unless we talked first."

"I know Mom but sometimes I feel like I need to do things my own way, you know? It's nothing against you guys or Nana or anybody else. I need to move on, and I need to know that I can do it on my own. I don't want you guys thinking that I don't appreciate everything you've done for me. There have been some tough times and without you, I would have sunk. People tell me that I haven't lived a normal life. You know that I'm even lucky to be alive and that I count my blessings every day. That's what Nana tells me to do so I do it every chance I get. The problem is, it doesn't change the past and it doesn't make me any happier. It just makes me realize that the road I've traveled has been a little bumpier than it has been for a lot of people my age. Pop, you've been through a lot and you don't talk about it. I don't bug you about it because it's not the right thing. If you wanted to tell me things you would've done it already. I'm not exactly like you and probably never will be. I just know that I've got my own stuff and, at some point in time, I have to be the one to deal with it my own way. So, when I look in the mirror, I can do the thing that you tell me is the most important Pop. I have to be able to like and respect the guy looking back at me. That's all."

As this tumbles out of me, I see a tear run down Mom's face and she begins to look down at the ground. I've upset her. I didn't mean to do that. When she looks back up, she quickly wipes the tears away. "Son, we might not like what you're saying because we think we've got the best answers for you. We're just trying to do the right thing. I guess we're just trying to protect you."

Pop has a big smile on his face. "If you think this is the right thing to do then ok. When I asked Nana if she thought it was a good idea, she just laughed and said, 'For God sake, it's about time that boy moved out. Besides, how far can he go anyway?'"

Whoops...wait until they hear. I guess I should have led with that. "Yeah," I chuckle. "Funny thing...the house that Steve found by the golf course...um...it's really not that far away. I mean, it's almost right down the street."

Mom and Pop have puzzled looks on their faces. Pop crosses his arms in front of him and says, "Define 'right down the street.' You mean like just past the Avondale's?"

"No...no...that would be silly," I tell them with a shake of my head. "No, I'm moving farther away than that. Geesh."

"Ok, so how far away? What's the address?"

Oh boy, here goes. "222 East Vernon Avenue in Northfield. Like I said, by the golf course."

Pop shakes his head and starts laughing, slapping his thigh with his right hand and reaching over to my Mom with his left, as if needing support. "Holy crap," he tells her. "He'll be home every night for dinner and you'll still be doing his laundry three times a week. Jesus Christ, you're crying over this. I'm going back to work." He turns and looks back at me. "You gonna be here for dinner tonight or are you actually working?"

"No Pop, I'm pulling a 12-hour shift, so I won't be here for dinner."

"Ok, well just let us know when you need help walking your stuff down to your new place. What do you figure…20 minutes to get you moved out? For God's sake Kate, he'll be so close we'll have to charge him rent here as well. You were worried. Ok son, thanks for clearing that all up. We can all go back to normal now."

God darn, Nana! All I did was mention it to her but, that was more than enough to get these two started.

With that slight bit of chewing out done, I run upstairs and get dressed for work. It's clip-on tie time. I better hustle or Steve will show up, get invited in and maybe he will get the interrogation that I faced. Come to think of it, maybe I should throw him to the wolves here. It might be entertaining. On the other hand, it could get a little bloody with my parents. Hell, I better pick up the pace.

I'm just about ready when I see the man of the hour pull up to the front of the house. I have to signal him before he knocks on the damn door, "Steve... Steeeeeve!" I'm waving my arms hoping he sees through the screen on my window. I catch him glancing up as he gets halfway to the front door, where he stops and gives a shoulder shrug.

"It's a parent trap. They're gonna grill you on roommate shit. Be ready," I warn him.

He smiles and throws me the 'ok' sign with his fingers. I hear the door knock and Mom greets him with a calm voice, kind of like she might be tired or sort of mad, but not really showing it. I know that voice. She isn't happy. I can hear the small talk starting as I approach the stairs. Steve is answering Mom's question about "what's new?"

"My buddy might be heading back here sooner than he thought. I wanted to thank Teddy for saying 'yes' when I asked him to help me out for a couple of months. That was cool of him because I guess I was kinda twisting his arm a bit. He likes it just fine right here, you know?"

WOW! Now that's how you tell a lie: you tell a big one and sound sincere. On second thought, is he lying or did his buddy really change his plans? If he did, where the hell will I go? Pop is probably already used to the idea that I'll be leaving soon. I can't disappoint him, can I?

"Hey Damian," Steve says as he spots me coming down the stairs. "We still got one stop to make and I don't want to be late for work!" Perfect set-up.

I bounce down the stairs and ask him what he was talking about with my parents. He turns to my Mom and winks at her as he says, "I'll tell you in the car. Let's get going!" Out the door we go. Not bad.

Time to load into the Javelin and make our first stop. "Where are we heading to first?" I ask Steve.

"Work, numb nuts. I had to get us out of there before any more in-depth questioning took place. The secret to lying is…"

"Knowing when to stop?"

"No -- never stop. Just get out as soon as you can, if you can. Otherwise, you have to keep going and you might lose your place, you know? We got out. My buddy isn't changing shit. You are though because, in about a week, you'll have to tell them that my buddy decided not to come after all and you're movin' in. Brilliant, huh?"

Oh yeah, real brilliant. The fact that he has no idea that they already sort of gave their blessing is just the absolute best for me. I can't really lose. Mom wants me to stay, Pop is ok with me going and I get to show how cool I can be when handling the bad news. This sets me up for a win when I break the news about actually moving in with him. I think...

"How do you do it, man? How are you able to look people in the face and just lie like that? I mean, I've told a few in my time but you, you have a gift. You're damn good at this shit - better than anybody I know, Steve."

"Yep, it's a gift, I gotta admit it," Steve agrees. "Practice makes perfect though, and nobody is better at it than my Dad. He is always pulling shit on my Mom like nobody's business and, even though I think she knows every time he's doing it, she just lets it go. She doesn't put up a fight or anything."

"Why not?"

"He pays the bills and he's a faithful husband. He just likes to have a drink now and then and maybe put a few bucks on the ponies. You know, stuff like that. Mom lets that shit go."

It makes me think about my own folks, how they are with each other and the fact that my Pop wouldn't ever think about doing anything stupid against Mom. He loves her and he protects her, no matter what. That's what I want some day.

"Damian don't forget, White House Subs, baby! Can't beat that at 4:30 in the morning, am I right? White House makes the greatest regular on the planet -- BAR NONE. I might get two and have the other one for early dinner before our next shift, you know? That's not a bad idea."

Steve turns up the "52nd Street" tape he loves so much and sits back in his seat, all smiles. He knows Billy Joel's songs word for word and sings every one of them. I guess you could say he's a Joel Freak. "He's got a new one coming out pretty soon," Steve tells me. "It's called Glass Houses. Can't wait for that one."

It's time to go to work and assume my new identity: Ted Damian, Bixby's Park Place Security Guard.

Chapter 16

Some of the posts I get stuck on are the absolute worst. Who the hell wants to watch a dead construction area...again? I've gotten this assignment more than a few times. Jesus not only is it kind of creepy, but it's by far the most boring thing I've ever done. I've been stuck on a few of these details. I think the worst was when a nor'easter blew in on us. I was told to "maintain my post" near the Boardwalk where they set up a temporary entry way around major construction. I couldn't let people divert off to the left or right. If they did, they might find themselves in a dangerous area and then we'd get the very thing we're trying to prevent. No, not injuries: lawsuits.

Lately, there has been a rash of lawsuits with the various casinos going up in town. It appears that there are folks that are quite adept at finding the weak points of entry and the law. In the end, I hear that the people get paid to go away and keep quiet. In the beginning, well, that's where guys like me come in.

"Casino entrance straight ahead" is something a security guard gets very good at saying. We have to be: it's part of a legal disclaimer that can be used in a court of law (we were told in "Security Guard Training 101") should we have to testify against the con artists/unfortunately injured visitors. What a racket. I wonder if they actually get injured. Do they sprain an ankle so badly that they need a doctor? Christ, faking an injury sounds like way too much work for me. I've had enough real ones. They hurt, especially the ankles.

My senior year was one of my worst for football injuries. It started off with getting my knee bent down to the ground in practice one day. We were doing live drills, defense against offense. I had position near the sidelines as Buddy Doerring came toward me with the ball, juked left, then cut right hard. Timmy Akers (the kid weighed about the same as a pair of wet sneakers) had him by the waist and got swung in midair, around and down on my left knee, which was locked in place. Ouch! It bent as I went down. All I remember was that I really couldn't 'walk it off' like Head Coach Schaler told me to do. More like limp-it-off, and that injury pretty much relegated my season to playing with an injury that wouldn't go away.

"Sergeant Smalley to Officer Damian."

Oh shit, Smalley wants me. This might get interesting. "Go ahead for Damian."

"Relief for your position is on the way. Move to the Employee Entrance when relieved until the conclusion of your scheduled shift."

"Copy that. Awaiting relief and then switching to Employee Entrance for shift duration."

"10-4...out."

Well, what do you know? I caught a break. Before long, Darlene Sellers shows up to relieve me. "Jesus Christ Damian, whose ass are you kissing to get my cushy job at the front? I got it made there. People are bringing me coffee, telling me stupid jokes and I get to sit down if I want. It's the best!"

Yep, it's a good gig if you can get it. She hasn't been very shy about how she influenced Smalley to score it, either. Ah, Smalley: the guy is about as unethical as it gets, and he's one of the bosses. Endzone doesn't like him very much. The two act a bit tense around each other. Smalley tries to look serious and professional during those times. He's a terrible actor.

"Listen Darlene, they probably have some new cocktail waitresses coming through tonight and need a 'man's man' to escort them around, don't you think? That's where I come in. I get all the tough duty. You? You get to watch people blow in off the boardwalk and make sure they don't get blown into a head injury, you know?" I grin at the 'blow' and 'blown' analogies, as does she.

"Well, I certainly don't want any injuries taking place over a little blowing. Nobody will experience anything like on my watch. You shouldn't get hurt while being blown, don't you agree?"

"Yep, it only lasts for so long and then it's gone. It should be a simple event."

We share a hard laugh as Darlene starts wiping tears from her eyes. "You are fuckin' funny, Damian. I hear those waitresses are blowing in off the street as we speak and it's your job to protect them, know what I mean?" She does the old 'lean in" move toward me, coaxing a response from me on that last set-up line. I have to think, and I have to make it clever.

I pause and put my finger up in the air, indicating that I'm working on it. I know I can do this. I know I... I got it! "I need to run to my blow... job!"

"Yes, you do! Now go!" This is the kind of stuff Smalley likes so I'll make sure to share it with him. Keeping him on my good side is my main objective. I'm there now but that could change and then I'll be like some of the goodie-two shoes guards he dislikes so much.

They always get basic detail and no perks. I score perks. Endzone and Agent Quaylz didn't have to spell this out to me, but they did anyway. "We need you to blend in, Teddy. Let's be upfront about what that means. Unless he's trying to get you to do heroin or throw someone off the top of the building, we need you to go along. You're going to get a little dirty. We need you to assimilate into what's going on and be 'one of the guys.' If it gets beyond what you think you can handle, we'll meet right away and do an assessment of the situation. It's very important that we all stay on track and keep everything moving. Are we clear on this?"

Once again, clear as mud. I'm supposed to blend in and, as I now understand it, be one of the "bad-good guys." That entails doing some pretty shady shit. I had to make sure Smalley thought that I was on the outs with Endzone and that he's really just a friend of my brother and parents. I bad mouth him every chance I get and act like he's some asshole to me. That wasn't easy at first.

As for this Smalley guy? Well, he steals, deals and uses drugs, runs interference for hookers getting work done -- he finds the empty hotel rooms list that can be used and gets a side piece of the action -- and makes sure anyone trying to run any games on us gets the shit beat out of them. Pickpockets, room thieves, petty drug dealers and even the occasional unruly drunk who comes in off the street… if these guys get caught up in his net, they pay a price. The guy rules with a smile and an iron fist. Nothing is done about it.

Sellers figured things out quickly. She did him a "favor" and because of that, gets good assignments. She did a business deal, plain and simple. "Guys are easy." she tells me. "Guys all want the same thing and if they get it, the world is one big party to them. All you need is a pair of boobs and the right attitude and a girl can get anything, don't you think Damian?"

"Yep, those two things are very important. I would have to agree. You gotta have those two together, though."

"Really? What if a girl had a bad attitude?" I thought about this one over quickly. She had a good point. "Hell, with the attitude, boobs win, so she wins. We love boobs - always have, always will."

I get closer to my new posting and, as I enter the corridor and walk to the front entrance, hear shouting. I find Smalley with three other security guards (Steve is one of them) and a big man they cuffed and have up against the wall. He's starting to get active, kicking and swinging his body.

As I get closer, the guy breaks loose and swings around, kicking at them as he turns toward me, "What did you say about my mother?" he screams. The next thing I know, he puts his head down and starts running toward me, like a mountain goat looking to head butt me. Holy shit, I walked into mayhem and I'm flat-footed with what looks to be a six-and-a-half-foot man (all 250 pounds of him) charging me or more like falling at me.

I slide to my right and turn my body sideways like I do when avoiding a check along the boards in a street hockey game. As I do, I grab my radio from its clip on my belt and jump in the air, coming down with a full swing, clobbering him on his head with as much force as I can muster. He hits the cinder block wall, bounces off of it and comes to a stop on the floor. Jesus Christ. A second later, he pops up into a sitting position and shakes his head from side to side, as if to clear it. "You pussy," he snaps at me. "Is that all you got?" He has blood coming from his mouth. He spits it at me, missing me short. What the hell is going on with this guy?

Smalley walks up, looks down at him and extends his hands forward with his palms up. "Are you done yet or do you want to take this into a private room? Before you ask, yes, we will keep you cuffed. It's your choice. Stop your bullshit and wait for the police to take you or go have more conversation with us. Your call."

"Fuck you, sheriff. I'm not gonna waste my time anymore. Bring on the marines and let me have a go with some real men. You rent-a-fags got nothing for me."

He seems to be fading a bit, but not by much. I think he's on drugs. Smalley laughs as he points to two of the other security guards, "Davis and Cantone: front and center. We'll escort him back to the front until the Atlantic City PD gets here. Cuff his ankles." Smalley pushes the man over onto his stomach and presses into his back with his knees while the other two finish cuffing him. "We got it from here. Damian and Zucker, go take your break and then report back to me. Davis, you take the front entrance for now and Damian will relieve you when his break is over."

I'll definitely take my break: gladly. With the guy spitting blood, I want nothing more to do with him. "You see that man? Jesus Christ Teddy, he was really coming at you! Smalley told me that he thinks the guy is on PCP or something like that because his eyes are crazy. We had a hard time stopping him. He got hit four times in the head with a radio before you hit him, so that might have done the trick. Well, that and him hitting the wall. The wall definitely helped. So, you hungry? Let's go grab something at the cafeteria."

We have a short walk since it's right behind us and down the hall a bit. I need a quick stop into a bathroom. The closest is the one on the casino floor. It's known as the "dealer bathroom."

"Don't bother those people," Smalley tells us. "Unless you hear gunshots or see dead bodies, pass through and keep going. We want to stay on good terms with the folks helping us get a paycheck. It's just good business." Fine, all I have to do is take a leak and get out. If I see a dead body lying around, I just might step over it to get to my urinal.

I push open the bathroom door and it is crowded but nobody is using a urinal. I'm in luck! Thank God, I really need to go.

As I step up, I notice something very odd: four pairs of shoes, er feet, occupying one toilet area with the door closed and hushed voices coming from behind it. This is weird. Four guys are boxed into a small area in a bathroom. I can hear the loud sniffing noises they are making, followed by "oh man" and "yes." It's a coke party and nobody's doing any sipping.

As I turn to finish, the door opens, and I'm face-to-face with guys who look startled and not sure how to handle the moment. The last guy out, I know and see him all the time. Nate Carlo always says hello to me when he sees me around. We've been talking about my craps schooling for weeks and he's given me great pointers. He dealt in Vegas for three years before he came out here and got a job as a boxman. In other words, he's a supervisor who sits at the craps table and watches the action. If this were baseball, he'd be like a coach. The floorman on the game is the manager. The Pit Boss is like the team General Manager.

Nate calls me Captain. "Captain, how are you doing? What brings you here?" The guys think I'm in here to give them a hard time or bust them so, if I handle it wrong, it might be bad for all of us. I have to think fast. "Who is that? I can't see very well. Who goes there?"

"It's Nate. What do you mean you can't see? What's wrong?"

"My fuckin' contacts slipped and I'm practically blind. These fuckin' things are worthless. All I see is shapes and shadows. This really sucks. Am I in your bathroom? Am I in the dealer's bathroom? Whoops."

I hear some murmuring from the other people. The room clears out, leaving just me and Nate. "Hey Captain, you don't wear glasses and you certainly don't wear contacts. I know because we talked about how well you see the felt and the game. So, my man, you're being cool. Cool is good. Cool takes you places. I like cool." He smiles big as he puts his hand on my shoulder and squeezes a bit, then gives it a little shake. "Ok, listen to me. When you get all done and you have that state license, come see me. I mean it. It helps to have friends and let me tell you my man, I'm your friend. You now have juice, capeesh?"

"I know what capeesh means but just what the fuck is juice?"

"It's as old as the hills in Sicily. It means you got coverage, that people look out for you and help you. You're 'juiced up' if you get that from a lot of different people, so keep being cool and you'll keep getting more juice. It's a good thing to have. I gotta go hit the floor. We'll talk some more later. Oh wait." He walks back to the toilet stall and flushes it by putting his shoe on the handle and pushing. "All that shit going on in there, somebody ought to at least have the decency to flush, know what I mean? Besides, no matter what, it's bad luck not to flush. I don't bring bad luck to myself. See you around Captain."

Off he went, away from the little bizarre meeting we all had. Christ, I need to remind myself to stay out of this bathroom. If I keep getting caught in these weird situations with these guys, I'm going to become as good a liar as Steve. I don't want that.

I wash my hands slowly and then count to ten to give all parties plenty of time and room to clear away from the area, then exit and head down to the cafeteria. I need caffeine. "Jesus Christ Damian, what were you doing in that bathroom, powdering everybody's nose?"

Here we go. "Nope, it wasn't me. It was some other guy that looked just like you! He was powdering everybody's nose in the stall for five bucks a piece. You sure you weren't in there?"

"Nope, but I was in the lady's room doing that. Made a mint. A chick would walk by and I'd powder her. It was great." I think we both have no idea what the hell we are talking about right now and we couldn't sound more stupid if we tried. Perfect -- it's why we get along.

Caffeine time. We walk into the cafeteria and grab a tray. I'm going to get some fries and a Coke. I want to keep it simple and not load up on food right now. The sub after work is worth waiting for. Steve well, he's different. The man can eat full meals six times a day and lose weight doing it. He's just like his folks. God, those people are skinny. I've seen them eat at a party. They are not shy, filling up several plates at a time. My folks think they have tapeworms or something. "Steve, save some for the other three thousand people that work here."

We move into the line to have our badge scanned. This is how the casino tracks your meals to make sure you are only eating the allowed two-per-shift full meals. On the other hand, they have so many snacks available it's ridiculous: popcorn, potato chips, pretzels, you name it! The place is a food factory.

I slide my small tray behind Steve's, marveling at the pile of food he amassed. I can't help but think that someday, they are going to have to start charging everyone for this. Giving food away is like inviting people to get fat. Well, maybe not, but there sure is an awful lot of it being eaten and Steve is certainly doing his part.

A new employee behind me asks where I got my fries. As I point the area out to him, I notice the server left the counter and there's no fries left. I offer him mine. "Here man, take these. I think my eyes are bigger than my stomach. I don't need them. There's ketchup over there if you need it."

I turn to hand my badge to the girl sitting down behind the desk. BAM! We lock eyes. Wow…she is…uhm…wow. I feel it pretty quickly. She is…well…at the moment…locked in on me. "Damian? Hello? You gonna swipe or what? Give the girl your badge, my man. Hey!"

I'm staring at her. She's staring at me. She takes my badge, gives it the required swipe, and reaches out to give it back to me, holding on to it as I grab it. Man, something pretty intense is happening. This is… new. "Your name is DAMIAN? You're a Damian?" I try to take the badge back, but she isn't letting go. She continues staring at me with gorgeous light blue eyes behind her glasses. Ooof. The glasses thing looks good on her. Her name badge says "KayCee." She has auburn-red hair and a hint of freckles on her pretty face. She's sexy looking and has this soft voice that carries her smiling confidence with it and right through my bones. I can feel this girl.

"Uh, yep. I'm a Damian. Guilty as charged."

Steve chuckles and offers up his thoughts. "I'll just go find a seat and you two can start picking out baby names for your kids. Jesus Christ…"

Just as I'm about to re-start our conversation, Glenn from the command center walks up with an apple and an iced tea. "Officer Damian, how are you? What's new, KayCee?"

"Oh, hi Glenn. I was just saying hello to Damian. We just… met… he just… I was…"

"Huh? It's Damian, huh? Does she have your first name yet?"

"Nope. We didn't get that far."

Glenn chuckles and seems to notice the electricity going between us. "So, KayCee darts at Prahshoot's after work? I'll bring Damian and we'll show him how we cut loose after twelve hours. That way, you get to learn his first name and see how he handles himself under the pressure of good competition and lots of alcohol. Ok if I take these two things on the house?"

KayCee hasn't taken her eyes off of me for most of the time Glenn has been talking. I'm actually trying to think about cold things and stuff I see on 'The World at War' to keep me, well, calm. It isn't working. "Uh...sure Glenn." Smiling, Glenn walks away to enjoy his snack.

"Hey, I'd like to get up, stretch my legs a bit and go grab a soda. Would you mind sitting on my lap...on my chair...and badging people in for a moment? It's no big deal. Just take it from them and punch it in here? Would you do that for me?"

"If I sit on your lap, would you show me exactly how to do it?" She gets quiet, puts her head down and closes her eyes, shaking her head slowly from side-to-side. "Ok, I'm going to go get that soda. Thanks." Off she goes, in a hurry. I don't think I offended her. I hope not.

I sit down and watch her walk away in her burnt-orange dress and…wow matching heels. She is slender up top but has some healthy curves that fill out her dress. Man, her walk is fun to watch. Yep - she has a great butt.

"Psssst. PSSST!" I look over as Steve is pushing his long french fry through an onion ring, back and forth and giggling at me as he's doing it. He's got his pointer finger extended toward me at the same time in case I wasn't sure that his sexual innuendo was aimed at me. The guy loves being sophomoric, but the point is made. She and I have something sparking here, and not just a small one. This is going to be an interesting rest of the day. I'm not so sure anything else can top the events that I've been part of. Most days are kind of boring, but not today. Today has been eventful, to say the least. I'm just not sure what can top it.

Probably nothing.

Chapter 17

My return to the front entrance brings more drama to the rest of my shift. All things considered, I'm not totally shocked. There is blood all over the walls. It appears that our friend caught a second wind and started bouncing and spinning around causing mayhem and, well, excessive blood spillage. He decorated the front entryway. It didn't help that Smalley cracked him in the nose and cut him above his eyelid. The blood went everywhere. Somehow in the midst of it all, Davis got head butted on his nose and more blood went flying. Jesus Christ, what a mess. Thank heavens a cleaning lady from housekeeping is having at it. She's probably gonna be here for a while. It's a pretty sucky job and I don't mean maybe. I watch her cleaning system: she wets the walls, wipes and repeats. Unfortunately, it seems like she is simply spreading it around more. Then, I notice her badge: new employee. It looks like it's her first day at this job and, if I had to guess, doing this kind of work. She needs a mop and a bucket. As I look around, I imagine that if I walked in here without knowing what happened, I'd think a horror movie was being filmed. Christ.

Another guard, Phillip Yelston, is walking my way. I hope it's my relief. "Damian, Sgt. Smalley wants to see you in the office right away. Why aren't you answering your radio?" I look down and notice that the green light is off. That means it's dead. "Oh yeah,"

Yelston says, "Zucker said to tell you 'gotcha,' whatever that means. That guy is a crack-up, huh?"

I shake my head. Really? "He sure is." I start to walk away and turn back to Yelston. "Radio Smalley that I'm on my way please. Thanks, Phillip." I can't believe it. Through all of the mayhem and bullshit, through the unreal moments I had with KayCee in the cafeteria, somehow... someway... he switched my battery with his dying one. Who thinks to do shit like that? Christ, the guy is really wired differently.

Time to leave the blood fest that is the front area for something better. In this case, it's Smalley's office. Generally, that's not the place to be. I mean, the guy keeps a messy place, but I'd rather be there than here. I head to the elevator and up to the fourth floor. Smalley is waiting for me in his office. "C'mon in," he says as he motions me into the room. "Shut the door." I step in and notice that his office is, well, clean. I mean, it looks like he paid a professional service to come in and take care of everything for him. It looks like a team of maids were set loose and told to go at it. My God, he even has some sort of family picture on his desk? What the fuck?

"Crazy shit out there, huh?" he asks as I stand looking around the room. "That guy went ape-shit and you, you handled yourself well with our visitor. So, I wanted to thank you and tell you 'good job.' Really, you acted decisively and forcefully. That's the only way to do it." He's talking like somebody has hijacked the real Smalley and replaced him with some strange twin. "Anyway," he continues, "let's talk about our report, ok? We need to coordinate what we saw so that the police get an accurate picture of how

186

everything went down…from our perspective… understand? We might have gotten caught in a tough one here, but we can adjust everything and make it all fine." He hesitates a moment. "I just need your help. Can you do that?"

"Sure Sarge, what do you need from me."

Smalley sits up in his chair and smiles. "It's pretty simple: everything stays in but the cuffs. That's it. It is as easy as that and we all move on to the next shift. The cuffs got left on by accident. That could be viewed as excessive force by some…by a lawyer that might get involved. This guy is ex-University of Miami football and he's got lots of friends. We want this to go away so we need this done right. I want your report to me in one hour and I want it done in pencil, is that clear?"

"Yep, I'll get it done and in pencil and back to you in one hour. No problem." Christ, Smalley screwed with the wrong guy this time. Now he has all of us on some sort of damage control. Why does he do this? Why does he always have to do the wrong thing and fuck people over? Now he has me lying on a form that can be used in a courtroom. Smalley is no good and never will be. He's an asshole.

I sit down and begin to weave a tale about a guy on PCP who suddenly broke loose from three security guards and came at me like a Rhino. I had to defend myself and knocked him down. I put down a six-foot-five, two-hundred-and-fifty-pound ex-football player on PCP. Yep. This report is already a joke and I haven't even written it yet. Fuck. Suddenly, I realize that the best way to do this is to think like my man Steve Zucker and write the lie that makes the most sense to me. You know, sort of make it like it was a movie. Now that will be simple. Good old Steve - he's inspiring in so many ways. I'll have to thank him in person. Maybe I will if I can get my radio battery changed.

The shift ends and Glenn meets up with me at the time clock. "Damian, let's go, my friend. It's time to leave the dusty and dirty existence that is this twelve-hour coffin in a construction site and drink alcohol until the sun is high in the sky. Translation: let's blow this popsicle stand and get drunk. You in?"

"Fuck yes, I'm done and ready."

"You better be. This just might be your coming-out party. Watch out."

I'm not sure what he means by that but Zucker follows behind him and asks, "Are you coming out? Really? I thought you were straight?" He pushes me and gives me a laugh, pointing to the outside. "It's still dark. I love that we get to act like there's still night left for us to have some fun in, you know. It's great. I'll head over to White House and pick us up a couple regulars and bring them to the Prahshoot. We can do our booze and breakfast act. Everybody will be jealous. Seven bucks -- cough it up!" It isn't a cheap breakfast, but it will be tasty.

It is pouring rain and supposed to get worse as the day goes by. There is a pretty strong storm blowing in. I drive over with Glenn who decides it is the perfect time to interrogate me about the bloody event at the front entrance.

"Smalley can be a dangerous guy if you give him the chance," he tells me. "Don't give him the chance. Stay out of his way and on his good side as long as you can. If you get pulled into his close circle, you might not like the job so much. I'm giving you fair warning: the guy is a wildcard. You better be on your toes. Be smart."

I appreciate Glenn's words and know he's looking out for me. I wish I could follow what he is telling me but that's not really my direction. I've signed on for dirtier shit and now Smalley realizes the same thing. He better -- my report was nothing but one big lie, all of it. Oh sure, I stuck to the PCP observation angle and wrote "he had a crazed look in his eyes and was speaking incoherently." I certainly didn't speak to him wearing handcuffs so yes, I lied big time. It's my admission into the club. I have to do it, so I did, and it wasn't hard…not hard at all.

"Ok Damian, darts are a big thing here but then again, so is drinking. KayCee comes over now and then. She's a pretty cool chick. I'm gonna let you in on a little secret so you know the deal. Her last boyfriend turned out to be a real asshole and she got hurt, even smacked around a bit from what I can gather."

"Yeah well, cowards hit women and I got no respect for any guy who does that kind of shit, you know? It's just wrong."

"I don't know the details, but I know she has been playing it pretty cool with guys since then. You know, almost cold. I think she's being very careful. I saw the way you two hit it off from across the room and know what I'm looking at. You look like you might get along just fine. I see it so here's the deal: I drove you here and I'll stay out of your way. Nobody will be bothering you because everybody is cutting loose and having their own good time. The bar rules are simple: no uniforms or name tags allowed so this shirt comes off and you hang out in your tee shirt, unless you brought a different shirt. The owners set this place up well. The Prahshoot is our place and we've been pouring cash into it since Bixby's first started going up. That's saying something because Mi Amigos is a lot closer. So, it's our bar and we like it that way."

"Sounds cool to me. I like it. I'm in."

"Yep, you are, or at least I think you are. Let's park and head in."

As we head into the front entrance, we are met by a bouncer standing inside the enclosed front doorway, out of the rain. Glenn greets him like an old friend. "Hey Jocko."

"Hey Glenn. Is he with you?"

"Yep, he's one of ours. Jocko, meet Ted." We shake hands. Jocko lets me know that there is a five-dollar cover charge to get in but, because I'm with Glenn, there is no charge for me today. Pretty cool. We thank him and head in. "Five bucks to get in?" I ask Glenn. "This guy must be raking in the dough, huh? It sounds like it's busy. Let's check it out."

I walk in and the medium sized crowd is lively and happy. There are a few dart boards on the walls, an arcade video game, a shuffleboard and lots and lots of smoke. One chick is passing around a small cigar. So far, this place is pretty fuckin' cool.

"C'mon," Glenn grabs my arm. "I want you to meet the owners. I'm sure that they're here tonight. They're always around for special occasions and tonight is a special occasion. So, to the bar, my friend." We mix through the crowd and work our way to the bar.

There are two guys behind the bar, laughing their asses off as they pour drinks. "Hey, you serve Irish here?" Glenn yells at them. As they turn, I recognize the face: it's Nate Calo.

"Fuck no, get your Mick ass out of my respectable establishment. But him," he says, pointing to me, "this guy drinks free all night." There are laughs all around and I quickly realize that it is, in fact, my night. Hell, it might even be my week. Glenn and Nate are old buddies and it's pretty obvious they've talked about me.

"Teddy, Nate is the man. I understand you two know each other, am I right?"

"Uh yeah, we've bumped into each other now and then. Sure, we know each other."

"Good, because he's my friend and is the kind of friend you want. Now, head up to the bar and let's see what surprise he cooks up for you."

I walk up to the bar and Nate extends his hand. We shake like old pals. "My man Mr. Ted, welcome to The Prahshoot!"

"Very nice," I tell him as I look around. "You even helped out the Medigans with the name spelling. I like it."

"My two brothers and I thought it was wise," he tells me with a wink. "Hey, I'm really a casino man these days but I come in now and then to help out butter-fingers over there so folks don't suck on broken glass instead of ice." He does a backwards thumb pointing motion and tells me, "that's my little brother, J.J." He turns and yells, "Hey Jay, meet my buddy over here." Jay walks over, shakes my hand and smiles at me.

"Good to meet you." He points back to Nate. "He offer you a drink yet? He won't go for ice water, this one." A little laugh and he turns to pour a drink for another customer.

"Kristi, hey Kristi, come over here for a moment. Kristi!" Nate yells at s pretty girl near the bar. She walks over and stares at him with a serious look, putting her hands on her hips.

"Don't yell at me, Nate. I don't work here anymore. Jesus Christ, I came to drink, not serve. What the fuck do you want now, you pain-in-the-ass?"

Nate leans into me and whispers, "Give that one some room. She's nothing but trouble, I bullshit you not. Word to the wise: she's a taker, know what I'm saying? She is fun though so I'm bringing her in on the game." Nate waves at Kristi to come closer. "Let's do some pillow shots, Kristi. New guy here…pillow shots!"

Kristi giggles, steps toward me and spins me around to face her. "What's his name?" she asks Nate.

"Well tonight, his name is Lucky. I dub thee Lucky," he tells me with a quick pat to the top of my head and a nod to Kristi. "Now, let's get our boy set up over here and ready." Kristi has a huge smile on her face as she tells me, "This is a cool little drinking challenge for you. Just trust me and listen to what I tell you to do. It is a lot of fun. I think you'll like it." With a quick movement, she takes off her shirt to expose what looks to be a cocktail waitress halter top. Her boobs are pushed up a bit and she reaches under to adjust and move them around.

Glenn chimes in, "Oh, this is the best part!"

"Well, I hear you guys like these, so I take them everywhere I go" she says smiling at Glenn and then turns back to the bar. "Nate, blindfold or no blindfold?"

"Blindfold, it's more fun that way." Wait, there's a blindfold involved? And I gotta trust this one: the one he told me to watch out for? SHIT. She wraps a blindfold around my eyes, tells me, "pillow time" and buries my head into her boobs. I feel a pillow go behind my head. Kristi whispers into my ear, "Lean back Lucky, far back. Lay your head on the bar. Trust me." What the hell is about to happen?

"Open your mouth," she continues. "It's shot time. First shot you swallow. Take a breath. Second shot, same thing. Third shot hold in your mouth. You got it?"

"Oh fuck. Sure, I got it. Am I gonna die tonight?"

"If you're lucky, you will! Wait...you are LUCKY! Now, head back!"

I do as she says and hear Nate tell me, "first up, Stolichnaya Vodka" as he pours it into my open mouth. I let it collect until he stops. It's a good amount. I steady myself and swallow carefully. Boom. Shot number one is done. "He fuckin' aced that one. Yes! That's a good start right there, my friend, a good start. Ok, shot number two: Dewar's White Label." He pours the second shot but this time, he makes sure he over-fills my mouth. I don't flinch. I'm not going to fail this. I hold steady as I begin to slowly swallow the liquid, little by little. It's not easy, but I get it done. Whew two down, I'm almost there. I've almost got this in the bag. It's not that hard. Besides, no one really likes to spill a drink, especially when it's alcohol. That really is the epitome of being wasteful. I've come a long way since the Senior prom incident, and I've learned a few tricks along the way. I will never again mix grape and grain and I always pound down the water when I start to drink. Those key elements have helped me develop a tougher physical and mental tolerance to alcohol. Needless to say, I can hold my liquor much better these days.

"Damn, Lucky here nailed that one as well. The kid is cruising through the game. He might just be a natural at this shit. Ok last one: Olmeca Tequila." I hear some shuffling around and Kristi whispers, "Remember, don't swallow this time. You must keep it in your mouth."

"Ok, I will." Here goes. Nate pours the tequila into my mouth. This time, he doesn't overflow but fills it to the top. I lay there, waiting.

"Ok, close your mouth without swallowing and sit up," Kristi tells me. I do so and she takes the blindfold off. "Turn to the bar, slowly fill the big shot glass and then drink it down without using your hands: teeth only. You have ten seconds."

What? Oh shit. I turn and realize I can't spit it quickly without spilling a bunch, so I have to let it drain with a little pressure to get it in the glass. "Six... five... four." As they count down, I empty my mouth, bite the glass and whip it up and back so that I can easily drink the fuckin' thing. "Two." As they hit one, I swallow the drink and release the glass from my teeth, catching it in my left hand. I did it: I fucking did it.

"You did it my man! You did it!" Nate comes around the bar and hits me on the back. Hell yes, I did. I like winning these kids of games plus, I'll start to catch a nice little buzz in a few moments. That'll be the bonus payoff: that and the fact that the drinks were free. Victory is mine!

I look around. Just like I thought, Glenn is already over at the dart board. He gives me a big smile and what looks to be a congratulatory, exaggerated head nod. I give it back to him, then he makes this sideways head nod toward the bar. My expression to him is "what? He does the same thing only this time, he moves his eyes so that they are looking at the bar area. Ahhh, ok. I scan the bar and I see the usual suspects plus a few new ones who have walked up. There is Nate at the end talking with *her.* It's KayCee. She pivots on her bar stool to face me, smiling and laughing.

"Lucky, huh? More like talented. So, any drops spilled or was that as clean as it looked from over here? I mean, that was pretty good. I think you've done this before. Have you?"

"Yep, but the first time was all spill and nobody rewarded me. Then, it was more like an ass kicking as I recall. You know what they say right? You learn from your mistakes."

"Did you?"

"I sure did and I learned so much I was able to skip college and go right off into the world. You might say, I encourage that kind of thing. My Pop has another way to say it. He calls it 'you're a fuck-up and you're gonna need to find any shit job sooner rather than later.' I think that is a generational thing though. You know, because he and his contemporaries beat the world's bad guys and saved us all. They get credit for that, so I cut him some slack. It's only right."

Nate comes back and briefly interrupts us. "Hey, you two I got two seats over here on this side. They are yours now if you want them. It's that high-top over there. You want it?" KayCee smiles and nods, then reaches down for a shot that was poured and downs it.

"I might not catch up to you if you keep going, but I can handle myself." Down goes another shot. "I like Jameson," she tells me. "I'm an Irish Whiskey girl. It's my thing. Do you like Whiskey?"

"Nope. Well to be fair, I do like it, but I get a little aggressive on it, so I watch myself, you know?"

She stops from getting up, pauses and then smiles at me with all her teeth showing. I must have struck some kind of nerve. "Nate, two Jame-ees?" she asks and shows him the "small size" with her thumb and index finger.

"And two BIG waters please," I add. I have to have my water or none of this will go well. Water is the savior when it comes to drinking as much as I want. I can do it, but I gotta work my system and I need some cigarettes.

"Ok then, whiskey, it is for us Mr. Lucky. Let's go grab our table, huh?"

We meander over to a spot that's just perfect for us: a high-top table in a corner that's out of sight from the rest of the place. Although, I'm betting they're too focused on their own good time to bother with us. The guy playing Pacman not far from our spot hasn't moved since I walked in so he's either spending a lot of quarters on learning the game or he's trying to establish himself as the king of high scores. Pacman is new so, whatever he puts up for a score will get broken fairly soon.

"You play?" KayCee asks me.

"I do, but I'm not great at it and I get bored after a while. Why is it that whoever is playing it is so damn good at it? Jesus, some of these guys should get paid, they put in so much time. It's a little crazy to me, you know?"

She nods her head, looks down and then leans on her hands and gives me a slight but pretty smile. She is a good-looking woman for sure, and her eyes sparkle. I can feel the ever-present current running between us. It's just so obvious. Even when we got up to walk to the table, it felt like we moved in unison, in rhythm -- like we knew each other's steps, each other's movement. It's quietly powerful. There is something completely uncommon about this woman, and although I've tried to chalk it up to a simple attraction, I sense something different from her. This is not your average girl. She's…unique. I felt it as soon as I started talking to her. I don't know how I know, but I know it, and something tells me I'm gonna find out sooner than later. Well, no time like the present. I'm ready.

Chapter 18

"I want to tell you something and it's very personal -- just for you and me. I feel I have to and it's not something I normally do. Would that be ok?" KayCee asks as she leans into me over the table. Of course, that is the moment that Nate decides to arrive with our drinks and ask us how we are doing.

"We're doing great. It ain't darts but we're having a good time, man. You got a great place here," I tell him, hoping he will leave as quickly as he came.

"Most folks like it here, and we do a great lunch and dinner crowd as well. Oh yeah, and remember, those drinks are on the house. Enjoy!" He turns around and walks a couple steps then turns back. "By the way, tomorrow you pay full price." We laugh.

The Pacman guy and his buddies are screaming. Apparently, he entered a galactic scoring zone. One member of the group walks over and passes us a cigar. "This is getting passed around, man. Hit it and move it. It's pretty good shit!" KayCee reaches for it, takes two big drags, holds it and passes it to me. I follow suit. We stare at each other and I hold up both of my hands to do a sort of 'count down' with my fingers, from ten to none. When we get there, we exhale and hardly any smoke comes out. Damn, she's good.

"I need to use the bathroom. Hold that drink until I get back." Off she goes. I sip some of my water, realizing I just smoked pot mixed into a cigar. Well, that's different - I'd like to see that factory.

Hell, I'd like to work there. I look over to see Glenn walking toward me, grinning like a Cheshire Cat.

"I'm on fire on the dart board. I'm up ten bucks. How are you doing over here, Teddy Boy? You guys ok? Wait, wait, don't answer -- I'm just busting your balls, man. Just checking in. Let me know if you need a ride or anything, cool?"

"Cool, thanks Glenn." He leaves and turns back as he's walking away to give me the thumbs up sign. KayCee strolls through the crowd, makes her return and sits back down. She looks a little stoned. "You have beautiful eyelashes, you know," she tells me as she stares straight into my eyes. "They're gorgeous. You *are* lucky, even more than what Nate thinks!"

"If I was a girl, I'd be lucky. I understand girls would kill for these, but they're just eyelashes to me, you know?"

"Well, when I saw them, I mean you, it did kind of stop me. You're...gorgeous. I think you're just gorgeous." As she talks, she stops smiling and gives me a more wide-eyed look. I have had girls tell me that I'm everything from funny to cute, but gorgeous sounds like her booze talking. "So, thanks for coming to get something to eat while I was working. I was very happy to finally meet you...I mean....to meet you. Cheers." We throw back the oversized shots and I lean over to touch her. She pulls back a bit. That surprises me.

"Are you sensitive, or am I being too aggressive?" KayCee signals to Nate for two more. It looks like she's trying to get us plastered. I'm not so sure I want that.

"You are definitely not being too aggressive, I promise. It's just that well, it's hard for me right now. I really like you, but I need a few drinks, that's all. I just like to drink a bit." She looks down at the table and starts pulling at the napkins. "So, no, you're not being too aggressive. I'm sorry, I really am. I just want to do it this way. I really need to." I think back to what Nate told me. She must have been treated very badly and still has problems because of it.

I lean in and try to get her to look up at me. "I won't do anything to hurt you, KayCee. I'm sorry. I mean, it's ok if you want to have some drinks and relax because so do I. I'm not gonna lie, I'm dying to touch you and it's hard not to right now." KayCee closes her eyes, leans her head back, takes a deep breath and lets out a slight sigh. She keeps her head back, sighs again, then leans her head forward and shakes it a bit, looking down the whole time. She stays quiet for a bit, then opens her eyes and smiles at me.

A girl from the bar breaks the silence as she puts two drinks in front of us. "Nate told me to bring these over so here you go. Oh yeah," she hands us another cigar, "this is making the rounds as well."

KayCee shakes her head. "I'm ok for now." So am I so we move the cigar over to team Pacman. KayCee takes a big gulp of water and then picks up the whiskey glass and shoots down half. I do the same with mine and then guzzle my water a bit. Whatever is going on with this woman, I want more of it because she's got my full attention. "Teddy, I'm not drinking because of pain or discomfort. That's not why I'm doing it. To tell you the truth, I haven't felt anything close to the way I felt when I first saw you in a very long time. I can feel it and I know you can too. That's it."

"What's it? What are you telling me?"

"It's simple and it's also complicated. I'm just...kind of sensitive...physically. Not just a little, but a lot. It's how I'm built, I guess. I control things and do just fine, but it's difficult sometimes. I decided pretty quickly after I first saw you that I was going to ease up and not fight what I feel for you, because it's pretty strong. You got my attention." I look around quickly and return my eyes to hers. "So, do we stay here, or do you want to get out of here?"

I reach out and touch her hand. She tenses up, tells me, "Don't -- not here," closes her eyes, and the noise she was making earlier is a little louder. And now, right at this moment, I'm finally realizing what she is trying to tell me.

"So, what happens if I kiss you, right here and now? Will that be bad?" She laughs a bit and lightly pounds her fists on the table-top to make her point, shaking her head the whole time.

"Oh...no, not here. It won't be bad...just...not here...please...let's get out of here...now. Trust me. My car is right in front. Let's leave and," she hesitates as she thinks for a moment. "We'll go to my sister's house. She's cool."

We get up and head for the door. Glenn and Nate are at the bar, smiling at us. Nate gives me a salute and Glenn gives me the mini wave. I take KayCee's hand and she takes mine and starts to walk faster and faster. We get to the door and she pushes it open. It's pouring rain. Shit. She tosses me her keys, yells, "Drive," and starts running toward her car: a cute white Mustang II with blue stripes. I go to put the key into the passenger door to let her in and press against her as I do. She whips around and grabs me...and holy shit, it begins. We couldn't even make it to the inside of her car. It's like a battle: a good one, but it definitely feels like there might be bruises afterward. We're just spinning in this frenzy… this dance in the rain.

Suddenly we're on the hood and she starts to peel my shirt off. I'm clawing at her dress top and starting to lose any control I might have had. I push off of her and say, "What the fuck are we doing?!" I fall off of her and we start laughing our asses off, getting soaked and splashed by a car as it goes by. We look at each other as we're laughing and slowly stop.

"Are we even going to make it home alive? Are we going to be this way in the car too? Jesus Christ."

"Yes, we'll die together. How's that?" We get into the car soaking wet. KayCee tells me where her sister lives -- way out onto the Black Horse Pike, outside of Pleasantville. Shit, I just don't think we'll make it. Here goes. I head down Atlantic Avenue and we're well, active, especially, at red lights. I get to Albany Avenue and things are getting out of hand. I glance in the rear-view mirror and see cop lights come on behind me. Shit. Why the fuck would a cop want to pull someone over in the pouring rain unless they were firing a weapon out of their window at passing cars? He must be hard-up for tickets. We're not even at the end of the month, so it's not like it's quota time. I pull to the side and watch as he approaches, then whips his car to the left and heads back the other direction. False alarm. Whew!

I look at KayCee to tell her and she reaches for me and pulls me to her mouth. Here we go again. Clothes are coming off fast and just like that, she climbs on top of me while I'm driving away. Now it's a rodeo and frankly speaking, we could die from this. The idea that "you only live once" crosses my mind as I strain to look around her. I have no idea how I'm doing it, but I manage to keep us on the road. I'm driving thirty miles per hour and somehow, we've managed to "screw" the flashers on. Ok, that's bizarre. She's pretty loud and Christ, she's biting my arm hard. I have to grit my teeth to get through it. What if we get stopped? Maybe another cop will see that I put my flashers on and think I'm being cautious in this bad rainstorm. You know, see the good citizen doing the right thing and move on. Or not. He could stop us and discover we're trying to tandem drive while screwing each other like a killer meteor is approaching earth. I mean, that's how it feels anyway. It's either going to be a meteor or one of these many cars that keep passing us at a high speed that I could easily veer into. KayCee isn't thinking about any of this, I'm pretty sure. She seems to be ok with dying this way.

Shit, I'm bleeding! She bit through my skin! What the fuck! The windshield wipers are on full blast and my vision still is pretty poor which is just one of the many struggles going on. I can't do this anymore. I push her off and over to her seat. She lets out a loud yell and punches me pretty fucking hard on my arms and chest.

"Hey...hey...stop it...time out, KayCee. Time out! Hold on! I'm going to pull over. Jesus Christ, we'll never make it to your sister's house -- never! We're going to die! I have to pull over."

"Fuck no," she screams back at me. "Are we stopping? I don't want to stop. No. Why are we stopping? You better not be stopping, Teddy."

"No, hell no, we're not stopping, we're just pulling over, that's all. It's just a stop, ok? Somewhere…anywhere." I see something to the left that is big and dark. Whatever it is, it looks closed and I'm going to drive around and park behind it. Thank God. I navigate my way around a strange little road and soon I'm on sand. I put the car in park, climb onto her in the passenger seat and push. The damn seat breaks and goes backward. KayCee doesn't flinch. We return to attack each other, like the movie we're in just got pushed to fast forward. It's a whirlwind. I can't believe how many fucking times she's slapped and bitten me -- God damn, hard too. I yell from the pain and she yells "louder." It gets louder than it already was. Jesus Christ, this is nuts. I can't take it anymore. I reach over and punch the passenger door open. We fall and drag ourselves out and end up right where we started: on her hood. It's pouring rain but I had to break out from that car before she killed me inside of it. It is ironic, considering I thought that could only happen while we're screw-driving.

The whole thing is out of control, and I can't stop. I don't want to. This is like other-galaxy sex or something. It's like the best fight I've ever had combined with sex that I couldn't even imagine. I'm bleeding from my arm and my lip where she bit down when we were inside the car. It's still loud and we've fallen off the hood and onto the sand. We scramble back to the hood, completely soaked. Somehow, we're keeping this bizarre battle going.

I ask her, "Back in the car?" and she answers, "Don't care." So, we drag each other into the backseat again. Holy shit, it's like we're doing another drug -- us. This 'us' goes on and on, seemingly in waves. The pace slows and speeds, slows and speeds. I'm lost in her.

When the battle finally ends, I stagger out of the back seat and back into the rain. I let out a loud scream that lasts for a while. I just need to scream. I don't know why. I stumble back into the car and I'll be goddamned, KayCee is sitting up, grinning and holding her head. She leans back and starts to punch the car ceiling.

"You kept trying to touch me in the bar and I worked so hard to stop you. I couldn't let you. I can, if we are alone but, you can't touch me in public, ok? It ramps up quick for me...all over...and I just...go. Drinks help some."

"Drinks and weed, I'm thinking." I climb back into her car and hand her dress to her and as I do, I see a car turning off of the Pike and heading our way. "Put this back on, fast. A car is coming and I'm not kidding. Where the fuck are my pants?" Shit, they're out in the rain, on the sand. I threw them out the door during the whirlwind. I go back out, put them on and climb into the driver's seat. I motion to KayCee. "Get up here into the other seat, fast. We're about to have company."

"What kind of company?"

"I see pretty lights, so cop company. Shit."

The car comes around and pulls up next to us. The car door opens and a cop steps out and into the rain. This will not be good...at all.

"Evening. Are you lost? I'm thinking you're lost because the Sandcastle is private property."

"This is the Sandcastle?" I ask him. "I didn't know where we were, and I had to park. We pulled over because of the rain. It was coming down pretty hard, not like now, and it was dangerous."

"You didn't know where you were because you didn't look. You were probably busy driving carefully to a safe spot until all this rain blows over. I get it. So, IDs...both of you"

KayCee and I have to dig around to find them. Mine seems lost and then I find it under a seat. Christ, this looks pretty stupid. We hand them to him, and he tells us, "be right back."

"We're screwed," I tell KayCee. "He's running our names. He's going to come back and write us tickets for being under the influence and trespassing. Your car could get towed. Not good. I think maybe we should have just fucked ourselves to death...either out on the Pike or back here. Dying might have been a better option than this."

"Maybe he'll just give us a warning," she replies. "I mean, he looks like a nice guy, don't you think?"

I shake my head. "I don't know any Egg Harbor Township cops and I don't know him, so I can't tell you."

A couple minutes later, he walks back to us and hands us our IDs. "I need you to get back in your vehicle and wait here, do you understand? You are not to leave. Sit tight."

"Are we being charged with something?" He looks at us both and laughs a bit, shaking his head and tells me, "You sit in your car and wait, understand? Otherwise, I will start writing you tickets and

I'm really not sure where I'll start. I have too many options. So, sit tight."

We sit in the car and sit some more. I'm starting to think that maybe this is all a way to help us sober up so we can just go home. He'll tell us, "I never want to see you again." I can hope. Well, maybe I can, because here comes another cop car. It looks different. As it pulls forward and turns, I can see the writing on the car. Shit - Atlantic City. He called my brother-in-law. Fuck, I'm really screwed now. This is really going to suck. The first cop pulls away and the second cop gets out of his car and walks toward us. It's not my brother-in-law. Who is this guy?

"Teddy Damian?" Oh, it's Billy Fry's dad. I played football with Billy in high school.

"Mr. Fry?"

"Sergeant Fry. I heard this called out and Officer Jefferson reached out to me privately. He was kind enough to let me intercede before he had to haul you off and the car, you understand? So, let's go back to my car and talk." Sarge steps forward and leans into the open door to talk with KayCee. "Young lady, good evening. If you would be so kind as to wait here, we'll be right back. Thank you." Sarge walks me back to his car and says, "get in." I do. "First off, you look like shit which tells me you two couldn't pass any tests right now and that would be really bad. So, I'm just going to make this simple for you. I'm giving you a one-time pass. You're getting off with a warning from me, do you understand? Your brother-in-law is off duty tonight, so he isn't going to be hearing about this. This is just between us. I'm doing you this one favor, one time, for a Mustang football player. This is it. You understand me?"

"Yes sir, I understand. It won't happen again."

"Bullshit. You two look like you like each other quite a bit, so I'm thinking it will happen again, just not anywhere near my jurisdiction, and I mean that. You copy me? And stay the hell away from the Sandcastle. This is private property with private security patrolling the grounds occasionally. You might get your ass beat and then the police will show up. Not good -- not good at all. Oh yeah also, and this is just from me, the next time you and your girlfriend decide to take a drunken joy ride, you might consider turning off the inside light in the car because you gave plenty of people a show. That's pretty much why you didn't get stopped, you entertained folks. Next time, that won't be the case."

Shit, we were being watched the whole time, or at least a good portion of it. The light was on. Really? Damn, I feel even more stupid.

"Listen Teddy, pussy ain't worth dying over. The next time you and your friend get ideas and you have no place to go, and chances are you will, just take her out here to one of the places on the Pike closer to my turf, you get it? The Venus Inn or the Sunset Motel are both cheap and safe. Now, how about you head down to Louie's Diner around the corner and get both of you some coffee. Make it strong. Then, get both of your asses home. Get out of here -- I got real criminals to deal with."

I exit the car and go back to KayCee. She looks worried. "What happened...are we in trouble? Is he going to arrest us? What did he say?"

"Well, for one thing no, he's not going to arrest us although he's well aware he could do just that. We get to leave. He even suggested a couple of places we could go to, you know, have our fun. I wasn't expecting that."

"That's it? That's all? Oh my God I thought we were in huge trouble, didn't you? Wow. We get to leave?"

"Yep, we do. I'm not taking all of his advice though because he suggested a Diner down the street for coffee. I don't like coffee, do you?"

"I love coffee! Come home with me to my sister's and I won't make you drink any coffee. She has a basement with a back entrance. She won't bother us. She needs to get to work anyway. Let's do that"

Ok, let's get out of here. We stay here any longer and you might end up in cuffs." KayCee giggles and pats me on my chest a few times. "Let's wait until we get into my bed before we do that."

Chapter 19

I punch in and see cocktail waitress Leena walking quickly toward me. She looks upset. Leena is what you might describe as Amazonian -- not the least bit of fat on her body, tall, blonde and very curvy. She's a veteran casino worker from Vegas and, if you ask her, she'll tell you that she has been around and back. She's the co-leader of the cocktail waitress pack at Bixby's, along with her friend Cafe, a gorgeous black woman built about the same way. The two make sure their 'girls' handle their jobs correctly. They are professionals and I respect them.

"Are you on duty?" she asks as she nears me. "I need your help right now. I just heard that one of my girls is having trouble with an ex-boyfriend who followed her down to our break lounge. They are arguing and he won't leave her alone. You need to get him out of here."

I tell Jody at the punch-in desk to call for security back-up and start to run toward the break lounge, checking to see if any other guards are in the vicinity. I don't see anyone so it's just going to be me there to start. As I enter the room, a waitress points to a back-hallway door. "They went out there - hurry. He grabbed her and they are fighting!"

I hear yelling and screaming from the hallway. As I walk through the door, I see a man slap one of the waitresses across the face. I quickly move toward them to put myself between the man and the waitress. As I do so, the man turns to me and throws a punch, connecting with my chest. His girlfriend quickly takes the opportunity to run back into the lounge. I punch back with my left hand, hitting the side of the man's face. We start wrestling and punching each other as we spin. I try to pull his shirt over his head (like I would in a hockey fight) but it's too tight. I'm going to have to battle it out with him and try to gain some advantage while avoiding any big blows. We slide off each other. I'm on the ground about to get up when suddenly, things change. Everything goes into slow motion as I see Leena appear with a round waitress tray in her hands. She grabs it tightly and swings it hard, connecting with the man's throat and knocking him back. As he grabs at his throat, she swings the tray up in front of his face with her left hand and, with her right palm flattened, she throws a punch that connects with the tray and into his face. Jesus Christ, I think she just broke his fuckin' nose. He is down on one knee, grabbing his nose and screaming as blood pours out. Leena drops the tray and assumes this battle-ready looking position, her knees bent and right leg forward. Her left leg swings up toward his head and delivers a strong kick. Down he goes. Leena destroyed the guy. Holy shit, Leena is a killer. She serves drinks in a casino? What in the fuck is going on?

"Are you fucking kidding me?" I ask her, the awe apparent in my voice. "That was fucking unbelievable. How the fuck did you do that, and in heels?"

She gives a small laugh and leans into me, holding onto my shoulder as she adjusts the high heel on her left foot. "I got lucky."

As she talks, Smalley and three other guards come through the door. Leena bends over, sounding like she is in pain. She winks and makes a stern face at me. "Oh, thank God it's over," she says, sounding as if she can hardly believe what she just saw. "I tried to do something but thank God, this security guard handled it. I guess I grabbed the right guy when I asked him for help. If it wasn't for him well, I don't know what might have happened. That asshole was smacking around one of my girls. Is she in there? Is she alright?" Leena asks, pointing to the break room. She doesn't wait for an answer as she walks toward the door and goes inside. Smally calls HQ and asks them to send for the Atlantic City police to come for the guy.

"You ok?" he asks me.

"Uhhh yea, I think so. I banged my head pretty hard, but it should be alright. It does hurt."

"Ok, I'll close this out. Go get yourself checked out. Nice work here." Smally sends me to the nurse's station. I walk there with Leena and the other waitress, Sonya. Sonya goes in first so Leena and I have a chance to chat.

"So, what in the fuck was that all about? Seriously, you go all ninja on him and I mean like Special Forces shit, and then point to me like I did it? Why? What the fuck is going on? You kicked that guy's ass and you're not going to tell anyone? What's the deal? Are you hiding something?"

"Oh sure, something like that. Anyway, let's get our story straight before it goes down on paper. Can we do that together?"

What choice do I have? If she doesn't get what she wants, she might kick my ass. I can't believe how super-human she is. The woman is unreal. All I can think about at this moment is having sex with her and, it suddenly dawns on me, I might die from it. She could kill me during sex. Is that even possible?

"Hey...hey...Officer Damian? Are you listening to me or are you going to keep staring at my tits?"

Do I even do that sort of thing? "What? No...no...I wasn't...staring...I was thinking. I don't like to...stare. I don't do that."

Leena grabs my face and pulls it up slightly to look at hers. "I need your help. It's pretty simple, it's actually very simple. I just need you to write what I tell you to on the report and everything will be fine. Do you understand?" I nod and smile. She continues, 'I'll make sure you get taken care of for this but only if you promise to keep this between the two of us, ok? It can never go any farther. If it does, I'll know, and I won't be happy."

All I heard was, "you get taken care of" and ask her, "Are you going to...take care of me?"

Leena frowns and shakes her head. "Jesus Christ, no. I'll make sure that you DO get taken care of. Now, shake and trust me on this. Shake." We shake hands.

I don't exactly know what is in store for me but I'm thinking it's going to be better than if I was sitting on Santa's lap and that's a real good thing.

I head over to Park Place and jump on the elevator to meet Officer Caroll on the seventh floor. I know he's got a cushy job and must love what he does up there. Although, I'm not sure if that would be my feeling. There's not much action wandering the halls. What the hell, though. If Smalley wants me to go to the hotel and roam around, that's what I'm going to do.

The elevator doors open, and I'm greeted by a grinning Phillip Caroll. "Hello, Security Officer Damian. What brings you to our fine establishment?" The grin fades. "Check that. What the hell are you doing over here in the hotel? Rookies usually don't get this kind of job. Who are you sleeping with?"

"Easy there Phillip my boy," I tell him, patting him on the shoulder. "It's my understanding that we're shorthanded tonight and by shorthanded, I mean there's only so many good-looking guys to give all these pretty girls the smile they deserve. Smalley says he wants the ugly people over by the exits. You're it."

"Fuck you Damian, you ass kisser. I'm thinking you fall asleep over here. Then, when I get sent to relieve you for your break, I'll find you and piss on you to wake you up. Now that's a shift worth talking about." Carol gets onto the elevator and gives me a wave. "Keep your eyes open Damian or the next thing you might feel is a stream hitting you on your nose. Sleep tight."

As the doors close, I give him the middle finger and we both laugh. I look around. So here I am on hotel roaming duty. How exciting. Since it's just past 10:30 PM, I probably won't see too many people around. I do get to go downstairs to the first floor and do a "fly by" on whoever is stationed there. That's always fun. You get to see what type of food is being served at Madame Mimi's

Café. More like Madame Mimi's house of overpriced three-piece shrimp cocktails.

I pick up my walkie-talkie. "Damian to first-floor, Damian to first-floor, over. Check-in."

The device squawks back. "First-floor back, it's Williamson. What's your 20 Damian? Over."

"I'm on seven now, making my rounds. I figure to stop by in about 10 minutes. Over."

"All quiet down here. I'll probably ask you for relief for five minutes. Over. Copy?"

"Copy that. See you in 10 minutes. Over." A-roaming I go. Look out drunk guests, Security Officer Damian is on the prowl. I carry a radio and a stern smile. I'll have them shaking in their boots.

One of the things we are trained to do as security guards is check the fire extinguishers every time we see one. They don't give us a quiz or anything. They just tell us, "Remember to check all extinguishers: the life you save someday may be your own." Bullshit. If there's a fire, I'll run my ass down one of the stairwells as fast as I can. Let's be real, they can't all be filled with smoke and fire, can they?

I work my way up to the 11th floor through the stairwells and notice several trays outside the rooms. Amazing -- people have already had room service. If it were me, I'd order a hot fudge sundae this time of night.

"Sgt. Smalley to officer Damian, come in Damian." Oh boy, I wonder what Smalley wants now? Maybe he'll give me a brief quiz on how many fire extinguishers I've checked so far?

I reach for my radio. "Damian here."

"Damian, meet me at the elevators on the sixth floor. Do you copy?"

"Sixth floor elevators, I copy." I make my way down the stairs to the sixth floor and hustle over to the elevator doors. Sure enough, Smalley is already waiting for me with a very, dare I say, stupid look on his face.

"I have Caroll's break time covered already. No need to worry about that. Hop on the elevator. We're going to pay a visit."

I do as he says and ask, "Are we going to visit an old friend?"

He looks at me, a big grin pulling at the corners of his mouth. "No, not an old friend. It's new friend time." The elevator stops on the ninth floor. We get off and hang a right, walk to the end of the hall and turn left, proceeding down the hall until we stop at door 915. Smalley turns to me. "I have a little surprise for you."

The door opens. We walk inside to see none other than the high-heeled assassin herself: Leena. She quickly catches my eye, winks and purses her lips together as if trying to shush me. Holy shit, what is she doing here? I'm pretty sure that she is supposed to be down on the casino floor helping all those wonderful people get drunk and lose a bunch of money.

"Well, if it isn't my hero Officer Damian! Welcome to the party. Remember, I told you that I would take care of you personally?" As she says this, her eyes widen and she nods her head slightly up and down as if to say, "I did say that, and you agree with me."

"Oh yeah, I remember that like it happened today. Come to think of it, it was today! Wow, I'm getting the feeling that you were serious."

"Okay Damian," Smalley interjects, "here's the deal. This is your party: yours alone. When you're all done, you make sure you talk to only me: nobody else." He raises his voice slightly to emphasize the point. "I mean...nobody...else. Do we understand each other?"

"Yes," I assure him. "We definitely understand each other. No problem."

Smalley walks back toward the door, opens it, as if remembering something important, turns with a smile to tell me, "have a good time and don't hurt yourself."

"Oh, Sgt.," I smile back, "you don't have to worry about a thing."

Leena drapes her arms around my shoulders and gives me a kiss on the cheek. "He's in very good hands."

Smalley closes the door. Leena lets her arms slide off my shoulders and gives me a serious look. "So, here you are. In a matter of hours, you went from a guy with some potential to man of the hour. Most important, Smalley believes in you and trusts you. That didn't take long."

"I guess I'm just a lucky guy," I tell her, the sarcasm dripping. "So, I expect that you are going to fill me in on all this, right?
"Leena walks me over to the bed and pats the mattress as if directing me to sit down next to her. I do.

"Now that we're alone I can explain a few more things. It's not what you think. I can't tell you in front of Smalley. I have to keep him in the dark, for many reasons."

I'm a bit confused. "What are you keeping from Smalley? Aren't you two working together? It looks to me like you guys are playing for the same team. Am I wrong?"

Leena looks down, trying to find the right words. "Here is what I can tell you: Smalley runs the action within the security department. Nothing gets done or pushed forward without his approval. That's a fact. He has heavy hitters backing everything he does. Getting on Smalley's good side is a beneficial idea no matter what." She looks up at me. "Let's just say I'm on his good side."

"Great," I tell her. "So am I. Unless I'm wrong, that puts you and me on the same team. Right?"

Leena smiles. "Why don't we just say, for the sake of argument, that you and I have a common interest and that it will be beneficial for both of us to work together from this point forward. How's that?"

"Ok," I agree. "That's fine with me." I look around the room. "Why am I here?"

Leena points to a door that joins a second room. "You're going to go in that room and meet Arianna. Just go in and be friendly. You'll understand once you are there. It's your initiation. Just understand that she will talk to Smalley. She's got pills, pot and powder so loosen up and have a good time." Leena puts her hand on my shoulder so that I look her in the eye. "But don't overdo anything."

"What does that mean?"

"It means don't get wasted, ok? Do a little powder and go from there. You'll figure it out pretty quickly." She stands up and motions for me to do the same. "Off you go."

I give Leena a look that says, "are you sure?" She shakes her head and tells me, "Go ahead. Get it done." I turn and walk over to the door. As I open it, I look back at Leena one more time. She gives me a backhanded wave and whispers, "Go." Ok.

I enter the room and am greeted by a woman's sultry voice. "It's about time you came in to see me. I've been sitting here for a while wondering what you are waiting for. Did you not want to see me?"

"Well," I tell the voice, "to be fair, I can't see you even in the room. Do you always entertain by candlelight?" I can make out a shadowy figure in the far corner. The figure reaches for the wall and works the light controls to bring the darkness to a soft, dimmed hue. As she begins to walk toward me, I can see her better.

She's tall, or at least tall in heels. She's wearing a long black silk robe, has dark brunette hair and gorgeous crystal green eyes. I'm not sure how many times I'm going to see stunning women today, but this one definitely tops the charts. Wow: she is an absolute knockout. Unlike Leena, she looks a bit more... feline.

"So, I understand you like to protect women," she tells me as she moves closer. "I admire that in a man. It's not everyday you find a guy who's willing to risk his own safety for a woman, you know. And you did it all by yourself? That's pretty admirable. Do you like being admired? You are a hero you know."

As she asks me the questions, she picks up a mirror and places it close to my face, positioning a rolled $100 bill at my nostril. "How would you like a little blow? Go ahead -- it's high-quality so it won't burn your nostrils. Enjoy."

I oblige and do the first line. She takes a turn and smiles at me, placing the mirror back on a small table. As she turns back, she asks, "So, Mr. Hero, what is your fancy?"

"Uhmm...this is working just fine. I guess you can say this is my fancy. You're absolutely gorgeous."

"You're sweet to say that...uh..."

"Ted, my name is Ted."

"Uh huh." She puts her hands on my waist. "I'm betting all the girls call you Teddy, am I right? If you were mine, that's what I'd call you. And those eyelashes...my goodness, what a Teddy Bear you would be for some lucky girl. Do you mind if I am that lucky girl for you right now?"

Before I have a chance to answer, she picks up the mirror, places it under my face again and points the bill at my other nostril. Wow, the first line is kicking in and feels really good and I'm starting on round two. Once more, she does the same and places the mirror down, giggling a bit. "Sit on the bed for me, please," she directs me.

I do so as she walks over to a cart with various bottles of alcohol next to a bucket of ice. "Vodka? Gin? Whiskey? Wine? What would you like?"

"I'm not picky," I tell her. "You choose."

Arianne turns to face the tray and, with a quick sweep of her hand, takes off the silk robe to reveal...well...whatever it is she's not... really... wearing. Strings -- lots of strings. They accentuate her curvy body, from her butt to her shoulders. Where do girls buy this stuff? Along with the strings, she is wearing high-heeled boots that go up past her knees. This is dangerous.

As she finishes pouring our drinks, Arianne turns and tells me, "Vodka -- straight up." Again, all I see is strings. Not that many, but strings. She looks like a semi-naked -- ok mostly naked -- goddess dressed to kill and, it appears, I'm on her hit list. She sits down next to me and hands me a glass. We take big drinks, and she touches my shoulder. "Do you like what I'm wearing? I call it 'blow his mind.' It goes great with cocaine, don't you think? It's a theme... sorta."

"Yes, I do," I assure her. "I like your theme a lot. If you're trying to blow my mind, it's working very well."

She smiles, takes my drink and places it on the table next to us. As she turns back to me, she places her hands on my shoulders, leans in and whispers in my ear. "Now it's time to blow you away."

Chapter 20

Three days ago, I had the on-the-job adventure of a lifetime but since then, it's been the standard boring security guard duty. It's not sexy but I had a safe shift and for once, I'm just going to go home and sleep. We're required to park our cars in the employee parking lot that was created way out on the Atlantic City Expressway. You jump on the shuttle and it takes you back and forth from work to the parking lot. It's actually pretty slick. They've done a good job keeping the extra traffic out of town. Still, there are plenty of cars in the city to occupy every available parking space. I'm pretty sure they're not all residents and gamblers. Since I have some time off, I figured I'd park close to have a quicker way out of town when I finish my shift.

I walk down Michigan Avenue and am approached by a man from my right coming out of the alley. "Get in the fucking car," he tells me as he pushes a gun into my rib, hiding it from sight. As he opens the back door, he shoves me in and tells me, "Scoot over behind the driver...NOW!" I do as I'm told. As I move, he jumps into the front passenger seat, turns and points the gun at me. Shit, it's the guy who got his ass kicked by Leena.

"Joel, what the fuck are you doing? You said you wanted to talk to the guy, am I right? You said talk. You didn't say nothing about pulling a gun and grabbing him. You narish tokhes putz." The driver seems quite agitated by all this. He isn't the only one.

"What do you want with me, huh?" I ask with as much bravado as I can muster. "You pull a gun on a guy you just want to talk to? Is that right? You plan on using that gun? Do you plan on shooting me?"

"Shut the fuck up, you piss ant little piece of shit. I should stick a bullet in you right now," he tells me, waving his gun in little circles.

"I want answers. You're not leaving this car unless I hear what I want to hear."

The driver quickly chimes in. "You do what you gotta do and get it done. I don't want this guy in my car any longer that he has to be." He looks in the rearview mirror and speaks to me. "Listen Tedd-ela, let's not be coy. My friend here, he's not so happy with you. I understand you can change all that by answering a few questions. There is no need for anyone to suffer any critical injuries like gunshot wounds, am I right? So, be a mensch and tell him what he wants to hear." The driver then turns back to his companion in the front seat. "There, see? I made nice and now our friend here will do the same. So, talk already. Go ahead Joel, ask the man. Go ahead."

"Ok security boy, it's pretty simple. I understand that you've been spreading stories around about a little encounter we had at your workplace. Stories that would impugn my integrity and good name. I will not let this stand." Aha, somehow this joker found out that he got beat up by a girl wearing high heels and a push-up bra. I'm thinking his friends and boss heard about it as well. With him training a gun on me, it makes perfect sense for me to tell him the truth he needs to hear, not the truth that really happened. Maybe he'll go for my story. I can only hope.

"Ok, ok. I think I know what you want to hear and I'm happy to share it with you. I wouldn't want any misunderstandings taking place. That wouldn't be right. It makes perfect sense for you to feel the way you do about this. If I were you, I'd probably feel the same way. So, let's get this cleared up so everybody can get back to their life."

That seems to calm him a bit. "Very good -- start talking."

"First off, let me assure you that I'm not spreading any rumors or stories that would negatively reflect on you or sully your otherwise fine reputation. Quite the contrary: I haven't said anything to anybody. Mums the word as far as I'm concerned."

The driver leans into his friend Joel and says to him, "See he makes nice with us and everybody's happy. Such a good start this is." The driver adjusts his rearview mirror so that I can see his eyes and a good part of his face and confirms for me what I already know: it's Mutzi Krabitz. "Do you know who I am?" he asks me.

"Nope, can't say I do. Are you somebody important?" This elicits a great deal of laughter and he wags his right index finger up in the air as if to say, "That's a good one -- that's funny."

"I'm important enough in this car to get a vote on whether or not your answers are good enough to stop my friend Joel here from shooting you. So yes, I am important. Understand?"

Joel looks more relaxed now and is waving the gun a bit as he talks. "Ok, so far so good. Tell me more."

"What would you like to know?" I need to feel this one out carefully. If I tell him that Leena was the one who actually kicked the living shit out of him, I'm thinking Joel might do more than just shoot me and Leena will have her cover blown. This could go bad pretty fast. If I tell him that it was me who did it, I'm not sure that's so great either. As I understand it, this guy is a bodyguard and a pretty good fighter. He might want another round to prove his point, whatever that might be. Everybody has an ego, especially guys who walk around like they are invincible, like this asshole. I just have to say what I have to say and hope for the best.

As I start to speak, Joel breaks in. "So, listen here security man. Here's how it is. I have a professional career to protect and I'll be goddamned if I'm going to have that skanky, good for nothing lying bitch ruin everything for me, do you understand? Here's what you are going to do. Tell my friend here what went down: what really went down. You know, how I was just trying to have a little conversation with my ex-girlfriend and yes, I had a few drinks and was a little blasted, but I did *not* hit her. I would never hit a woman. Did you see me hit her?"

Oh shit, this guy has a gun on me and all he wants is to sweat an answer out that works for his boss. The worst part is his boss seems to be going along with it. What the fuck is up with these two? "Well yeah, that's exactly what happened. You nailed it. You guys were talking and then my sergeant and some of his henchmen decided they wanted to push you around. They basically jumped you. I thought it was pretty messed up because I could tell you and the young lady were having what I would consider a private conversation. That's all. That's what happened." Holy shit, I thought this guy was going to push me in a whole different direction. Not the case. Still, it was pretty easy considering they stuck a gun on me. What kind of bullshit is this? Is this guy going to shoot me?

"Teddy...bubulla...you did well. You did very well. See Joel, such a mensch this fine young man is. I never doubted him for a moment. Now, let's put the gun away so we all can make nice. Agreed?" Joel stops pointing the gun at me. The men look at each other and give a slight shoulder shrug as if to say, "ok, we are done."

"So gentlemen, everything is better and I can go?"

"Not quite," Mutzi tells me. "There is one more thing. I'm having some friends over to my club this Saturday night and I'd like you to be my guest. Join me. You'll have an opportunity to tell them what you just told us. I want you to let them know that Joel is every bit the gentleman that you described here, ok? Simple as that. You come do that and it will end this whole story. Everybody goes back to their lives and the way things were."

"Why do you want me to do that?"

Joel turns back to look at me. "These are business associates and a few members from the local press. Right now, this story is bad press. That's bad for business. Bad business makes bad money. You're going to fix it. You do this and we're done. Are we clear?"

"Sure, we're clear."

Mutzi takes the lead. "Ok kid, here it is you be at Dogface Dancehall at 8:30 pm sharp. Follow my lead and this will be over before you know it. Do we have an understanding?" He turns and looks me directly in the eye and repeats, with additional emphasis, "Do…we…have… an…understanding?"

"Yes, we do. Saturday night, 8:30 at the Dogface," I tell him.

"Perfect, you can go." I get out of the car and they drive away. Great, now I have trouble with Mutzi Krabitz and his flunky henchman Joel Jenkins. I need to get out of it. How the hell does this shit happen to me?

Chapter 21

My family tends to stay around the southernmost part of New Jersey, within 30 minutes of our house. During my second year in Little League baseball, the All-Star game was held in Wildwood. It was like the greatest road game ever: a long drive down the Garden State Parkway to a place we all heard a lot about but had never visited. We felt like celebrities.

"French Canadians go to Wildwood, Kate. It's a foreigner's paradise," is what Pop told Mom before the game.

"Frank, it's not just a foreigner's place. My God, they even have a Zaberer's down there! Since you love the boardwalk, let's go early, have a nice walk and get some pizza and a Coke. What do you say?" Mom asked.

"Sure, just no frog legs or crap wine, ok?" I think Pop was just teasing her.

Occasionally, we took a real cool road trip that would take us past the Wildwood turn-offs on our way to Cape May. Once we arrived, we would hop onto the Cape May-Lewes Ferry to go see my Aunt Lori, Mom's sister. We would say, "Are we going to the ocean?" Pop would reply, "Sure, if the Captain makes a left turn, we'll be in London before you know it. Sit tight and hold on for the big turn!" It never happened.

My Pop's brother, Bob, lives in Egg Harbor City with his wife, Sally. We only go to see them once in a while. From what I have been told, a big fight took place over Richard Nixon and things haven't been the same ever since. Mom says Uncle Bob called Pop a 'Communist' which was a really bad idea. I agree.

This morning, my sister Dori called to ask if we could take a little road trip and have some chat time. Hearing that familiar tone in her voice tells me we are on the same wavelength: it's needed for both of us. We've been driving for a while, but she hasn't told me where we are going. We crossed over the Beesley's Point Bridge and into Marmora but that's about as much as I know. Maybe we're going to 'down beach' Ocean City.

Nope, she passes those turn-offs as well and we continue south. Finally, she hangs a left turn and, aha, now I know. "It's interesting that you chose to bring us to Strathmere Beach, Dori. I've been up, down and around every beach in South Jersey but not this one." I gaze out to the ocean. "Someone might think you have a secret fishing spot here. Of course, I could be wrong."

Dori shuts her car door and gives me a silly frown. "You don't know all the good fishing spots, just the good make out spots. Let's see if I have them correct: the helicopter landing pad at Shore Memorial Hospital; the back way secret parking spot past Bargaintown Lake off the Garden State Parkway; and, God knows why, you even have a spot almost all the way out near Price's Pit." Dori says as she's staring at the three fingers she counted. "That's sad Teddy," she adds with a disappointed look on her face. "If I was your girlfriend and you told me we were going to park out by the world's biggest toxic dump, I might have you detour over to Dairy Princess for a banana split and a ride right back home."

"I see, you're going to name the well-known spots that Danny and Jerry used to take their 'hippy chicks' to and then pretend those spots are good enough for me. Uh, wrong." I reply with a confident smirk on my face. "You got a couple of them, but I haven't been there in a long time…like days…so there." We both laugh at this comment.

I learned a long time ago that parking with a girl is an art form: maybe more like a science, considering how much thought I've put into it over the years. I say this because there are so many elements involved. If you screw up, you look stupid. I had to learn that the hard way.

First, if you are picking the girl up at her parents' house, you both have to have your story straight. The old "we're seeing a movie" is the WORST idea when you don't have a clue what the supposed movie you saw was about. Did that. Stupid mistake.

Second, you both better agree on a course of action. Parking without preparation means birth control is left to chance. YIKES! Be smart and be ready. The old "it was just a spur of the moment thing" is absolute bullshit. We're all amateurs here, but we don't have to be idiots as well.

Next, and this is probably just as important as the other two, NEVER park in a spot that hasn't been tested or checked out. That means a friend or family member has been there already, and it was all "smooth sailing." No cops or random citizens were around.

Getting walked up on is nobody's fault but your own. That's just how life works. You have to park like you mean it.

Fourth, and this is HUGE, know your exits. Simply put: how are you getting away? It's a complete approach, because you have to be able to move at a moment's notice if things take a turn. (On the other hand, if you planned well, they won't.) The keys must be in the ignition or close by. You must have those keys ready to go to work. And, most important, being fully naked means, you are fully exposed. You never want that. Be ready to "pull up and pull down" clothes so you can make your move out of there. Naked people are panicked people and panicked is not how you want to be.

Finally, it's all about positioning. There is a lot of talk about action that takes place in the back seat. That's not the way I look at it. This isn't a hotel you've checked into -- it's a Detroit V-8 with an AM-FM radio and a cassette player. Sometimes, the front seats lay back, and that's a good place to be right there. Back seats delay recovery and get away time...not good.

Needless to say, I've parked enough times to know how to handle myself. I'm not an idiot. Dori, well, she's good at razzing me about this kind of stuff. She gets it. For today, if nothing else I just want to get out of the house and give Mom and Pop a chance to make up, disagree or giggle at each other for some silly thing they do seemingly over and over again. I can't tell if they are really mad at each other or just happy they're not mad anymore. Either way, they are always ready to make up.

One time when I was little, Uncle Bone threw his napkin at Pop at the dinner table and said, "Enough already. You two get a hotel room!"

Mom shot back, "We've got our room right here, why don't you go get a hotel room?" That was funny. Uncle Bone was sleeping over that night because he and Pop were driving to the Poconos the next morning to do some "gunnin," as Pop calls it. They don't do much hunting. For the most part, they hang out, drink lots of beer and shoot at cans, bottles and whatever works at the time. I get to do the same thing with Uncle Bone and Luca each summer, but only for a couple of days. Mom knows that we're not camping, roasting marshmallows, and singing all those silly songs. She knows we are shooting guns. When I come back, she's very good at asking me, "Did you have a good time? Don't tell me any more than I need to hear. Do you have all your toes and fingers? If you heard any dirty jokes, you better make sure you don't tell them in this house young man. You're never to be too old to have your mouth washed out with soap."

She's right. I save those jokes for Pop. Funny thing is, he'll say something like, "I told Bone that joke. Is he taking credit for my jokes again?" Wow, Pop knows some real dirty jokes.

Dori breaks into my thoughts. "Let's go out on the beach and sit for a while. I want to talk to you about several important things. It's something I've wanted to do for a long time. All things considered; I have a feeling now is the right time. Come on." Dori starts walking to the beach.

Over the years, Dori and I have talked about all kinds of important stuff. A lot of it has had to do with our family. Lately, Frankie has been our main topic of conversation.

We decide to take our shoes and socks off and enjoy the feeling of the sand between our toes. There's a light breeze so it's comfortable. The sand isn't kicking up into our faces and eyes. That's the worst. We walk about three quarters of the way down to the water when Dori drops her shoes and takes a seat by falling back into the sand, laughing and waving at me to do the same. Ah, a crash landing. Ok, down I go.

Ouch!!! I landed right on a seashell turned with the pointed edges up! What are the odds? "Smooth move, Ex-Lax!"

No kidding. The first thing you are supposed to do is check out the sand behind you so that you don't get impaled with bi-valve cover. Wow...I'm still using Niner's stuff. That kid's sayings never get old.

"So, Teddy, I know you've never been to Strathmere. You would've told me, or I would've found out. This isn't on your usual path, like Ocean City and Longport." Dori begins to look out to the city, "It's different here, and to be very honest with you, it's a special place. I know we're not going to get interrupted. That's good. I have a lot to tell you, and I think that less distractions will make it even better."

I pick up a shell and toss into the water. A bunch of seagulls about 20 feet away scatter: scare-dee gulls. "Yep, it's just us and all these birds. I sure hope Alfred Hitchcock's not around or this might get bloody." I say sarcastically as I look around. "I don't think of seagulls as attack birds, but they sure can pester the hell out of people. I'm not sure which one is worse."

Dori picks up a handful of sand and lets it slowly slip through her fingers. "Teddy, you've gotten into plenty of trouble over the years for not paying attention or listening to instructions. It felt like Mom and Pop had to meet with Mrs. Winston on a weekly basis when you were in 5th grade. Man, you were a handful." Dori sighs and smiles at me. "You eventually figured it out though. I'm sure you learned how to fake it better."

"Yep. I cheated a lot. I used to look at Terri Martinez, smile a lot and then look at her paper. She was smart: straight A's all the time. When eighth grade came around, I was planning to ask her to a school dance. Unfortunately, she hurt her ankle during a dance competition. I couldn't believe my bad luck. I knew a cool girl that was really pretty and could dance but, I couldn't ask her to be my date. I got stuck hanging out with all the other losers leaning against the wall. On the other hand, Terri did help me get good grades. So, I guess you could say I paid attention. I promise to pay attention now, though. We'll see what grade you give me."

Dori chuckles and tells me, "This won't be so hard to pass, Theodore. It's not like you can really fail anyway. The reason I wanted to talk to you was because I thought it might be important to tell you a few things. Nana is pretty good at watching out for you and telling you things. She does the same with me, but those conversations are private. I'm not going to break confidence and tell you our business. That's not right."

"Uncle Bone says that kind of stuff isn't cool, so I get it."

"He's right, Teddy," she agrees, "it isn't cool. Folks who have private conversations should keep them private. In my opinion, you bring bad things to your life when you don't act honestly and show integrity. It's that simple for me. So, we'll keep that where it belongs and start our own private conversation."

"Sounds like the way to go," I agree with a nod. "I figure you brought us here so we could have a bit of privacy. Other than the occasional metal detector guy and those seagulls, not much is going to interrupt us, am I right?"

"Pretty much. Soooooo...listen Ted, awhile back I discovered some things about our family. I want to share some of it with you. It makes sense to get this out on the table and I think it will help you understand a few things."

I'm not entirely sure where Dori is headed with this, but she has always looked out for me, so it doesn't really matter if I understand or not. "Ok."

"Good. I'm going to tell you what I know but not how or where I got it from. If you have questions later, I'll do my best to answer them without breaking any of the rules we respect and value. I'm going to talk. You don't have to agree or acknowledge anything I say. I just need you to listen. Deal?"

"That's a deal." We both understand that there is a possibility that whatever information she has, came from the same source I get mine from. We're careful to keep things general though and not name names. That wouldn't be right.

"So, there is family on Dad's side with roots in Northern Italy. They are an interesting group, to say the least. They lived in a village with a lot of cultural diversity but, most of the people were religiously traditional with an allegiance to the Roman Catholic Church. As you know, that's pretty standard for Italians. In this particular village, there was a small group of Buddhists from the Himalayan region of Asia. The families had originally come to the village for trade and then some decided to stay and make a new life for themselves. Their new life didn't, however, include joining the Roman Catholic Church. The families practiced their own faith and were happy to share it with their new neighbors. Our family was very taken by these new thoughts and traditions. Our great-great grandparents were the first to be introduced to the Far East culture and the way of higher-consciousness."

"Higher what?" I ask. This isn't going the way I thought it would at all.

Dori smiles, understanding my confusion. "Higher consciousness. Our great-great grandparents had prayed and followed the doctrine of the Catholic church; however, the new approach appealed to them. Over time, it became a part of their everyday existence. In addition to their daily prayers, they began practicing meditation."

"What, like that Kung Fu guy on TV?" I ask. "Did they shave their heads too?"

"Uhm," Dori hesitates for a moment, trying to decide if I am making fun of her. "I'm not sure but I think probably not because that might have been a bit much, don't you think?" She smiles at me and continues. "Their introduction into the new doctrine brought them strength and inner peace. It must have been pretty remarkable. The problem was, it made them stand out and look different from the other villagers. As you probably understand, sometimes being different or doing things that other people don't understand makes you a threat." Dori looks very sad as she tells me, "They became a threat."

"Just because they meditated?" I ask. "Why? Did it piss off the church folks? What kind of threat can you be when you are calm and peaceful? That doesn't make sense."

"It does if the people in charge maintain control by having everyone act and think the same way," Dori explains. "People who get in line and do as they are told make good citizens if you are the one in power. For our great-great-grandparents, you did what the church and village authorities told you to do or there was trouble. Unfortunately, that seems to be the way the world has worked throughout history. Our family didn't play along so things went from bad to worse."

"How much worse?" I'm not sure I really want to know but for some reason, Dori thinks that it is important that I do.

"Our great-great-grandma began to speak about things she would 'see' in her meditations, including what local henchmen were doing to children in the area. She knew that there was horrible abuse that was being ignored or covered up by those in control. That meant that the church was involved as well. After our great-great-grandmother spoke about her visions, several of the henchmen showed up dead. It seems that our great-great-grandparents found a way to form a vigilante group -- a death squad, if you will. That's the best way I can put it. In short, the bad guys started to disappear. Believe it or not, this didn't sit well with some of the villagers. So, the people who migrated from the Himalayan area were labeled heretics and put to death. Our great-great-grandmother apparently met a similar fate. The story is that her husband was burned alive, yet the truth is, he escaped and eventually traveled to Scotland. A new life and identity were created for him and the rest of the bloodline."

I have so many questions and Dori seems to know so much. I figure Nana told her everything she needed to understand. Then, out of the blue, various memories come together and the pieces of the puzzle start to fit.

"I'll be damned. Well, I'll be damned. Venice...your Venice trip.... your two-week trip with the Italian Club at Mainland High. You went to Venice and around Northern Italy and Nana was one of the guides. Nana went with you." I sit back and smile at Dori. "I'll be damned. Wow, I'll be goddamned. I get it now."

"Easy there Theodore," Dori tells me, laughing as she tries to calm me down. "All we did was hang out and study Italian culture…"

"…and Italian history. Shit, no wonder you're such an expert. Man, Nana is…"

"…special, Ted. Very special. We BOTH know that, and we need to keep it right here. She's sent from heaven for you, me and so many others. We need to leave it at that. She's a guardian angel, with burn marks on her wings. That's where I stop...no more. Let's get back to...us...and you."

"Sure, what about us?"

"Let's talk about it. I'll lay it out for you, plain and simple. It won't exactly make sense, but the way things are well, that's just the way it is. That's the only way I can say it. It is why we are here today. I'm going to tell you why you are different: why you feel and think differently. You've wondered why you feel so uncomfortable in some situations and why you feel...strong and calm...during more stressful times."

"You mean to tell me I'm not slowly losing my mind?" I ask, thinking that she really has no idea what it is like. "It's normal to feel this way? It's normal to enjoy..."

"Chaos...craziness...danger...pain? You mean that stuff?"

I laugh and shake my head. "I don't particularly ENJOY pain, but I understand I can take it. It's a little weird, but it's how I've been since I can first remember. When I injured my knee during my senior year, I handled it pretty well. It killed my speed, but I was just as..."

"...angry? Ready for a fight?"

I look at her with surprise. "YES... that's right on. I knew if anybody tried to mess with me, no matter how big or strong they might be, I could take them down. I could find a way to hurt them. I lived for it."

"So, basically speaking little brother, this is where it starts to get a bit more interesting. Whatever our great-great-grandmother found, whatever she developed, was passed on to our great-grandfather. He was known for being highly intuitive. He was a good cop and earned his way up the ladder quickly to become a Detective. He was a 'case-cracker' and known for his gentle approach. The more he did, however, the more pressure was placed upon him. Eventually, it became too much so he decided to pack up his family and bring them to America. Nana was born here." Dori stands up and stretches then looks out at the ocean. "I've heard stories about her being different for years and believed them. Nana just seems to have 'it,' whatever 'it' might be. She's special."

"She is pretty cool," I agree. "It's like she knows stuff. She always has good advice and answers for most of the questions I ask. Mom trusts her a lot. So, do I. What do you mean by 'it' though? That sounds a little weird."

Dori shakes her head as if she is confused and looking for an answer as well. "I know she prays and meditates, so I think she taps into a higher level of thinking. That's the best way I can put it. I know because…"

"…because you're like her. I know it. I've always known it, Dori. Hell, it's not just the dreams that you talk about. It's almost like sometimes you see things before they happen. You would kind of hint at it when we were growing up. Remember the time we talked about my upcoming field trip to the Dunes off the Ocean City causeway? You kept talking about smells and about everything being very smelly. It didn't make sense to me because that part of the bay doesn't get that way? Do you remember that?"

"I do. Your class ended up finding a rotting humpback whale 10 minutes after you got off the bus. Some field trip, huh?"

"I'll say," I agree, wrinkling my nose at the thought. "Usually, those events lead to shell collecting and the occasional horseshoe crab remains. If you are lucky, you may be able to watch a fisherman pull in a keeper. Generally, it's just a cold day at the beach. That day made the papers."

"Whatever I see and feel, it's not something I really work on," Dori tells me, a calm coming into her voice. "It just comes to me. There's something else you should know: Pop has this too. Or at least, he 'did' have it. He has fought the visions ever since the war. He and Nana have argued over and over about it through the years. Although I've heard some of the discussions, I didn't fully understand it until I got older. Having this ability really bothers Pop." Dori pushes the sand around with her feet, as if trying to find an answer in the grains beneath her. "I understand that there was a lot going on with him when he was on the islands in the war. He was able to lead his men through some pretty dangerous experiences, but it was very hard on him. I heard Pop tell Nana one time, 'I don't need no ghosts or voices trying to direct my everyday life. That's some sort of sickness and I'm not giving in to it. I've gone through it all once and that's enough. I don't want that crutch. Whatever is going on isn't going to be part of my morning coffee and that's that. I left the war behind me. I've been better ever since.'"

"Pop is pretty stubborn," I agree with Dori, "and he doesn't talk about the war at all. That's just not Pop. I've seen Pop and Nana really get into it. Sometimes, it's almost like they don't like each other much. I know they love each other but they don't talk that much. It's too bad. Do you think that will change?"

"I don't know Teddy. That is one thing that I just can't see. I am going to tell you what I do know. It's time you heard this, so you understand things better."

"Ok," I tell her. "I think I'm ready." I hesitate for a moment. "At least I hope I am. Shoot."

"Whatever this consciousness or 'knowing' is, it seems to move through our family generation by generation since the story began with our great-great-grandmother. It moves like this: girl, boy, girl, boy, girl. The last one on the list is me."

"Wait, that means..."

"Right, my son Dante will be the same way if this stays true to form. He'll be a 'knower' like me," Dori turns and looks me in the eyes, "and like you."

I stare back at her. "But that doesn't make sense Dori. I don't fit the pattern. I'm not supposed to be this way. How did this happen?"

"The best way I can figure it is this: that time when we were little kids and we almost both died together...then somehow miraculously recovered," she hesitates and looks at me. "I think we gained a piece of each other."

"So, you came back as you and I came back as.... a freak."

"No Teddy, you're not a freak. Of course not." I can hear the frustration in Dori's voice. "Don't say that. You're not a freak."

"Really?" I can't seem to get through what she is saying. "I'm the only one who doesn't fit the family pattern. I know it's all kinda strange: I get that but, what's stranger: being like this or knowing that I'm not supposed to be like this...that I am completely different...a freak?"

Dori raises her voice. "Stop saying that. You're not a freak."

"Then just what am I, huh?" I respond, my anger rising. "What exactly am I?"

Dori stops and breathes deeply. "It's all pretty simple, Teddy. You're not the freak. You're something much more special than you can ever imagine."

"Oh yeah...and what is that? What is this special thing I am?"

"It's simple. You're the enigma."

Chapter 22

"Love you, Teddy." I know how much my sister Dori means it when she tells me that and it never fails to give me a lift and somehow, makes me feel stronger. After our Strathmere Beach time, I need it. I understand that we are more a part of each other than I ever thought possible.

Dori drops me off at Mom and Pop's house because I need to pick up mail and, as Mom told me when she called in the morning, "There's food. Eat it before it gets thrown away." Dori drives off with a wave and a little horn music, giving me the tempo to hop up the stairs onto the front porch and in through the door. No matter what, I always love coming down Vernon Avenue and seeing this house. In my mind, I can still see woods to the left, the right and down and across the street where we jumped hills and built forts for hang outs with the gang. My rugged fort overnight stays were always an adventure. These days, an opportunity similar to that includes a feminine presence. The old days were much simpler times and, in many ways, a much simpler life. Life developed a harder edge over the years -- much harder than I expected.

The sound of the phone ringing breaks into my thoughts. I double-time it into the kitchen and to the corner where the phone is anchored. If I miss the call, at least I'll be closer to grabbing something cold to drink and my hustle won't be wasted. The ringing dies before I pick up the receiver. My chance to display my voiced sense-of-urgency to the caller is snuffed out. The old trick of speaking loudly and a little breathless "HELLO?" always makes an impression. Not this time.

I open the fridge and check the contents. Maybe there is a cold Coke waiting for me? I seriously doubt it although it never hurts to look. Besides, there just might be something else that catches my eye. Maybe Mom is trying to hide some Tastykakes behind the mayonnaise jar in the back. It could happen. I see her famous tuna so I'm guessing that's what she is telling me I can finish up before it gets discarded. I'll pass for now.

RING! "Damn!!!" The frickin' phone jolts me a bit, just as I was about to go on my Tastykake search. I grab it up.

"Hello."

"Damian, where the fuck have you been?" This is the way Luca talks on the phone: like your whereabouts have been a mystery or that you are part of some missing persons case and he just solved it. He cracks me up.

"None of your greaseball business. What do you want?" I chuckle into the phone.

Luca does a double throat-clear sound: his "code" for letting me know that he's about to talk in code. We have never officially established ground rules but, after years of practice, we both have this down. Uncle Bone does it too: like father like son. Luca will throw in a random number somewhere, which equates to the base time for our meet. Then, I know to add three minutes, hours or days (depending on the meet) for the Father, Son and Holy Ghost.

That part he told me directly when we were young. It's a 'Catholic thing' I guess.

"A friend of mine is in from out-of-town and wants to catch up," Luca tells me. "He really digs baseball, so I figure we do Jo-Jono's for a slice. How about it, can you meet us?"

"Sure." Luca tells me, via code, that it will be in about an hour, so I have a little time. As I hang up, I chuckle a bit. Code: we speak in code for what…so the secret police don't hear? I mean, who really needs to speak in code? Luca does because he likes to and, since his Pop does it, again the whole apple not falling far from the tree concept comes into play. Basically, we aren't planning to meet at Jo-Jono's. Jo-Jono's doesn't "rate" with all of us, just me. So, that means I'm heading to Palmizzi's in Pleasantville because it's the opposite of Jo-Jono's. That's the basis for the code stuff and, since it works, we stick with it. The out-of-town baseball-digging friend is also obvious to me so I'm all set.

I'm going to pass on Mom's tuna salad mix and since I don't see a Coke in the fridge, I look around for something else sweet enough to tempt me. All I see is Tab. Hell no, not Tab, not ever. I walk into the dining room and sit in one of the squeakier chairs and glance out the window. There it is -- Lisa's Pinto. It's become my bitter chariot, occasionally carrying me to places near and not-too-far around South Jersey. Although I appreciate having a car, this one will have to go sometime soon. It's tough to drive for a number of reasons: the first being that it is actually tough to drive. No power, bad brakes, bumpy ride and the AM radio absolutely sucks.

Christ, how did I get in this situation? Seriously? With all the shit that happened earlier in my life, I still managed to try and see the world correctly and adjust myself so I could deal and enjoy things. I don't need rainbows and unicorns. I built up strength and resolve and acted like a big boy to keep moving everything forward. Then, Johnny C happened...out of nowhere. It was horrific. It still is. I was numb for days. Add to that the GTO burning up and almost killing Mom and Dori and things couldn't get much worse. Losing Lisa in my life, not even getting a chance to try to help her after the horror she endured, was a gut-punch that I still feel. So much shit happened and there have been times when all I could do was react and keep going...keep jabbing. Deep inside, I ache to do something about it. I'm not exactly sure what to do as I continue to search for life's answers but the time I had with Dori today certainly helped.

As I continue to stare out the window, the remaining part of Luca's "code" enters my mind and brings a smile to my face, a small one but a smile none-the-less. I might not have all the answers and be a little short on solutions, but at least I know someone who is good at finding them. If he can't help me, nobody can. Our "code" conversation about the out-of-town friend who likes baseball well, that means one thing and it's a very good one.

We're meeting with Geno.

I walk into Palmizzi's. Sure enough, Geno is sitting with Luca and sipping on something. Judging by the glasses, it's probably Dago red wine. As I approach the table, they get up and big hugs are offered all around, with no words spoken. A glass of wine and a

Coke sit in the spot I am to occupy. Geno gives me a wink and a head nod as if to say, "just in case you didn't want wine" and points to the fresh bread on the table. Beside it sits a dipping plate filled with olive oil and balsamic vinegar. We have the proper set-up to talk business in a casual way, a little breaking of bread together. Our octogenarian host sits in the far corner, minding his own pony-playing business with a cigar and newspaper, apparently circling his choices as he reads.

Geno and Luca are all business, keeping their voices low and their hands folded together when they lean in to make a point. We chat for a bit about the most current events and moving pieces of my life these days. and begin to explore possible solutions. Geno fills our glasses with more wine.

"I didn't just lose a car, you know," I tell him. "I almost lost my Mom and sister. And just like that, the two assholes that did the shit, pull a disappearing act, like they have IQs high enough to get away clean. I think about those two every day, sitting somewhere in, I don't know, Alabama, laughing at me. I had just gone through all that Johnny C shit and now even Lisa has decided to go away. I'm telling you this right now: what went down with Johnny C was evil shit. How he went out...how this family ended...it wasn't right. Not right at all." I tap my fist on the table which gets a quick look from our host who quickly buries his head back into his newspaper. I calm down a bit and return to a lowered voice. "There's got to be something I can do about this without sitting around with my thumb up my ass hoping it works itself out. That's a jerk-off move and I'm no jerk-off. I want to do something about this. I want..."

"Payback. You want payback Teddy, right? That's really what you want and that's really what you gotta have. I understand. That's why I'm here. I think I've come up with something that will help. Listen up." Geno walks me through the plan and the way he can make it happen.

Luca shakes his head up and down in agreement. "It's a good plan. It's rock solid.," he tells me.

"It's also dirty work Luca," I tell him. "As long as you are sure about all of this, then I am too."

Luca sits up a bit straighter and glances over at Geno. The two have probably talked quite a bit about this very issue: how far everybody is willing to go. It can't be halfway on anything this time around. It's got to be the real deal. I know it and they know it.

"Listen Teddy," Luca says to me, leaning in as he does so and looking me straight in the eyes, "I'm in. It's as simple as that. I'm in."

"You must be, otherwise you wouldn't be here my friend. Hell, none of us would be. This ain't a Florida baseball camp, fellas. Not by a longshot."

"It's not," Geno agrees, "this is different -- way different. The way I see it, this is your home Teddy, right here in South Jersey. That means the choices you have are pretty simple. The first choice is to live like a victim and the second choice…" Geno's voice trails off as he sits back and takes a swig of his wine, putting the glass back down on the table and slightly nodding his head. Luca does the same. "The second choice is to make a move," he continues, "simple as that. Am I right?"

"You're right, my man," I agree, conviction strengthening my voice and resolve. "You're right. Only this time, we play for keeps and no bullshit. None. It's the only way."

Luca and Geno grab their glasses and hold them up for a toast. I raise mine to clink and chug the wine. Everything we've talked about so far makes perfect sense to me.

"So, Geno, let's go over your plan in detail."

Whatever he's come up with, whatever the plan, our move will be permanent. It has to be because things are different, and like he said -- this isn't Florida.

This is South Jersey.

Chapter 23

"Hey, Ben, there's that Lincoln Continental again. Right there. That's the car I couldn't get a clean plate number on before, because they probably switched 'em. Those plates came up off a stolen '78 Seville. And there it is. Look -- the plates are different again. What do you bet those plates come up good for this car now?"

George Morrison and his fellow off-duty Somers Point cop buddy Ben Bobbet are cruising the back parking lot area of one of their favorite diners, "Roman Hollandaise." It's one of the best breakfast places in town, and lunch is just as good. Dinner crowds tend to head more south and east in the city, because that's where the Italian and seafood selections become more world-class. Somers Point is to "good food' what Cape May is to "bird watching." It's just like no other. Typical cops -- casing the joint before they walk into a front door. Oh well, you never can be too careful. Even in a town where arrests totals for drunk and disorderly outnumber the nabbed murderers by, like 3000 to zero each year -- caution is always a good idea.

George is feeling very cautious right now. The last time he saw that car, he just happened to come face-to-face with the gentleman who eventually drove away in it. These guys were not locals. Not even close.

"A couple of gumbas outta Philly" is how Ben labeled them after George described his encounter with them, and George remembers shaking his head in agreement.

"These aren't your typical green-beer drinkers. These 'charming young men' do dirty work -- that's what I'm thinking."

They park the car and decide to chat up a strategy for entering the place, because they realize it might be better to observe these guys' movements and learn a little bit more about them. Something is up if they've suddenly been turning up in Somers Point. Something must be up.

"I have an idea. Go in and flag down Janice -- get her out here to talk to us. Just tell her it's important and she should just say she's taking a coffee break."

George frowns at the suggestion, because it just isn't going to work for him. "You do that. You. Not me. I go in there and start talking about important stuff, and she brings up me standing her up for Junior Prom. Still. She still won't drop it, Ben. For Christ sakes -- she even brings me warm coffee every time. I think she spits in it. So, no, I'm not going in."

Ben shakes his head and just points to the old Chevy Malibu parked about 6 cars away. "That's her husband's car, and that drunken bum just got a job here as a cook. I'm telling you, there's no way I'm walking through the back door by him and meeting up with his wife. It wouldn't go well, do you understand? Just trust me. I can't do it. You gotta do it. No badges, no breaks. You are the best option on this, pal. This is yours."

George looks up to the sky and blows out his breath pretty hard as he slightly bangs his head against the half closed window. "I was going to go to Trenton State and take business classes...get my degree and eventually move to Miami. MIAMI. I had it all figured out, I really did. It was all so simple. Expensive for sure and I would have had to work two jobs while taking classes, but no...you talk me into this life."

Ben lets out a chuckle and slaps him on his shoulder. "Go get her, Champ!"

George exits the car and heads toward the back door, and as he goes to reach for the handle, it slowly opens and out walks Janice with a cigarette in her hand. They lock eyes and as she's about to say something snide to him, he blurts out, "Ben wants to see you -- it's REALLY important!"

Janice looks over and raises her eyebrows a few times and then nods over at him. "OK, I wanna see him too. Turn your back and give us privacy, will you? You won't mess up that plan, I'm hoping?"

"Enough Janice -- we both gotta talk to you. Seriously. Both of us. TRUCE. I'm calling a truce, ok?"

"You're a cop, for fuck's sake, George. Cops don't call truces unless they lost their balls. Should I wait while you look for them, or can we just skip over there together?"

Janice begins to walk toward the car and Ben flashes her a big smile and mouths, "Get in the back," and makes the 'shhhhh' sign with his finger against his lips. Janice likes the idea, but figures the back seat action will be pretty much a pretty boring oral approach, what with the talking and maybe even arguing. Considering George is going to be in the car, the arguing just might be a guarantee. She strides over and winks at Ben and mouths back, "Join me," and winks.

These two are enjoying each other's secret company these days, and it might be sooner than later that their secret gets out. That clock is ticking. She climbs in the back and George returns to the front, and she just stares at the back of his head.

"Is George going to organize and run this little meeting, or do we need someone more, you know, reliable? I wouldn't want to waste anybody's time here. Just pointing out the obvious."

Ben points at George and Janice and says, "Not now and not here, you two. Seriously. Not now. Agreed?"

"Oh sure, I agree and I'll keep my commitment. And uh....Georgie...what say you?"

George just looks at Ben with a very disgusted look on his face as he's nodding, and Ben turns to Janice to make his point more emphatically. "We have much bigger trouble brewing for all of us in this town, and that trouble is personified by the two big bruisers that came in this morning. They are driving that car right there. The big Continental. Ring any bells?"

Janice sits back and fuddles with her hands as if to think through what she is about to tell them, takes a deep breath and exhales pretty hard. She looks a bit concerned. "Look, whatever is going on, it's moving at a fast pace. I saw these two last week chatting up the owner, Gionni. It was smiles and back slaps all around, you know? Next thing I know, they're coming in from the back door and sliding into that booth he keeps for special occasions, you know? Real private and nobody walks by or bothers them. It's like they have their own booth to themselves, and I've never seen them before. Something is up, I just know it."

"Are they there now?"

"Yep. Stuffing their faces with round three of their infinity-course meal and talking like kids under a sleepover blanket-tent. They speak so low only dogs can hear them."

George gives Ben a slight nod and then opens his door and makes a bee-line for the back entrance. "Wonder-boy is gonna get a closer look, ok? How've you been?"

"Since last night? Hungrier. I'm hungry for you. When can we get together again, hmm?"

Ben smiles in the mirror at her as she makes a pouty face back at him, then slides her finger up and down the back of his neck. "I miss you already, Benny-bear."

They do the back-and-forth with each other, talking about their 'adventures' and how much they are enjoying them....but now George is working his way back to the car to disrupt their little verbal nirvana-chase. He looks like he found something.

He opens the door and climbs back in. "That's the Frick and Frack I remember. They look like they picked up about 20 pounds each. Do they eat here everyday Janice?"

"Pretty much, the fat fucks. They're wearing out our bathrooms as well. I don't like them. Gionni serves them personally, so we don't talk with them at all."

George shakes his head as he is thinking through some ideas, and he decides to share one with the group as he looks out the window and off into the distance. "I say we talk with 'Gio' and find out what's what with these two. He's catering to them like co-owners, so let's just call him on it and see where it goes. You know, make a strong move. That way, we show our hand and he either helps or we turn up a little heat on him and his new taste-testers. It's bold but I don't see another way to get information. What do you think?"

George continues to stare out the window but notices...silence. Absolute silence. He's getting nothing back. "Hey, I said what do you..."

As he turns to see what the reaction is, he's stared back at by two people with smiles on their faces. Like they just heard a joke. It's a little...confusing.

"Ben. Did you even hear what I said? C'mon...how about a little input here. How about it?"

The smiles continue and now Janice has a little bit of a giggle going, and she sits back in her chair and begins to break out into laughter. She's laughing and George is pretty darned confused. Ben puts his right hand up on George's shoulder and starts to laugh a bit too.

"Did I ever tell you about my shitty divorce.? I did, I'm pretty sure. I think I did. Man, did it suck and I mean big-time SUCK. What a fuckin' joke that was. She kept finding every angle and every opportunity to make me look like crap, so that when we met or went to court, I got the "L" and she got her "W." That lawyer she hired and fucked came right here to this very....very....restaurant. This one. They loved coming here and always got a special booth. Didn't they Janice?"

Janice leans forward and now her laugh has calmed down to a slight chuckle. "Yep. Sat back there working on how to screw Ben in every way possible, because he didn't have a pricey lawyer and she did, and she was more than happy to screw-off some of her bill. Piece a' work, that bitch. Real piece of work."

George looks at Ben, then at Janice, then back at Ben and begins to wag his finger at them both. "Wait a minute...wait a minute...just a minute here. Just wait. You two. YOU TWO. You two spied on them, didn't you? You found a way to spy on them and turn things a bit, huh? You did. I know you did, just tell me. You did, huh?"

"Nope. Not me, George. I'm a cop and that would be wrong, you know? That would be some sort of ethics violation and I'm just not gonna stoop to her low-life way of living and doing things, just to make sure she didn't get all my antique train sets I inherited from my great-grandfather, or the 1950 Thunderbird convertible that I had mostly restored and was worth a mint...or my granddad's coin collection that we discovered by accident, that she was claiming was given to her by her family. On and on and on with this woman it was going. On and on and no screw left unturned that she couldn't, or wasn't, finding to pick up and put in me. Lies and hateful stories about me hitting her as well. All lies. But still, I wouldn't break the law. I wouldn't spy on her."

Janice leans even farther forward and pats George on the shoulder as she makes her point. "But I would. And I did. Me and my goofy whiz kid cousin Norton. Good ole' Norty. That kid can rig up a sound recording system anywhere and you'd never discover it, you know? Still haven't."

George drops his jaw a bit and just shakes his head at them both, trying to find the words to say to them, but he's speechless, but not for long. "You...you cheated. You fuckin' cheated. You...."

Ben cuts him off with his hand up in the air and raises his voice. "HEY. FAT EENIE and FAT MEENIE are in there plotting God knows what, because guys like us...all of us in this car...have to play by the rules and they don't, understand George? They don't and never will. Our badges give them reason to lie to us and better for them, find ways to avoid us all together. Ok? They're above and around any laws and YOU and I both know it. YOU FUCKIN' KNOW IT!"

"So do I George...so do I" Janice offers.

"We can do something to these assholes. Us. We can beat them at their own game, and all I gotta do is call Norty down from Rochester for a while. That's it. He'll stay with my aging grandma who has gout and can use the company. She's hard of hearing and sleeps a lot. It won't be trouble. He's quiet and he's brilliant, and he had fun last time. He'll really have fun this time, what with these guys being mobster types and all. I'm telling you, it worked once before and it will work again. He's got Grandma's van and he converts it to his little workshop pretty quickly. The guy just parks and stays on the job. Don't ask me about bathroom breaks, though. Just don't. It's disgusting."

George gets out of the car and begins to walk around a bit, looking everywhere to make sure he isn't being noticed, and all he can think about is screaming. He really wants to just let it all out and if he doesn't, he might just burst. Minutes go by and he can feel the calm coming back to him, so he turns to the car to see those same two faces staring back at him in anticipation. They look like teenagers waiting to hear if they can stay out an extra hour tonight. They look...a little bit pathetic. He turns and speaks to them.

"I've never cheated on a test. Ever. When I got accused of that in 5th grade, I cried for a whole week. I ran my paper route so honest and clean, I didn't collect the full amount for the week if I ran late that one day. It was rare, but when it did happen, I felt good about it."

He looks down and has a few tears in his eyes that he's trying to fight back, but they are noticeable and Janice gets out of the car and walks toward him. As she reaches him, she touches his shoulder again and he picks up his head...then touches hers.

"My Dad...prom night...got drunk and hit my Mom...hard. He knocked her down and even broke things, ok? He hit her and so I punched him in his drunk stomach and his drunk chest and he passed out. He just passed out. My Mom begged me to leave her and go, but I couldn't...I just couldn't, Janice, and I never was going to ever tell anyone, ok? I was never going to talk about it, just act like I was a screw-up about the prom and take my medicine...or in our case...eat shit from you for years to come. It's all I've ever been able to do. But I would never leave here...never just run from it all. This is my home and I love it here, you know? I love South Jersey. And my Dad? Well, he was a bully, and I don't like bullies and I became a cop to protect people from bullies and bad guys, because that's the right thing to do. It's what I know. It's who I am. I'm honest and I really hate bullies."

Ben gets out of the car and joins them both, having heard the whole story. "Listen, George, You're more than my friend, you're my best friend and I'm telling you right now, we don't have to do this like this, ok? We don't. We got badges and we have the law, and when the time comes, we'll get these bastards the right way. Ok? I'm sorry about pulling you into our little caper and even telling you about what we did before. It was wrong to do it and wrong to burden you with it. I'm really sorry."

George hears the words and they soothe him a bit, and they all stand around together and then lock arms together in a bit of a semi-group hug and begin to laugh. As they do, the back door opens and the subjects of their interest walk out and glance over as they move toward their car.

"Don't move. Nobody move," Ben whispers. "Act like we're doing a little group prayer thing. Don't look at them."

As he says that, one of them perks up with comments that can easily be heard. "Look at 'dis over hee-ya, for Christ sakes. It's the gay brothers and their make-up consulatant doing a group love-in. Fuckin' fags. These locals aren't just soft, they're queer-soft."

They get into their car and speed off away from them, kicking up dust and gravel as they go. The dust cloud envelops the three of them and then passes by like something from a silly cartoon. It goes away as fast as it comes. George begins to laugh a bit, and they all begin to slap and pat the dust off of their own bodies, bending and turning as they do. George leans forward and grabs both of them by the shoulders, then pulls them a bit closer. With a wink and a slight grin on his face, he lets them know what he's got on his mind.

"Count me in. Let's take these asshole bullies down."

Chapter 24

"Jennifer...JENNIFER! Can you come in here please?" Jennifer Mausenbacker has been with Halston Realty for two years now and never has her boss called for her as emphatically as he was doing at this moment. It's no surprise -- he probably came in and read the note about her new big impending sale and wanted to congratulate her right away. The commision on this one is huge. He may have his own parking spot and get to come through his own back-door entrance, but she's been making some real headway with new clients and sales this year.

Those Nevada people just seem to keep on coming, and they have cash to burn. Lot's of it. She's on a roll, and never has it been so evident than now, because this new one she landed is, well, pretty impressive. Joan Caley had so much gold and diamonds on her body when she came into the office yesterday, she might be smart to travel with more than just the two friends that were with her. This lady was loaded and much more local, hailing from South Philadelphia. The heavy accent gave her away. "My husband is in construction -- times are even better than they have been, so we figure to move down here and get settled closer to the action, so to speak. We've got our eye on that abandoned property at the end of Broadway. I'm pretty sure it just came on the market."

Jennifer was sure that was a mistake, so she made a few calls and just like that, what do you know -- the property is listed. Odd.

"I'm coming, Tim. I'm thinking you have a handshake and some champagne waiting for me?" Tim Foles has neither in mind. Quite the contrary.

"Jennifer, I'm afraid there's been a misunderstanding and a pretty big one at that. The Broadway deal is mine to close with the husband, because he hired me two days ago. His wife jumped the gun a bit -- believe me, he's none too happy about it, but what's done is done. I'm going to meet up with him today and smooth things over with him, so this sale can go forward."

Jennifer's jaw practically drops, and she sinks into the chair in front of Tim's desk. She's stunned, but more than that, she's pissed. Real pissed. She stares at Tim as he fumbles around with his paperwork on his desk. He's made his statement and seems content to let it stand, but that won't suffice. Not now. Not with twenty five thousand dollars sitting on the table that she can no longer get to.

This is bullshit, she thinks. "Bullshit. My client, who I walked the property with, and my sale. Mine. That's my sale, Tim. Whatever conversation you may have had can't possibly override my work and time...LOOK AT THIS...look at ALL THESE NOTES! Jesus Christ, Tim. Are you kidding me? All this work and time schlepping Miss South Smelly around that god-forsaken white elephant of a mess that she just HAS to have, and you're telling ME no sale? I worked this already. I did. It's MY SALE and god-damn it it's MY COMMISION!"

Before Tim even has a chance to respond, Jennifer gets up and in an instant, pulls her blouse open to reveal her chest, seemingly stunning Tim and as he adjusts back quickly, he falls out of his chair.

"THESE! RIGHT HERE! That's REALLY all you give a shit about, Tim. THAT"S IT. You hired me because you like these and figured the eye candy helps you get everything you want. EVERYTHING. You got me softening up the deal and then you come in and put on your straight-laced charm and all-business attitude and what do you know? It's YOU handing them the pen to sign, huh? YOU. I get "finders fees" and "split commissions," but never a "nice job" or even recognition. NO RECOGNITION. EVER. I WANT MY RECOGNITION...and god-dammit, I want MY name on one of those Atlantic County Realtor top-sales plaques. ME! My sale...my FULL COMMISION!"

Jennifer storms out of his office and heads toward the bathroom around the side-front of the office, then slams the door, knocking off some of those very awards that have Tim's name on them, causing a crashing sound and broken glass to get scattered. The peace in the office...the appearance of fair team play and family-like attitudes, has also crashed and shattered and to top it off, it was all punctuated with an angry boob-flash.

"What...the...fuck...just...happened?" Tim murmurs out loud. "Did Jennifer just flash me?. Holy shit". He gets up off the floor, trying to mentally brush himself off, but that visual that she just provided -- the entire scene that came and went like a hurricane, won't leave his mind. He glances at his watch. "SHIT." He's gotta go -- he has to go do the meeting with the husband, and this guy is not a patient man or even a kind man and you just don't want to keep people like this waiting.

"Christ, what's happened to my Somers Point?" is what Tim says under his breath as he approaches the front of the office, preparing himself to talk to a bathroom door. He's second wife has been known to show her temper now and then, so it won't be his first time staring at a door knob and trying to impart wisdom...and won't be the last.

Oh boy. "Jennifer. We'll clear this all up when I return. I have to go meet this husband now -- I HAVE to. We'll talk and I'll work it all out with you, ok? Trust me. We'll get this fixed, but for now, I gotta go out to the place. Please wait here and when I get back, we'll go to Happy's Clam Dock and have a few and work this out -- I promise. Can we do that?"

Silence. Absolute silence and it's pretty awkward for Tim,and he's not sure what to do. As he leans in to say more to Jennifer, he hears some rustling in the bathroom, giving him hope she'll be out soon to accept his apology. "Tim" "Yes?" "Go fuck yourself"

Tim pulls his '79 White Chrysler Cordoba to a stop at the end of Broadway where the old Flockhart property begins. Old is a relative term because this entire project started to great fanfare 7 years ago, then went through 2 years of legal-family wrangling after Mr. and Mrs. Flockhart died mysteriously in Montreal, just before it was all completed after a full 18 months of construction. Surprise-approved variances, or as most people understood, 'pay-offs' to state officials made this secluded property more unique than anything else in South Jersey. It's a bit of a slow- winding road to get to -- oftentimes a bit flooded -- and the view out onto Great Egg Harbor Bay is semi-obstructed by all the trees growing out on the tiny artificial islands that were built up just for that purpose. Privacy. Lots of privacy. This place is a perfect get-away location. You might say it's the perfect hide-out.

"Ah, Mr. Foles -- great to see you!" Tim recognizes the voice right away -- this must be his client's attorney, Mr. Yazmene.

"Ned Yazmene. Thanks for coming down on such short notice. When my client inquired about it and then found out about its sudden availability, well, he just had to see it."

"No problem Mr. Yazmene. I have to tell you, I was very surprised to hear about it going up for sale like this. The Flockhart Trust has been in flux for so long, we thought those two kids would never be able to settle on a solution. This whole thing is a very pleasant surprise"

"Indeed. Now, we're clear on all the points I've raised, correct?"

Yazmene reaches into his suit jacket pocket and pulls out an envelope. "There's Five Thousand in there as a show of good faith and gratitude from my client. The name goes down as Mark Johnson. Mr. Johnson is one of our associates in our firm's Montreal Office. I have authority to sign for him on all matters, and I'll provide you with all documentation as we move forward."

Tim takes the envelope and buries into his own suit jacket, then looks around as if searching for a missing pet. "I don't see your client. Are they here yet?"

"Oh, they've been here for about an hour, giving themselves a tour of the house and grounds. The door was open, strangely enough, so they just wanted to get it all moving. No time like the present, am I right?" As Yazmene finishes his sentence, a group of voices begins to be heard coming from the property, and soon enough, six people emerge from inside the house and start to walk toward them.

Tim glances and recognizes each and every one of them, because, well, they are all easy to recognize. He'll play it cool, because he really has no choice. Business is business, even if it is a little dirty, and in Somers Point, things are about to get filthy and there's just no getting around it. Dirt is gonna get under his fingernails.

As he smiles to prepare to greet them, the sound of another car that's coming up the end of the winding road to the property catches everyone's attention. The black 1980 Triumph TR7 that just pulled up quickly and came to a sliding stop can only mean one thing -- Jennifer Mausenbacker didn't stay put.

"Oh Shit," Tim says out loud. "Is there an issue Mr. Foles?"

"Uhh, no, no issue...I just..."

"Who the fuck is this broad?" snaps the biggest man in the group, walking toward them both with his lady escort on his arm.

"That's the one I talked to yesterday, hun. She was, you know, 'nice.' The big guy looks at Foles and points at him.

"She with you? I sure hope she's with you. I hate surprises, my friend."

Foles turns toward the car and begins to walk fast to greet Jennifer, trying to save her from a bad situation that she's not ready for while keeping up appearances.

"Jennifer, did I forget something? What brings you here?"

Jennifer smiles as she adjusts her sunglasses. "No. I came to close my deal, Tim. Simple as that. Hi everybody!" As she waves to the group, Tim steps closer to her as if to block her view, then slightly turns to also wave to the group as if to signify solidarity and calmness.

"You need to go. This is not a place you want to be right now. Please, Jennifer, I beg you. Leave. For your own good"

"Hell no, there's Mrs. Caley right there. Hi Mrs. CALEY!" Jennifer begins to walk toward the bigger group and realizes that Mrs. Caley looks quite disinterested in engaging with her.

Tim walks by her side, smiling and whispering as he does. "Jennifer...you can't do…"

"Do what, huh Tim? What? Bullshit. RECOGNITION. I told you already. Recognition. You can't stop it. Now, leave me to my…"

Jennifer stops dead in her tracks, as if she hit a pane of glass that was put in front of her. She freezes and removes her sunglasses slowly, then bends her head toward Tim. "Oh my God. Oh my God. Oh my God. It's..it's………..him."

As she does this, the big man whispers into the ear of his lady companion, and she turns and walks back to the house with two other men; he steps forward with the other two.

"Ahhh...this is the young lady Geenie had a little misunderstanding with yesterday, huh? It's Jennifer, am I right?"

Jennifer can't get words out of her mouth, because she's a little scared and a little shocked. Maybe more of a little of both. "I can clear this up, just you and me, ok doll? No problem. Let's me and you talk. Fellas?"

The two men with him nod at Yazmene and Foles, letting them know that the area needs to be cleared for a private conversation. Tim looks at Jennifer and says, "Perfect. Perfect. Jennifer is a wonderful representative of Foles Realty and I'm sure she can work through any issues that might have arisen." Tim turns to her and says "You wanted recognition, you got it. Now act like a businessperson and do what you gotta do, understand?"

Jennifer stares at him for a moment, then smiles slightly, letting out a nervous 'sure' as she does. Tim smiles and walks away. "Ok Doll, here it is."

The big man reaches into his pocket and pulls out a wad of hundreds, peeling off 20 of them and handing them to her. "You take this. Then, you drive my man to your office and hand him all your notes from yesterday. I just need to review them for legal purposes. Capish?" Jennifer nods her head and the big man says "Good. After that, our business concludes. Easy enough, am I right?"

"Yes, easy enough."

"Very good, very good. Hey, Yazmene. Go with her. She'll explain everything to you and then bring you back here."

Yazmene nods at the big man, so the plan is understood. "Tell me something, little lady. What brought you down here today, huh? It's my understanding that my man over here had this all sewed up for us and everything was in the bag. You causing trouble? You and him, you know, an item or something? What gives?"

Jennifer finds the question a bit odd, but quickly feels a need to explain it to him, so she does. "My sale. Mine. I've been doing this long enough and it's time I get recognition. That's all I want. Recognition. I worked for it. I deserve it. That's all. That's the only thing I want -- what I worked for and what I deserve."

The big man smiles and gives out a bit of a laugh as he does, because he respects her conviction and drive to get what's "hers." That means something to him.

"Hey, come here." Foles sees he's being summoned and walks right over to join these two, hoping it will all come to a happy ending sooner than later. He's in for a bit of a surprise.

"Recognition. That's what this is all about today, am I right? So, we're all gonna put away the bullshit and just cut to the chase, you understand? No more bullshit. Tell me you understand. Both of you." Jennifer and Tim both nod their heads in unison. "Good, very good. Here's how this plays out. She gets the full commission and decides what to kick over to you. Her sale, her call, capish?"

Tim smiles and shakes his head emphatically. "Absolutely! I was going to suggest that! She's earned it, so yes, absolutely. That's good business right there. 100%"

The big man leans in to speak to Tim and wags his finger as he does. "That, my friend, is recognition. By you, her and me. That's how it is." He points toward the cars and everyone begins to walk away, Jennifer leading Yazmene to hers. Tim also gets in his and then drives away to anywhere else but here. Probably the Prime Diner.

As they are driving toward the Point Circle, Yazmene is making a bit of small talk as they approach the Circle. "Recognition," she says out loud.

"Excuse me?"

"Recognition. He said recognition. He saw that I knew it was him. He saw me recognize him. Fat Freddy Callo is not a man you wouldn't forget easily, Mr. Yazmene. He's in the papers a lot, especially these days. It was on the front page just last weekend, and I read it. The article said, 'With Joey Shells eliminated, we've gone from 'Fair Duce' to 'Don Callous.' Things will be getting bloody."

Yazmene smiles and just stares out the window as he collects his thoughts a bit, but knows just what to say to her. "He likes you, Miss Mausenbacker. He really does. So, don't worry about what you are reading. Fred and Geenie Callo are reasonable people, you'll find. They just want a home that's private. You're selling them that home, so you are now in their business circle. I believe you'll find that position offers opportunities that will be quite beneficial. That's my opinion. You'll be just fine." Yazmene is used to lying to people about this kind of thing. It's his job.

Jennifer contemplates the statement he has made, but she can't help but think about the reality of the situation. Things, it seems, have drastically changed in Somers Point, and fast. Once, there was a bad-boy 'Prince' who ran around the local streets and everyone knew him because, well, he is the son of the former mayor -- her Boss. This "Prince" was more of a nuisance than real trouble. Some Prince.

But now, things have changed at the very top. A new violent King has appeared and is replacing the old and gentle King. Now, Somers Point has that very King -- the new 'Mob King' of the entire Delaware Valley. Fat Freddy Callo is taking up residence in South Jersey. Fat Freddy Callo just took up residence in easily one of the best and friendliest cities in the entire state, and it isn't going to be a moment celebrated by anyone from the local or surrounding Chambers of Commerce.

The new King has arrived.

Long live the King.

God help us all.

Chapter 25

It was like a dream come true, because when he got the call from *Atlantic City Big Fish Tours,* he could hardly believe it. "You've won an all-expense paid trip for two," the woman on the phone informed him. Apparently, an anonymous friend entered his name into a contest and wanted his identity to stay a surprise until the trip was done. Maybe it was a work buddy? Who knows? It's a free trip so what the hell?

He pulls the car up to the address he was given and sure enough, a clipboard-wielding man is standing on the sidewalk, waiting for his customer, as advertised. The man is wearing a t-shirt with some kind of logo on it. As they park and walk toward the dock, he realizes that the logo is an anchor surrounding a life-preserver with the "The Philly Connection" printed on the life preserver. Cool name for a boat.

The guy with the clipboard waves them over and introduces himself with a handshake. "I'm Larry Smith, but most folks just call me Lucky. C'mon, I'd like you to meet our captain." Lucky walks them up the sidewalk, onto the dock and to the boat where a curvy blonde is handling gear. She gives Lucky a wave, turns and walks away. Her t-shirt has the same logo, only the neckline is much lower, and her shorts are very short. The blonde wig she has on secretly hides her natural red hair.

"She's impressive," the man whispers into Lucky's ear.

Lucky whispers back, "...and deadly," with a wink and smile.

Lucky turns their attention to a man standing at the boat controls. "That's Captain Plata. Let me tell you, you are in excellent hands today. Captain Plata navigated waters up and down the eastern Atlantic seaboard and throughout the Caribbean. We're promising a trip full of excitement and surprises. Captain Plata will share the first surprise with you. I think you are going to like it."

They carefully step from the dock onto the boat and the captain greets them with a heavy Cuban/American accent. "Captain Plata, where are you from?" the man asks. The captain explains that his family came to America from Cuba many years ago and settled in the Miami area. He has friends in New Jersey and visits often. He also picks up a little extra cash leading the charter trips, so it makes it worth his time.

"Where are jew frum, my friend?" Captain Plata asks in return, his accent thick.

The man gives a smirk and shakes his head a bit. "I ain't no Jew, Captain Cuba. I'm from the good ol' U. S. of A."

The awkward moment elicits slight laughs and shuffling of feet as Lucky steps inside the cabin and reappears with a small tray. "For good luck, Captain would like to share a special tradition with you. It's an honor and will bring you fortune. This," he continues, raising the tray as in tribute, "will start your destiny for today," He puts the tray down on a small table, grabs four cigars and holds them up. "For good luck!" He tells the group. "We'll light these and take seven puffs for the Seven Seas! Don't worry, you don't have to inhale deeply, it's just ceremonial. On the other hand, the deeper the draw, the bigger the haul!" They take seven puffs. The guests only cough a little bit.

"Ah, experienced puffers, Good. Now, a toast with a concoction served at many a Cuban-themed party," Lucky tells them as he reaches back to the tray for the beverages. "Don't mind the red Solo cups. We try to keep breakables off the boat." Lucky raises his cup to the rest of the group. "To life," he toasts. The two guests raise their cups in return, then take big gulps, barely tasting the sweet concoction. As they do, Captain Plata softly speaks the words of his people, almost to himself and not audible to the rest of the group, "L'chaim."

"Ok, let's sit back and enjoy those cigars," Lucky instructs the guests. "We'll get you out of port and on your way. The view is gorgeous, and the punch is endless. Also, give me your car keys so I can secure them for the trip. Trust me -- it's just a smart precaution when you're boating".

"Wow, to think we come over to a Hebe-town like this and find a Cuban-run operation. That's kinda funny," the man tells his companion as he hands over his car keys. Lucky smiles at the man's anti-Semitic comment, fills their cups and points to where they can sit. "More good luck for both of you -- drink up!"

They take their seats and relax, puffing and sipping as Captain works his way through the back bay and toward yet another surprise. It's a pretty day with puffy white clouds in the sky. It would take a lot to ruin a day like this.

They make their way past Longport and head for the northern tip of Ocean City Island. "Ok," Luck comes back to tell them, "we're gonna make our first stop and pick up our other contest winners for today. It should only take us a few minutes to get them on board. Then, we are on our way out to a prime location we've personally selected for you. Believe me, it's the spot."

"You're picking up more people?" one of the guests asks Lucky, obviously not happy. "We thought it was just the two of us."

"The promotion that's being run includes a few contest winners that sometimes overlap on availability," Lucky explains. "These two guys can make it today, so we are going to make it happen. Don't worry, it's a big ocean. We will make sure you two don't miss out on a great experience. Besides, the more the merrier right?" Lucky receives reluctant nods of acknowledgement and the boat continues on.

Before long, they pull up to another dock. Lucky waves at two gentlemen, standing at the end, excitedly waving at the boat. They look a bit "red-neckish."

"How y'all doin'?" The men greet the two guests already on-board as they settle themselves in. "I'm Bobby and this my brother Billy. He'll try to get y'all to call him William 'cause he thinks he's fancy and all that but he ain't." Bobby slaps his thigh. "Shoot, I'm just funnin' with you. He doesn't talk all that much. It's nice to meet you." Lucky takes them aside and brings out the tray with 2 more cups and 2 more cigars. The guys take sips and begin to chew and puff on the cigars, making it tough to understand them when they speak. It makes them even more annoying than they already are.

"Alright then," Lucky calls out to the Captain. "Fire this baby up and let's go find that perfect spot!"

The Captain eases away from the dock and into the Great Egg Harbor Inlet. As he passes through the inlet, he runs extra power into the motors and off they go due east and out into the deeper Atlantic Ocean waters.

"So," Billy tells the group, "me and Bobby travel 'round and do construction. Right now, we are workin' on a new Casino Hotel they's buildin' in Atlantic City. It's called the Penthouse and it's gonna be big! We also do small projects when asked. We was just doin' this job in Linwood for a fella. He needed his garage enclosed, so we did that." Listening to the story, the guy can feel the drinks hitting him just a bit. He looks over and his trip-mate smiles. The cigars and drinks are making for a happy time.

"One day," Billy continues, "that fella wasn't acting right, you know? He was really distraught. We didn't know why. Anyway, we was finishing all the extra work he had us do and when it came time to pay us, he just handed me his wallet and told me to take whatever we wanted, with this blank stare in his eyes. He wasn't right, I'm telling you. Imagine that? The guy just hands us his wallet and walks away. What do you think about that?"

The man thinks everybody in the story is an idiot, that's what he thinks. "So," Billy turns to ask the man, "what would you do if someone did that to you? You know, like even a real drunk friend? Do you take his money?"

"Well," the man offers. "I wouldn't take his money…ever. That's not right. Only an asshole takes money from somebody in that condition."

"BINGO," says Bobby. "Only an asshole does something like that. A friend, a real friend, would never do that. Never," he adds with emphasis. Bobby turns away from the man but he can tell, both of them are probably feeling a bit woozy from the special concoction that was mixed for them. He also knows that the cigars hid the taste of extra ingredients. He and Billy wait a couple of minutes and then stand and approach Lucky for a brief meeting. "It's time, Luca," Bobby tells him.

Teddy and Geno discard their hats and wigs and turn back to the two remaining "winners." Looks of horror cross their guests' faces. They've been duped and now they know...they are also in deep trouble. Fighting back the fog that seems to have enveloped them, Edward and Tabatha realize they have been drugged as well. They're screwed.

Tabatha screams at Teddy. "I know you! I KNOW YOU. You came to my house: you were in my home. What the fuck is going on!"

The two stand frozen to their spots, in shock. Suddenly, Tabatha begins to weep quietly. "Crying won't do it," Teddy tells her calmly. "Save your energy and tears. We have questions and we know that you have answers. Stop your fuckin' crying."

Geno reaches into the storage bin on the side deck, pulls out a 36-foot logging chain with two heavy-duty hooks on the end and begins to wrap the chain around their waists, tucking and wrapping them so they are secure. About 6 feet of the chain with the hooked ends is hanging loose so Geno secures each end to a cleat on the railing. "This will hold you two punch-drunk assholes in place," he tells them as he pulls out duct tape and wraps it around their ankles, so they are connected there as well. The two will not be going anywhere.

Teddy watches Geno as he completes his task. "You know what?" he asks Edward and Tabatha, "I know for a fact that the police would love to talk to both of you. That would go REAL bad." This elicits sobs and begging from both. "Shut up," Teddy snaps at them, "no one is shooting you, so talk. You were Johnny C's friend, right? YOU WERE HIS FRIEND. So why? Why did you fuck him over? Edward would you like to answer first?"

"It was all his idea," Tabatha sobs out. "He made me do it...all of it. I didn't want to, but he made me."

The two begin to scream at each other. Teddy shakes his head and shouts, "SHUT...THE... FUCK...UP." He points his gun at Edward. "You, you fucked him over. YOU DID. Why did you do that? He took care of you and made sure you got a good job when you followed him here from Vegas. He helped you. Why did you fuck him over?"

"I was told what to do," Edward screams at Teddy. "That's why. I had to. I got approached. Jesus Christ, I had no choice. Three nights before I first met you, Zirkov's guy approached me for the takedown. They wanted to make sure that if Johnny tried to leave, I would get him back into the building for the little "dosey-doe" they pulled. I heard about them and the little girls they use. When the time came and Johnny came outside to get his car, he was in bad shape, I couldn't do what they wanted, I just couldn't. So, I left with him and got him to our house. It was the right thing to do. We got him home and into bed safely."

"Yep, he was safe," Teddy tells him. "But somehow, they still found a way to lower the boom on him, didn't they? Then, when I came to get him you, you piece of shit, you failed Johnny's test. You're a scumbag piece-of-shit low life."

"What...wait a minute, what?" Edward stops flaying around for a minute and looks at Teddy with a puzzled look on his face. "What test? We got him into *your* car, and you took him home. You were responsible from there on."

"That's true...but Johnny C was no dummy, not even close. He knew something went wrong two nights before. He knew you had fucked him over. You don't know, do you...about the test? It was really pretty simple. He left me a clue in plain sight, right where it was easy to see."

Tabatha has gone from upset to angry and interrupts, "Fuck you. FUCK YOU. It's all bullshit. ALL OF THIS IS BULLSHIT. Take these GODDAMN CHAINS OFF OF ME RIGHT NOW!"

"Nope, we'll get to you in a few," Teddy tells her calmly. "I'm not done with him yet." He turns back to Edward. "You see, Johnny C knew the character of a man by the way he acted. He handed you his wallet that night...and you fucked up. You took some cash and winked at me as if it was the 'cool' thing to do, the right thing between friends. WRONG. That's a scumbag move. He set you up and you fuckin' took the bait. It was a test...and a clue.

You failed. He wasn't your friend. He was simply another cashbox for you and your partner here."

Teddy nods to Geno who pulls a tarp off a pile to reveal four cinder blocks. Geno places two on each side of the captive audience, running the chain through them and then using the hook to secure them onto the chain. The blocks are balanced part way over the boat and part way over the side. Edward screams at Geno, "WE DIDN'T DO SHIT TO HIM. LET US GO!"

"Pretty good punch, huh?" Geno asks Edward, unmoved by the rant. "It works wonders. It is an old recipe, handed down to us."

Edward turns his head and spits at Tabatha, "You bitch, you caused all of this" Tabatha dips her head in silence.

"So now," Teddy continues, "I want to know: if Zirkov's guys didn't do the little picture taking session, who did?" A deathly silence fills the air. "C'mon," Teddy urges, "Tell us what we know already. It's not like you have any place to go. Certainly, you don't with dead weight chained to you."

Geno steps over to Tabatha's side and readjusts the cinder blocks. "Damn, these fuckin' things are heavy. You stay still now, ok? I don't want you bumping them and knocking them…well…over the side because that's a LONG way down and that fuckin' water looks cold to me."

"We didn't do anything, I swear," Edward blurts out. "We just took him home, that's all. We would never hurt Johnny C. You're wrong about me, about us. He was a friend. He got me a job and I didn't forget that. I know how to repay friends."

This elicits a sarcastic laugh from Teddy. "You do, huh? You know how to repay friends? Really? What about you, Princess Tabatha? Are you the same way? Do you take care of your friends?"

"Why the fuck are you asking me these stupid fucking questions, asshole," Tabatha hisses back at Teddy. "Get these goddamn chains off of me. All this talk about friends and other bullshit. What the hell do you want to know? You want to know if we have friends? Of course, we have friends and we're good to them. Jesus Christ."

"Like your neighbor, the cocktail waitress? That's one of your friends? You even watch her little girl, don't you, like a good friend?"

"YES," Tabatha answers quickly. "That's what I told you. I'm a good friend and she needs my help, so I help her. I watch her kid. I do that. Can't you see?" The slurred speech makes the words even less convincing.

Teddy gives Tabatha a slight smile and then looks over at Edward and does the same.

"I think you are both full of shit," Geno tells them. "I think you would sell your mother for beer money. Or, in your case Tabby-girl, your own cousin. You are both pieces-of-shit. That's the truth."

Teddy nods his head in agreement. "Tabatha, I asked you before if she was your friend and you told me she wasn't, that she was just a cash box. Do you remember? You don't give two shits about anybody and neither does your scumbag hubby over there. You're worse than parasites, sucking on the blood of others so you can go get a thousand-dollar fucking TV system for your living room. I also saw some newer appliances as I looked around." Teddy pauses and then starts again, resignation in his voice. "You see Edward, there is only one way that you could have pulled this off and bought all those nice things: one way. You figured it out together, didn't you? You got Johnny C home and into the bed where he passed out. Just like that, it came together in your sick little minds. You both did it. You took the Polaroids to Zirkov and got paid handsomely."

"NO, THAT IS NOT TRUE," Edward yells out. "THAT'S JUST NOT TRUE!"

"THAT'S A LIE! THAT'S A GODDAMN LIE! JESUS CHRIST!" Tabatha joins in. "You can't prove that. You prove it or LET US THE FUCK GO!"

Geno reaches into a side storage pocket and pulls out an envelope that he hands over to Teddy. Teddy reaches in and pulls out several Polaroid pictures. He holds two of them up for Edward and Tabatha to see. "Do you recognize that little face?" he asks. "It kind of looks like your neighbor's daughter, doesn't it? It's not hard to tell, even if you did play dress-up with her. You know, give her a little adult-looking disguise." Teddy turns the picture back and looks down at it. "She has makeup and everything." He steps forward and places the pictures in front of their faces. "Take a good look," he commands. "There it is. YOU...DID...THIS. BOTH OF YOU, you sick-fuck pieces of garbage."

Edward and Tabatha protest loudly, screaming and squirming. "FUCK YOU. THIS IS ALL BULLSHIT. IT'S ALL A SET-UP. IT'S

A LIE. THAT PROVES NOTHING." Teddy lets them go until they stop to catch their breath. As if considering what they said, he asks, "I'm wrong, huh? You're telling me you didn't do this?"

"WE DIDN'T," Edward screams back. Tabatha shakes her head "no" as she begins to cry louder and harder. Teddy leans in between them and moves the picture back and forth. "Just one problem with your story: I got a good look at the headboard on your bed, your custom designed, hard-carved headboard. Take a closer look at the pictures." He gives them a moment to focus. "That's right, it's your bed in the pictures. When we went inside, the little girl was standing outside the room staring at it." His voice takes on a harder edge. "Sure enough, there it is...right there, behind Johnny C's head. It's your headboard. There's your proof. You two pieces of shit did this and got paid. You ruined his life." Teddy begins to pace back and forth as he's talking, getting more animated with each turn. "He's gone and so is his wife. DEAD. You two caused that. To top it off, you fucked up his daughter's life and now she's a mess because of what you put them through. Johnny C, his wife, Lisa and that poor little girl -- you did all that...you two fucking worthless MONSTERS."

Edward and Tabatha lean into each other, crying hysterically. Luca joins Teddy and Geno to discuss what to do.

"So, are you shooting these two or what?" Luca asks. "I mean, what's the move now?"

They turn and as they do, Edward speaks up.

"Please...PLEASE don't shoot us. PLEASE. You said..." his voice begins to fade. The punch has kicked in for both of them. Tabatha can barely keep her head up as she says, "Fuck you."

Teddy addresses them. "I told you before, we're not shooting you. I'm not a lying piece-of-shit like you are." Teddy and Geno stand on each side of Edward and Tabatha and toss the guns into the water. As they do, Teddy turns to Luca and nods at him, "This is the move." With a swift turn, the two heel-kick the cinder blocks into the water. They splash hard. After a few frantic moments of violent thrashing and gurgled screams, it is over. There is only ocean and wind. Teddy looks over the side to see barely a ripple. It's as if Tabatha and Edward were never there.

"I said I wouldn't shoot you," he tells the ripple. "No need for that when we can just let you swim your way to hell."

In the Captain's room, Philly Silver looks out over the ocean. As Luca enters the cabin, he asks him, "So, no fishing today?"

"Nope, not a good fishing day," Luca replies. "It does seem like a good day for swimming though."

Philly smiles at him. "Good day, bad day: for some people, it's all the same." He pauses and then asks, "Should we head back now?"

Luca pokes his head out the door and shouts down to the boys, "Are we finished?" Teddy and Geno nod their heads in unison. Geno folds up the tarp and takes the tray and glasses to the galley. It's always good to clean up after a day of fishing.

Teddy remains on the deck, looking down at the water. They got rid of these two, but there are two more out there...and more after that.

"All finished...for now."

Ted Damian isn't finished – Actually, he's just getting started. Follow him as he travels deeper into the exciting Atlantic City Casino world to find new adventures and new dangers in Book # 3 of this action packed series:

"South Jersey Casino Boy 3: Somers Point Royalty"

www.ingramcontent.com/pod-product-compliance
Lightning Source LLC
Chambersburg PA
CBHW060304260626
47160CB00007B/2495